NIGHT C

By Joan Hall Hovey

ISBN: 9781926965567

PUBLISHED BY:

Books We Love Publishing Partners (BWLPP)
192 Lakeside Greens Drive
Chestermere, Alberta, T1X 1C2
Canada

Copyright © 2011 by Joan Hall Hovey

Cover art by Gary Val Tenuta Copyright © 2011

To Lynne
much Love
mom Hovey

Joan Hall Hovey
Sept/2011

vulnerable heroine." —**Harriet Klausner**

"...a thriller release from the pen of the very talented writer, Joan Hall Hovey, who once again demonstrates her ever-increasing skill at designing tales of psychological suspense and terror." —**Jill M. Smith – Rave Reviews**

"Wow! Riveting from the prologue to the hair-raising conclusion. Highly Recommended." —**Cindy Penn, Wordweaving.com**

"...Joan Hall Hovey is a mistress at description and in bringing characters alive...a chiller of a book..." —**Shirley Truax, Ivy Quill Reviews**

"...a taut, edge of the seat thriller...certain to inspire readers who love the thriller genre to demand more from this writer." —**Patti Nunn—Charlotte Austin Review**

"...Start reading this book on a Saturday morning. That way, you'll have all weekend to read it, since you won't want to put it down." —**Martine G. Bates Inscriptions magazine**

"Extremely well structured, good plot, impossible to put down until the last page is reached." —**BASTULLI MYSTERY LIBRARY**

"...highly professional thriller...more than a series of twists and turns..." — **E.E. Cran—Telegraph Journal**

"A fast moving suspense thriller, it will keep you up all night to finish it..." —**Kathy Thomason Book Reviewer The Butler County Post**

"...a riveting thriller that will leave you breathless. Hovey is a master of this genre..." —**Deborah Shlian, Author of Wednesday's Child, Shou**

"...a gripping style that wrings emotions from everyday settings. Oh and by the way ...is your door locked?" —**Linda Hersey—Fredericton Gleaner**

LISTEN TO THE SHADOWS

"Joan Hall Hovey packs a terrifying punch as her first novel, 'Listen to the Shadows', spins a chilling tale of revenge, murder and madness..." —**Jill M. Smith—Rave Reviews, N.Y.**

"...will appeal to fans of romance, gothic and suspense novels. Hovey's scenes focusing on this deranged psychopath are razor sharp, and one is reminded of author Ruth Rendell." —**Evening Times Globe, Saint John, NB**

"LISTEN TO THE SHADOWS has shades of the old gothic stories, complete with the scary old house. This story has the makings of a classic." —**Reviewer, Yvonne Hering**

"...This one will put goosebumps all over you...chilling. I read it during a thunderstorm and found myself jumping several times. Excellent!" —**Huntress Book Reviews**

NIGHT CORRIDOR

By Joan Hall Hovey

ONE

October 1973

He noticed her as soon as he walked into the bar. She was sitting with another girl, a blond; pretty, he supposed, but his attention was riveted on the dark-haired one. He ordered a beer and took a table in the far corner where he had a good view, while he himself was safe from watchful eyes. She had satiny hair to her shoulders, high cheekbones, was slender in a silk print top, black slacks, like a woman on the cover of a magazine. She was laughing at something the blond said, flashing perfect white teeth and his heart tripped. She's the one, the voice told him. Excitement surged through him as he recast her in the movie that for years now, replayed endlessly on the screen of his mind.

When the two women rose to leave, he left his unfinished beer on the table and casually, so as not to draw attention to himself, followed them outside. She had put on a jacket and it shone bright white in the lights from the parking lot.

After chatting briefly, the two girls gave each other a quick hug, then parted and went to their respective cars, parked a good distance from one another. There was a rightness to it. They might just as easily have come in one car, or parked closer to one another. But they did not. The stars were finally lining up in his favor.

He came up behind her as she was fitting the key in the lock of the red Corvair. "I'm Buddy," he said softly, so as not to frighten her. Despite his best intention, she whirled around, eyes wide. "Jesus, you scared the shit out of me. What do you want?"

He felt the smile on his face falter. A mask, crumbling. "I just want to talk to you."

"Fuck off, okay? I'm not interested."

With those words, her beauty vanished, as if he'd imagined it. Her mouth was twisted and ugly. Disappointment weighed heavy on him. Anger boiled up from his depths.

"That was wrong of you to say that to me," he said, still speaking quietly.

Belying the softness of his voice, she saw something in his eyes then and he saw that she did, and when she opened her mouth to scream, he stuck her full in the face with his fist.

She slid down the side of the car as if boneless. He caught her before she hit the ground, then dragged her around to the other side of the car, blocking her with his own body in case someone saw them. Not that he was too concerned. If anyone did see them they would just figure she was his girlfriend and that she'd had one too many. But there was no one in the lot. Even her friend had already driven off.

He lowered her limp form to the ground while he hurried round to the driver's side and got the key out of the door. He put on his gloves, and opened the passenger door. After propping her up in the seat, he went back around and slid into the driver's side. Then he turned on the ignition and the car hummed to life.

Shifting the car into reverse, he backed out of the parking spot. He gave the wheel a hard turn and she fell against him, her hair brushing his face and filling his senses with her shampoo, something with a hint of raspberry. He pushed her off him and her head thunked against the passenger window. A soft moan escaped her, but she didn't wake.

He drove several miles out of the city, then turned left onto a rutted dirt road and stayed on it for a good ten minutes. Spotting a clearing leading into the woods, an old logging road no longer used, he eased the car in, bumping over dips and tangled roots. He went in just far enough not to be seen from the road on the off-chance someone drove by, but also taking care he wouldn't get stuck in here.

The headlights picked out the white trunks of spruce trees, spot-lighting the leaves that seconds later receded into blackness, as if this were merely a stage set.

Beside him, the woman moaned again then whimpered, her

hand moving to her face where he had struck her. Blood trickled darkly down one corner of her mouth and her eyes fluttered open. He knew the instant she sensed him there beside her, like the bogeyman in a nightmare. Except she was awake now. When she turned to look at him he felt her stiffen, could see in her eyes that she knew she was in big trouble. He almost felt sorry for her. Almost.

"Who are you?" she croaked, more blood leaking from the corner of her mouth, eyes wet with tears.

"What does it matter?"

"Please…please don't hurt me. I'm—I'm sorry for what I said to you. I shouldn't have. If you want to… I mean, it's okay. You don't have to hurt…"

His fury was like lava from a volcano and his hand shot out, the back of it shutting off her words in mid-sentence. "Shut up, whore."

She was crying hard now, heavy, hiccupy sobs, helpless, terrified. But her tears meant nothing to him. She was right to be afraid. He slid the knife from its sheath that hung on his belt and let her see it.

"Oh, God, no please…" She was choking on her tears, wriggling away from him, trapped, like a butterfly on the head of a pin. He smiled when she reached for the door handle on her side, and then drove the knife into her upper arm. She screamed and he wound his fingers into her hair. "Be quiet," he said, while she held her arm with her other hand and wept like a child.

As he had wept. As he wept still.

"You can't get away," he said. "There's no place to go."

TWO

On Monday morning, Caroline Hill woke with such a sense of dread that it was a struggle to get a full breath, as if there was a clot of air trapped under her ribcage. The smell of eggs wafted up from the kitchen and made her feel sick to her stomach. Pushing herself up in the narrow bed, she took a few deep breaths, the way Nurse Addison had shown her, and by the time she left the room, she felt calmer, but hardly calm. She dressed and went down to breakfast, knowing she would eat little this morning.

Just the thought of walking through the big oaken doors of Bayshore Mental Institution (formerly called The Lunatic Asylum) and out into a world that no longer knew her, nor she it, struck terror into her heart. Nine years since she had been a part of it all. Her hands were sweaty. She was anxious, yet at the same time a small part of her was excited at the thought of freedom.

Not that it was so bad in here now. Not like it used to be. Olga Farmer, one of the old ones who had been here forever, said it was a thousand times better than in the early days. Warmer, for one thing, since the central heating went in, and the food was edible most of the time, and there was more variety. Meat and cheese were often served at meals, for example. That wasn't always the case. Olga said she remembered when a patient had to have specific doctor's orders to be allowed such luxories as an egg or a glass of milk.

Olga turned eighty-five last month and they had a cake for her in the big hall, and Mrs. Green, who'd once been a school teacher, banged out Happy Birthday on the out-of-tune piano the way she did for all their birthdays, even those for whom birthdays meant little.

She stood at the long, barred window looking out beyond the high reddish-brown fence to the world on the other side, to the wooden houses in their greens and browns, climbing hills. Higher up, the church with its clock steeple, farther out the blue water of the bay.

The people looked small, like the ones she'd read about in Gulliver's Travels. But she could see them well enough, scurrying here and there, going about their daily business, oblivious to her here in the window, watching them. As she stood there, a fresh wave of apprehension washed over her, swamping all anticipation of leaving, filling her with a terrible sense of foreboding. She shivered involuntarily.

"Cold?"

She looked to see Nurse Lynne Addison at her shoulder, smiling, her eyes questioning.

"No. I'm fine, thank you, Nurse Addison."

"You don't have to pretend with me, Caroline. I know you're scared and I don't blame you. I'd be scared too. But don't worry. It's going to be fine. We've arranged a bed-sitting room for you in a very nice rooming house," she said, "and you have that dishwashing job waiting for you at a restaurant called Frank's, not half a block away. You'll be eating most of your meals there. I've been there with my husband; the food's great."

"Really?"

She grinned. "Really. You'll do great, honey. Later when you're feeling more confident you might decide to do something else with your life. Maybe even go back to school. You're a smart girl, Caroline. You can do anything you want to do. Not right away, of course. It'll take a little time getting used to being on the outside. But you will. The dishwashing job will be a breeze for you. God knows you've had lots of practice in here. Oh, did I tell you, there's a nice park not far from your building, with benches and a lovely fountain. You can sit and read on days you're not working. You love to read."

She was about to say something else when one of the office staff waved to Nurse Addison from across the room, just outside the office. The wave said it was important.

When Nurse Addison was gone, Alice Barker, a patient, headed for her, her moon face full of purpose. Her flowered dress hung loosely on her short, plump frame, shoelaces tapping on the dark green tile floor.

Caroline could smell the ever-present Juicyfruit gum she was always chewing. According to Martha Blizzard, if the gum was putty there'd be enough in Alice's mouth to seal a good sized window. Caroline tried not to smile as the image popped into her mind.

"You going home, Caroline?" she asked, talking around the gum. "Martha said you were going home. "Will you tell my mother to come and visit me?"

"Sure," Caroline said, knowing Alice's mother had been dead for years. Caroline's mind replayed the words *going home* and the faint smile fell to sadness. She hadn't a home anymore. Not really.

Down in the grassless yard, male patients endlessly retraced their steps, as they'd done yesterday, and the day before that. Sometimes fights broke out and the burly men in white coats would come running and drag the ranting offender away. A divider, made of the same dull brown fencing that cut them all off from the world outsider, separated the women's yard from the men's. She sometimes took a book outside with her, and read.

She thought about sitting in the park, reading, and felt better about things. Her mother had taken her to a park once. From time to time images would leap to her mind; her mother's smile, her father's bent head as he read from the Bible, the pale amber light from the lamp fallen on the printed page. Sensations too—the smell of green grass, the warmth of the sun on her face. She wasn't altogether sure if her memories were real or imagined. Perhaps fragments of dreams.

The strong scent of Lysol broke into her thoughts, overwhelming the egg smell and she turned to see Raina, who had a foul mouth and wore loads of chunky jewelry that always announced her, washing the floor. They used a mop nowadays. When it was Caroline's job she used to scrub the dark green floors on her hands and knees, creeping over shadow-bars when the light was just right. Her knee had swelled double its size and throbbed with pain all the time and the doctor who checked it said she had water on the knee, and drained it and wrapped it with a thick bandage under her special brown stocking. All the patients who were capable were given jobs to do. It was part of the therapy. Some worked in the kitchen, the laundry, or did other jobs, including working in the vegetable garden on the other side of the building, which produced the food they ate. When Caroline could no longer scrub the floors, they put her to work in the kitchen washing dishes where she'd been for the last three years. She liked immersing her hands in the warm suds, and listening to the chatter of the other women that went on around her. She seldom joined in, but it was fine just to listen to them talking and laughing. She often felt like a child among adults, which made her feel safe and comforted.

But this would be a new kitchen, with new people. Strangers. Her body thrummed with fresh anxiety and fear. Her skin itched. Would her room have a lock? Would other people have the key?

Now with her worn black suitcase packed and sitting in the lobby, she smiled and said her goodbyes to everyone. Some of the patients laughed and clapped for her.

Martha Blizzard hugged her, her warm brown eyes swimming in tears. "You're gonna do fine out in the world, Caroline. You a good girl. You were always nice to me and I ain't gonna forget you. I gonna miss you bad, girl. You stay close to Jesus, you hear?"

"I will, Martha. I'll come see you," she promised, hugging the slight, bony frame and fighting her own tears. Martha held her at arms length and looked hard at her. You could see she was pretty once, now there was a fierceness about her, though her inner beauty shone through. "You get outa here, girl, you stay out. You forget this place. And be careful. I'm not the only one who killed someone, you know. The devil is alive and well on the streets of St. Simeon."

"The devil? What do you mean, Martha?"

She gave her head an impatient shake. "Don't pay me no mind. I shouldn't have said nothing. You just be careful, Caroline."

Martha was a petite black woman who bludgeoned her husband to death with with a baseball bat because he beat her when he was drunk, and he was drunk more than he was sober. She weighed about ninety pounds and she was either very strong, or else very mad when she did it, because she always seemed very calm and rational to Caroline. She was also religious and read her Bible every night before bed, though she was never one to preach. Unlike Caroline's father, who had been fervent in his preaching.

When Martha first came to Bayshore, they said she washed her hands all the time trying to get rid of the invisible blood on them, just like Lady MacBeth. But Caroline didn't believe that was true. Caroline thought she was probably fine once her tormentor was dead.

Martha's husband was asleep when she brought the bat down, cracking his skull at first strike. "He waved to me before he died," she told Caroline. But Caroline thought that must just been his body reacting to the blow, though she didn't tell that to Martha. Martha said he lived separate from his soul, and in killing him with the bat, she'd rejoined him to his soul and delivered him up to the Lord.

When Caroline had said her goodbyes to Ella Gaudet this morning, her roommate for the past five years, Ella merely nodded at her, and gathered up her imaginary wool from the skeins in the imaginary basket on the floor. Ella, who had a mole on her chin that sprouted white hair like cat whiskers, was not a talker. She kept to herself, mostly just sitting in that chair in her room, rocking, rocking…*creak…creak…creak*…hour after hour.

Once, Caroline told Nurse Addison that it was driving her nuts and they both laughed at the irony of that. She told Caroline that if she could make jokes at her own expense, she was indeed getting better.

"You ready to take on the world?" Nurse Addison asked now, as if Caroline's thoughts had summoned her. Her voice was filled with cheer and brightness, but it didn't sound quite true to Caroline's ears. "Ready to live by your own rules? The cab will be here in twenty minutes or so."

A cab. Taking her away. To somewhere.

"I…Would you go with me, please?" The fear took hold of her, making her head spin, her heart pound.

The nurse smiled. "I'm afraid I can't do that. But I'll carry your suitcase to the cab. How's that?" After a pause, she added, "There's a trunk that belongs to you, Caroline. It was sent here after your parents died. I believe there are photograph albums inside, personal effects. That sort of thing. The doctor thought it would be too difficult for you to deal with at the time, but I think you'll be okay with it now. We'll be sending that along to your new address."

A different kind of fear welled in her throat, making it hard to speak. "That's okay. You can just leave it here for me."

The nurse let on she didn't hear her and handed her a squat brass key. She was trying to be cheerful. Happy for Caroline. Caroline could see that. "And this too," she said, reaching into her uniform pocket and producing a small blue book with gold lettering. "This is a bank book. You have two-thousand dollars in the bank, Caroline. Your parents left it to you. It's not a fortune, but it'll be a nice little cushion for you if you're careful with it. Don't let anyone else have them. They are yours. Your private property."

She fought back the fear, forced her voice calm. "I won't let anyone have them." She tucked the bank book and the key to the trunk inside the zipper pocket. "Thank you for the new purse, Nurse Addison. I really like it. The leather is so soft and the blue goes with my suit." Someone had donated the suit, which was practically new and fit her perfectly.

"And your eyes," the nurse teased lightly. "It goes with your eyes, too. You're very welcome, Caroline. And you already thanked me for the purse a dozen times. But I'm glad you like it."

"I do. I love it."

"You'll be fine, kiddo. Got everything?" She slipped the shoulder bag off Caroline's shoulder. "Okay if I double-check? I'm like a mother hen, aren't I? But I worry."

"Sure. I'm glad you're like a mother hen."

Laughing, the nurse took a quick look inside the bag. "You've got your case—five crisp twenties. Your meds. These are mild," she said, holding up the small bottle of pills. "Enough to help you sleep, if you need to take one. "Or if you're feeling stressed. Maybe you won't even need them."

But they both knew that wasn't likely.

"Good. Good to go, then," Nurse Addison said, dropping Caroline's meds back into the new blue bag. She stood back to appraise her. "Well, almost."

Taking a comb out of the bag, she fussed a little with Caroline's brown, wavy hair, newly washed and shining, then she took out her lipstick and touched a bit of coral to her cheeks, blending it with her fingertips. "Perfect. You just needed a bit of color."

Caroline stood passively, allowing herself to be fussed over. She wished she could just stand here and let herself be fussed with into eternity, even though she was perfectly capable of brushing her own hair and applying rouge to her own cheeks, and they both knew it.

Nurse Addison was taller than Caroline, square-shouldered, with a laugh that sounded like music. She could be tough if she had to be, but gentle too. She really cared about the patients. Most of the attendants were kind and caring, but Caroline had also known others who were devious and cruel, and made the patients sicker than they were when they came in. She didn't like to think too much about it. It was not so bad in here now though.

"Your cab's here, honey."

She could only nod as she preceded Lynne through the big doors. She would not have been able to speak past the thickening in her throat.

Lynne gave the taxi driver directions and waved goodbye to Caroline, whose face reflected the fear of a child set adrift on an ice flow. She'll drown, Lynne thought, as the dark cab rolled slowly down the narrow paved road like a car in a funeral procession. Despite the blush she'd added, Caroline's face was ghostly pale in the back window. When her hand rose in a small wave, Lynne's heart contracted.

No way in hell is she going to make it out there on her own. I should have given her my home phone number. She'd thought of it. But her phone would be ringing off the wall if she gave every patient who was discharged from here her phone number. Joe would end up leaving her out of self-preservation. She couldn't be held responsible for what happened to patients after they left her care, could she? She was already stressed, what with her mom being diagnosed with Alzheimer's. For that reason, she was glad to be retiring. Her mother needed her now. Mom, always so vibrant, so mentally sharp, now often seemed confused and vague. One didn't have to be a psychiatrist to know that she was terrified. The fear was in her eyes. She knew what was happening to her. The phone call earlier was from a neighbor who happened to look out the window and spotted her mother wandering in the middle of the road and rushed out to bring her back home.

I have decision to make, Lynne thought. But not yet. Dear God, please not yet.

The taxi was gone now, and Caroline with it. Even Lynne's own personal sorrows were not enough to allay her fears for the child-woman who had just been cut loose from all that was familiar to her.

I'll check on her, she promised herself as she envisioned the lost teenager she'd been when she was admitted. She's much better now, Lynne told herself. She wouldn't have recommended her for release if she didn't believed that.

Escaping the chill morning air, she went back inside the building. It seemed so quiet here now. There were far fewer patients, so fewer staff. The place was emptying fast since the bureaucrats decided to close it down.

THREE

"Pretty fall day," the cab driver said over his shoulder, and Caroline jumped at the sound of his voice and turned around in the seat. She'd been looking out the back window, watching the prison-like structure of Bayshore Mental Institution, gray and sprawling against the cornflower blue of the sky, grow smaller and smaller. The man's voice had startled her. But for Doctor Rosen, no man had spoken to her in a very long time.

The cab driver's shoulders were wide in a maroon blazer of some soft material. His hair was a mass of gray curls and he wore dark sunglasses; she could see them in the rearview mirror. She couldn't see his eyes but knew he was looking at her, waiting for her response.

She must say something. It wasn't like he'd asked her some difficult or personal question, only commented on the weather. Speak up, Dr. Rosen had told her. Hearing your own voice strong in your ears will give you confidence.

"Yes," she said. "Yes, it's very lovely."

She settled back in the blue-gray plush seat, enjoying its soft, luxurious feel. The car smelled of new leather, pleasant and mildly reminiscent of something that nudged the edge of her mind. Ah yes, William's leather jacket. William's leather jacket. So long ago.

Outside her window, the maple trees flashed by in shades of gold and rust and scarlet, bright as in a Technicolor movie. A few leaves borne on the wind, danced past her eyes.

"You been away a while?" the cab driver asked.

"Yes. Nine years."

His head turned slightly in her direction. He shook his head. "Long time."

She said nothing. Folded her hands on her lap. Then she unclasped them and ran her fingertips along the plush arm rest.

"You like music?" the cab driver asked from the front seat.

"Yes, sometimes. I like Frank Sinatra. And Ella Fitzgerald."

"Ya got good taste, kid. Didn't figure anyone young as you would even remember the great ones."

She felt warmed by his approval, and began to enjoy the drive as he switched on the radio and turned the dial until he found a station that was playing blues. She liked that. And jazz, too.

Martha Blizzard had some old LPs in her room and would sometimes play them for her: Ella Fitzgerald, B.B. King, Louis Armstrong's recording of Blueberry Hill and others. She even had an old record by Billie Holiday. It had a crack in it and skipped, but Martha would just give it a little tap and it would play fine again. Caroline could feel that music deep down inside herself and sometimes it made her want to cry. But it made her feel good too in a strange way. Like Billie Holiday did. Like she was singing your blues too. Like she knew all about them, even better than you did yourself.

"Ain't Frankie," the cab driver said, "But not too bad, eh?"

"It's nice. Thank you." She didn't know the tune, not one she'd heard before. A man singing about a lost love. She knew all about that.

"My pleasure. I most always listen to music when I'm driving," he said. "Some people don't like it though, so I turn it off."

"I do. I like it."

He nodded again, seemed to smile to himself.

They drove past the park, and the sight of it tugged at an old memory. A woman was sitting on the green-painted bench watching two little red-haired boys running about in the grass. Yes, there was the fountain Nurse Addison told her about. The smell of grass on a certain summer's day suddenly rose up in her senses, overriding the leather smell of the car.

The cab slowed as they passed a small crowd of people spilling into the street. Two policemen were directing traffic. Yellow police tape was stretched across the mouth of an alley across from the park. Like a scene in a movie.

"What happened?" Caroline asked the driver, continuing to stare out the back window even after they left the scene.

"You sure you want to know?"

She turned around in the seat. "Yes, please."

He gave a brief nod. "Guess they wouldn't have let you out if you weren't up to hearing bad news," he said. "Plenty of it around." He hesitated. Then, "Young woman murdered. Body dumped in that alley there. It's the second murder in a month. The first was a nurse on her way home from working her shift at the hospital. Too late to be walking alone. Poor kid. There's talk about all those nuts being let out of Bay…sorry, Miss, I didn't mean you. No offense intended."

"It's okay. I don't mind."

He raised his dark-glasses and peered at her in the rearview mirror. "I got it on good authority both those girls had dark hair and blue eyes," he said. "Like you, Miss. Not trying to scare you or nothin' like that, but you wanna take care."

FOUR

The landlady was standing in the window when the cab pulled up at the curb and the young woman in a blue suit, stepped out. She looks a little lost, Greta thought. Poor little thing. She let the curtain drop back into place and hurried as fast as her heavy limp would allow, to greet her newest tenant.

Widowed for the last twelve years, she had learned to adapt to most situations, knew how to take care of herself. This house, which she had purchased with her deceased husband's life insurance, provided her with a decent living. She had a soft spot for strays, as long as they paid their rent on time and didn't give her any problem. And this one looked harmless enough.

She opened the door wide, a smile on her face. "You must be Caroline. I'm Greta Bannister, the landlady. Please, come inside. My, they didn't tell me what a pretty little thing you are. You hardly look no more than sixteen."

"I'm twenty-six," Caroline said quickly, panicked that the woman might not let her stay because she wasn't of age. She had no place else to go. Unzipping her blue bag, she rummaged in it for the wallet that held her birth certificate. "I have my papers," she said anxiously.

"No, dear, settle down now, please. I know how old you are. My goodness, I was paying you a compliment. Never mind. Come in, the wind is kicking up; you'll blow away. A beautiful fall day, though. Supposed to rain tomorrow. Already starting to cloud over. I'll make us a cup of tea and then I'll show you to your room. It's on the second floor."

She closed the door behind Caroline, turned the lock with a sharp click. "The washroom's at the end of the hall, same as on the floors above us. You probably noticed, this is a three-story house. Oh, I'm rambling, aren't I and keeping you standing here in the hallway. Come along. Just leave your bag in the hallway for now. Harold will bring it up later."

"Harold?"

"Harold's my nephew, he lives with me."

Caroline followed her through to the large kitchen which smelled of good cooking mixed in with another, less pleasant smell she couldn't discern, until she saw several cats eyeing her from various corners the rooms they passed. In the living room, lace doilies rested like crocheted shellfish on the arms and backs of sofas and chairs, reminding her of the parlour of her childhood.

Mrs. Bannister walked ahead of her, her ample bottom waddling unevenly beneath the navy housedress, imprinted with small white sailboats.

There'd been kindness in her face, and her hair was the color of the leaves on the maple trees they'd passed on her way here. Caroline felt much of the earlier tension leaving her.

In the big, cluttered kitchen, Mrs. Bannister motioned her to a chair at the large square table covered with a yellow and white-checked oilcloth.

Steam escaped the pot cover on the cast iron stove, the source of the good smell.

At the landlady's invitation, Caroline sat down on one of the chairs, held her purse in her lap, and watched her bustle about tending to this and that.

"Did you hurt your knee scrubbing floors?" Caroline asked tentatively.

"What?" The landlady turned a puzzled look at her, then she chuckled as she took down two cups and saucers from the cupboard. "No, dear, that's not what happened to me?"

"Oh. I got water on the knee a couple of years ago from scrubbing floors at the hospital," Caroline said. She extended her right leg to show her. "They had to bandage it up and then they put me to work in the kitchen. I liked it a lot better."

"Ah. Well, I'm glad. No, I fell on the ice last year and broke my hip. Right at the bottom of the steps, wasn't watching what I was doing. Thinking about something else, wouldn't you know, instead of paying attention to what I was doing. Feet went out from under me and I landed bad. If someone had had a camera at the time they might have made a pretty penny on that picture."

Brown crockery Teapot in hand, with a white daisy painted on the side, Mrs. Bannister hobbled to the table.

"Hurt like the dickens," she said, pouring the tea into the cups. "They're supposed to replace the hip, but I'm thinking I might just not bother. This one will probably last as long as I do." She gave a big horse-laugh at this, and Caroline dared to smile.

"You walk fast," Caroline blurted, too loudly, startling both herself and the orange cat who leapt from the windowsill, where a moment ago it had been curled up asleep. Now it looked up at her with disdain. She didn't blame the poor animal for being annoyed. Her voice had boomed in her own ears and apparently in the landlady's, too, from her expression, though it melted quickly into her easy smile.

Doctor Rosen said she should always speak up, but she would have to be careful about that, because you could speak up too much and frighten people. And animals. Make everyone think you were crazy.

"Not so bad," the landlady said, returning the teapot to the stove and sitting across from Caroline, acting as if her new tenant had spoken in a perfectly normal way. "Old legs still get me where I'm going. What's the matter, Sally?" she asked of the cat who had cautiously bounded back up onto the windowsill, but was keeping a wary eye on Caroline.

"I think I frightened her."

"Oh, posh, Sally's just shy of strangers. Aren't you, Sally. She'll be fine when she gets to know you better. So what was I saying? Oh, yes, I've usually got eight roomers in all. The bathroom's at the end of the hallway, same on all three floors, like I said. We're generally filled up, but the tenants do change from time to time. The room across from yours has been empty for quite awhile." She was silent for a few seconds, sipped her tea. Then, "Girl that used to live there was murdered. It was all the news this morning. Terrible thing." She shook her orangy mop of hair for emphasis, and went on. "People come and go. Everyone minds their own business. Don't allow no funny business, of course, you understand. This ain't that sort of place, so you don't have to worry your head about that."

"Oh, I wasn't."

She envisioned the milling crowd the taxi driver had driven past, police cars in the street, yellow crime tape stretched across the alley.

"Well, no need if you was. Got one young fellow on the top floor teaches piano, so I'm hoping the noise don't bother you too much. No one's complained though some of those students ain't got much talent, God bless 'em."

For the next half hour Mrs. Bannister rambled on while Caroline listened, speaking only when asked a direct question and then in careful modulation.

"I'm used to noise," Caroline said when the landlady brought up the subject of the piano player again. The woman's friendly chatter was pleasant to listen to and Caroline felt lulled by it. Sort of like being in the hospital's kitchen, except that this woman was actually talking to her, not over and around her.

"Of course you're used to noise, dear, in that place." She stopped abruptly, looking concerned that she might have offended her new tenant. "I'm sorry…"

"Oh, no. I didn't mean that. I meant Mrs. Green at Bayshore. She likes to play the piano in the big hall. She's not very good but it's not totally her fault. The piano's out of tune. Been that way forever. I like the sound of it anyway though."

"Oh. Well, Mr. Denton's piano is electronic. One of them Yamaha keyboards, so I guess it's not a problem for him. Sometimes if the student is very bad, he'll even turn down the volume a little and that's a mercy. Since you're a fan of the piano, maybe you'd like to meet Mr. Denton. His first student isn't due for…" She glanced at the cat-clock on the wall. "Well, it won't be un…"

"Oh, no, thank you," Caroline said, stricken at the thought of meeting yet another stranger.

The landlady shrugged. "Sure, honey. Whatever you like. I keep forgetting what a change this must be for you. By the way, in case I forget, there's a phone out in the hallway if you need to make a call. I don't suppose you'll get too many will you? With this hip, you understand, it's a hassle for me to call people to the phone. Though I don't mind if it's important. Of course, you can always get your own private phone installed in your room if you want to pay the extra."

"No, it's okay. I wouldn't know anyone to call."

The landlady smiled at her, then got a bowl down from the cupboard and set it in front of her. "You'll have some of my delicious soup before I show you your room." The simmering meaty smell rendered Caroline helpless to refuse.

"Nothing like a hot bowl of soup to keep body and spirit together," the woman said as she ladled out the soup, thick with chunky vegetables, into Caroline's bowl. "This is Harold's favorite."

Caroline noticed how the landlady beamed whenever she mentioned her nephew, and thought how lucky he was to have someone who cared so much about him.

"It's very good," she said of the soup, consciously trying not to eat too fast despite her enormous hunger. "I don't blame him-- Harold."

"Harold works at *Big Bakery*," she said, returning the pot to the stove, her face flushed from the heat. She set out two shamrock rolls and butter on a plate, then sat back down slowly, as if the effort caused her pain. "That's the name of it, but it really is pretty big, supplies the entire city with its bread and sweets. It's right across the street from Frank's Restaurant where you'll be working a week from today. Don't look so surprised, dear. I know everything about you, you see. It's going to be a whole new life for you here, Caroline. I think we're all going to get along just fine. I supply all linens and towels, fresh clean every Tuesday. For everything else, tenants are on their own. There's a laundromat just up the street. But I do know this is all new to you, dear, so if there's anything you need, or you have any questions, you just knock on my door. Not too early, though, mind you." She laughed. "You want some jelly for that roll?"

"No, thank you. It's very good with the butter." Finishing the soup down to the last spoonful of broth, the roll to the last crumb, a grateful Caroline dabbed at her mouth with a napkin, and thanked the landlady. She couldn't remember when she'd eaten anything so good.

She suddenly remembered the rent cheque in her bag, already made out. Nurse Addison had shown her how.

Barely glancing at it, the landlady nodded and set it on the refrigerator. Then she got two brass keys from atop the counter and placed them in Caroline's hand. "This is the one for the front door," she said of the longer key. "The other one is the key to your room. You might want to put them on a key-ring so you don't lose them. We wouldn't want them to fall into the wrong hands, especially with a killer on the loose."

At the note of warning, Caroline heard the cab driver's ominous words: "…they both had dark hair and blue eyes. Like you, Miss."

***

The man walked past the alley again. At the corner, he turned and came back, like a moth to the flame. There was little to see in the aftermath of his handiwork, but the jackals were still hanging around, hungry for scraps of whatever juicy information that could get.

No one paid him any mind. Not even the woman clutching a camera who had pushed past him, muttering 'scuse me' on her way to the front of the dwindling crowd, leaving a flowery scent in her wake. What would she say if she knew he was the one the cops were looking for? He smiled inwardly.

Not that he had meant for things to turn out the way they did. He'd just wanted to talk to her, that was all. He wasn't the monster the papers said he was. He was a good person, a victim himself. Why couldn't she understand? It was her own fault she was lying on a stainless steel slab in the morgue right now.

But choosing her as the one who could make things right, was his mistake. Just like the girl before her was a mistake.

He would have to be more careful, look deeper into his selections before he revealed himself. Of course you couldn't always tell about a person until you got to spend time with them, and found out what they were really like.

Cruising a bar had been a dumb idea. His perfect woman wasn't likely to be hanging out in bars, was she? Though the girl in the bar had been beautiful to look at, he hadn't been mistaken about that. It was only when he had tried to talk to her that her ugliness had spewed out like vomit from that lovely mouth, contaminating the good intentions that had been in his heart.

The bitch deserved what she got.

A cop with lazy, black eyes moved through the crowd, telling people to go back to their homes. "Nothing more to see here, folks."

He moved on.

FIVE

Caroline followed the landlady upstairs and stood behind her as she opened the door to what was to be her room from now on. No need to share it with anyone. Though she could have. It was much larger than the room she and Ella had shared at Bayshore. A big, square room with brown linoleum on the floor, the walls painted a cream color half way up, and blue flowered wallpaper to the ceiling. It was a nice room. She could smell the new paint smell. Had Mrs. Bannister had it painted just for her?

Lace curtains hung on a tall window overlooking the street below. She remembered there'd been similar curtains in her parents' living room windows. She could still feel their starchy texture in her hand.

"Well, go on in, dear, make yourself to home," the landlady said with a smile. Inside, she gestured to the beige sofa flush against one wall. "This pulls out into a decent sized bed. The closet's small but more than big enough to accommodate what you got in your suitcase." She chuckled softly, opening the closet door so Caroline could look for herself. Wire hangers dangled along the bar. There was a shelf above it, on which were folded sheets and a blue blanket.

"It's fine, thank you. Yes, more than big enough."

"Sheets, pillow cases and a blanket on the top shelf," she said unnecessarily, before closing the closet door. "Well, I'll leave you to get settled. Like I said, Harold will bring up your suitcase when he gets home from work."

"Please tell him thank you."

"You can tell him yourself when you see him. I expect he'll knock at your door."

And then she was gone. Out of old habit, Caroline found herself listening for the turning of the key in the lock. But there was only the soft, uneven step of the landlady's feet as she descended the stairs.

Caroline eased the door open, looked out into the deserted hallway, her eye deliberately skipping past the door across the hall, and closed it again. She liked it that she could bolt her door from the inside.

You are the keeper of the key now, she told herself. Not the only one with a key, but it was enough. And even that fact didn't seem quite real.

There was only silence outside her door now. The landlady had gone inside her own flat.

As quietly as possible, lest someone realize she was a patient and needed to be locked up, Caroline slowly slid the bolt home, shutting herself in, and others out. Then she went to sit down on the sofa, folded her hands in her lap like a patient child and looked about her. Her own private place. No Ella Gaudet knitting imaginary clothes with her imaginary knitting needles for grandchildren who never came to visit.

Except for a quick visit to the facilities at the end of the hallway, trips taken while looking neither left nor right, ducking back into her room like a thief in the night, Caroline remained in her room for the rest of that day.

Once, returning from the washroom, she saw her suitcase outside the door and brought it inside and unpacked it, hanging her few items of clothing on the wire hangers. She put away her blouses, stockings and underclothes, in a dresser drawer.

For long periods of time, she sat on the sofa and tried to orient herself to her new life. Sometimes she wandered to the long window—a window without bars—and looked out through the part in the lace curtains, at people walking along the sidewalk. At the cars passing by. She had a flash of herself looking out of the window at Bayshore, at these houses, these people, of which she was now a part.

With the room still bright with daylight, she was able to hold her demons at bay and all things seemed possible. The doubt and fear did not begin to steal over her until the sun went down and shadows crept across the brown tiled floor. But fear can only hold you in its grip for so long, as it had held Caroline, and after awhile the tentacles loosened and Caroline rose from the sofa and opened it to its full double-bed size and made it up, taking down the extra warm blanket from the closet shelf. Changing into her long, white nightgown, she climbed between the cool sheets.

As tired as she was, in both mind and body, she lay wide-eyed in a bed that felt like a raft in a huge ocean, the sheets drawn up to her chin. As she stared at the ceiling her eye traced the stain that the longer she looked at it, the more it took on the shape of a menacing dog. Mercifully, as darkness deepened outside her window, its edges blurred becoming one with the rest of ceiling.

She wasn't in complete darkness, however, owing to the light from the utility pole out on the street, which sent its pale light into her room. She had imagined it would be a great relief not to have to share a room with Ella Gaudet, but right now she would have gladly welcomed the sound of Ella's snores emanating from her narrow bed across the room. Even her occasional ravings in the night would have offered comfort.

She hadn't really minded that Ella didn't talk, and that she spent much of her days knitting with her invisible needles, content within herself, needing nothing more from the world. She had not thought she would miss Ella, but here alone in this big, shadowy room, she learned she was quite wrong about that.

Here there were no screams in the night, no wailing or mad bursts of laughter traveling down corridors, finding her. But she had known their source and understood that these were lost people whose minds had simply turned on them. Here, the smallest sound above her head, or on the stairs outside her door, seemed amplified, threatening. Every creak and moan of the building settling. Every car that passed by down on the street seemed so loud, and when it began to rain their tires made a hissing sound on the pavement, as if a million snakes had been let loose.

The rain tapping at the window was almost pleasant at first, but now it took on a frenzied rattling sound as though someone was wanting in.

Slipping out of bed, she padded across the cool floor and checked that the window was still locked, even while knowing she was thinking nonsense thoughts. It was locked. Anyway, who could climb up here? The branches on the naked tree outside her window did not look strong enough to hold one of the landlady's cats.

She checked the door. Locked. Now she was rummaging in her purse to be sure her keys were still there, where she had put them. That she hadn't dreamed this whole day. A part of her was still listening for someone walking the hallway, jangling a ring of keys, like a taunt.

The quiet was something to get used to. Strangely enough, the jangling of those keys might have made her feel safer. Taken care of.

But only children should need to be taken care of, she chastened herself. Or the infirm. I am neither. I am a woman. A healthy woman with a future ahead of me, she thought, mentally parroting Doctor Rosen's words of encouragement. I can pay my own way in the world and come and go as I choose.

Doctor Rosen, a cherub-faced man with sad eyes, said it was natural to be afraid at first, but if she didn't give into the fear, if she went about her days with a brave face, the fear would go away after awhile. Was he right about that? It had seemed very right when she was sitting across from him in his office. She'd felt confident then. Fight those fears, Caroline," he'd said. "Rise above them and live your life as you deserve to. Don't let the world steal more from you than it already has."

"I'll try," she whispered into the semi-darkness of the room. I'll try.

SIX

Lynne Addison was also having trouble sleeping, while her husband Joe was lying on his side, away from her, snoring softly. She envied him. She couldn't rid herself of the memory of Caroline waving to her from the backseat of the cab. Of her ghostly face in the glass.

Many patients had come and gone in the years Lynne had been at Bayshore Mental Hospital, but only a handful stayed with her, haunted her. Caroline Hill was one of them. She'd seemed so lost when she left in the taxi, so vulnerable to the outside world, even though she'd been doing her level best to put on a brave face.

She'd been through a lot in her short years. Her parents tearing her away from a boy she loved like they had, and a few months later having her baby ripped from her arms, and all by the time she was seventeen. Caroline had told Lynne she'd held her little girl just long enough see run her fingertips over the blond peach fuzz on her perfect little head, see one tiny fist raised in the air, as if in protest. And then the woman from social services came into the room and scooped the newborn up in her arms, and Caroline never saw her again.

Caroline said the baby's cry reached back to her, from the hallway, sounding like the mewling of a lamb. How that sound must have tormented her, breaking her heart like shattering a piece of fragile china. So often, Lynne had heard her crying in the night, begging them to bring her baby back, always to be answered with a needle in the arm. And oblivion.

It was after that that she slipped into a deeper, darker place and remained there for a very long time. The primal wailing, the thrashing about, eventually grew silent, still. Her tears dried, she drifted through her days eating little, sleeping as long as we'd let her. Someone would finally come and raise her from the bed, wash her face, force food into her. Give her her meds. Sometimes that person was Lynne.

She didn't fight us. She took her medication without complaint. Sometimes the pills were a different color, or size, but she was too far out of it by then to notice.

Lynne had tried to get the dosage reduced, but was quickly put in her place by the doctor on staff at the time. She was just a nurse; he was the doctor, he reminded her. She was grateful when Doctor Rosen came on staff. Things began to change then.

Caroline said she barely remembered those days. They were a blur. Though she did have a vague recollection of her mother and father, he a stern-faced man and she a weepy woman in a black, veiled hat. An odd memory to have of one's parents. Lynne remembered them too, and Caroline's description was apt. Such sad people. Guilt-ridden, probably. And then one Sunday afternoon on their way to their regular Sunday visit with the daughter who was unresponsive to their efforts to touch her or talk to her, they were killed instantly in a head-on collision with a truck. At the time, the accident appeared to have little effect on Caroline, but of course it had to have had. At some level anyway. *What will happen when she opens that trunk?*

SEVEN

The knock on the door the next day had frightened her at first. Then a deep but young voice called through the door. "Miss Hill, it's Harold Bannister from downstairs. We've brought your trunk up."

She hesitated a heartbeat, then walked tentatively to the door, unlocked and opened it. She moved back by the window as the two men carried the trunk inside, scraping it lightly over the threshold. The sight of it was a blow to the heart. She wanted to tell them to take it away, please, she didn't want it, but they would just think she was crazy, so she remained silent.

"Where do you want it?" Harold asked, giving her a shy smile.

"Anywhere. Uh, right there, by the sofa is fine. Yes, yes, that's fine. Thank you."

Harold's helper was a taller, bigger man than Mrs. Bannister's nephew, unshaven, wearing a faded plaid shirt under his jacket. Older than Harold, she thought, as she averted her eyes from the trunk.

"We took the early lunch hour," Harold said, "so we could bring this up to you."

When the trunk was settled in place, she thanked them.

"Got to get back," the man with Harold said. "We'll be late."

She was about to thank him again, but he had already slipped out the door, and was on his way downstairs.

"That was Danny Babineau," Harold said. "He works with me at the bakery, rents a room a couple of blocks from here. He goes home to Petite Ridge on weekends. Lotta French people live there. Danny's French. I guess you know—from his name."

"Yes." She paused, then said, "I know a woman who's French, but I don't think she speaks it. Just English. Though she doesn't say much either way. Her name is Ella Gaudet."

She also once knew a French boy, and he spoke it beautifully, and English too, but she wouldn't talk of William, not to a stranger. It had had been a while since she thought of William, who, in a way, seemed like a dream from which she had finally woken.

She became aware of Harold standing there looking at her, nodding, waiting for more of the story. When none was forthcoming, they both directed their attention to the trunk as if it were a third person in the room and might have an opinion on the matter. No point in ignoring it; the trunk was here now. Familiar. Hard to look at, like looking into the eyes of your betrayer. Like Jesus must have felt when he looked into Judas' eyes. But she was being silly. The trunk was an inanimate object, incapable of thought or intent.

"It's a nice trunk," Harold said. "Got those fancy brass hinges."

"Yes, it belonged to my parents. They're gone now."

"Oh. I'm sorry."

"It's okay. It happened a long time ago." The trunk was their legacy to her, along with the money in her bank account. They intended you no harm. They did what they thought was right. Doctor Rosen's voice.

The trunk was black and flat-topped, with the brass hinges Harold had mentioned, and hasps and other bits of brass on the corners. They'd carried it in by two worn leather strap handles. She knew it was very old, once belonging to her mother's mother, Caroline, for whom she was named. She visualized the key in her purse that would open it. Pandora's Box came to mind.

"My parents are divorced, "Harold said, drawing her attention from the trunk. That's why I live with my aunt."

"She loves you a lot," Caroline said, surprising herself at her boldness. But she almost felt as if she knew him. "I could tell."

He reddened slightly and gave a shy smile, shrugging his shoulders as if to say she sometimes fussed over him, but nothing he could do about it.

She took notice of the tee-shirt he wore beneath the jacket, with John Lennon's likeness on the front. Harold looked a little like the murdered musician, with his rather long, pleasant face and glasses with their round frames. He had nice hair, thick and dark blond, parted in the middle. Like a poet, she fancied. Like John Lennon, she thought again. She probably looked odd to him, too. A mental case, living in his aunt's rooming house.

He was shy like her and she was made brave by his shyness.

"I knew you worked at the bakery. Your aunt told me. Do you like it there?"

"It's okay. Yeah, I like it, I guess."

"I used to be able to cook," she said. "When I was a girl. I've forgotten how though. Anyway," she laughed lightly, "I have to buy food. I don't have any."

"You can get stuff at the store. It's not far. I don't do no baking at work. I just help out, washing pots and pans, cleaning up and stuff. Sometimes they let me pour batter into the pans. I like doing that." He ran a hand across his chest, like it was dirty and he was wiping the dirt off on his shirt. The trunk probably was dirty; it had been locked away in some corner of a dusty old basement room at the hospital, for years.

Picture albums inside, Nurse Addison had said. Other things. She looked back at the young man. I don't want him to leave. I don't want to be here alone with the trunk. Maybe he would tell her about the place where she would be going to be washing dishes. The landlady said it was right across the street from The Bakery. What was it called? The name was written on a piece of paper in her purse. Frank's. Yes, that was it. Frank's. But before she could think of a question, he had his hand on the doorknob. "Well I gotta run. I gotta get back to work."

"Oh." She fought a moment's panic. "Okay. Well-- thank you again."

And then he was gone. She hadn't known how to stop him. So much in her life she hadn't known how to stop.

She turned her back to it and looked out the window. A woman was walking past the building pushing a dark blue baby carriage, puffs of pink satin peaking out around the edges. She had a memory flash of her own baby daughter, who would turn nine in July.

Does she know about me? she wondered. Know that I exist? But then, who would be cruel enough to tell her about a mother who spent all those years in a mental institution? No. Best she didn't know. But that did not lessen the sense of loss that never left her. That had left a hole in heart.

Feeling a need to breathe in fresh air, Caroline tried to raise the window. It struck at first, then creaked upward, letting in the smell of rain. The mist was cool on her skin.

She had resisted taking a pill last night. She needed to stay alert in this new and strange place. She had lain awake a long time when she heard someone playing the piano. Raising herself up on one elbow, she listened to the notes raining softly down on her through her ceiling. It was not a tune she recognized, but the melody had a haunting quality that reached deep inside her. It sounded far better than when Mrs. Green played in the big hall. In a way it was almost like listening to Billie Holiday sing. She knew it had to be the piano teacher Mrs. Bannister had mentioned to her. Apparently, he hadn't been able to sleep either.

As she stood in the window, the woman pushing the carriage had moved out of sight, and a fair-haired man in a tan trench coat emerged from the building and proceeded down the rain-slicked street, in the opposite direction. Was he the piano teacher? Had it been his hands that produced the lovely music that swept through her like lovely entwining, ribbons of sound, and soon lulled her to sleep? She had not heard him pass by her door, or go down the stairs. Maybe he's on his way to lunch, she thought, and the thought made her realize she was hungry. At the hospital, she would already have eaten her breakfast in the dining room with the others. It would be lunchtime. Yes, Harold Bannister and his friend had been on their lunch break.

She glanced over her shoulder at the toaster sitting on a four-shelf metal table in the corner. Her mother's toaster had been the kind where you toasted the bread on one side, then had to turn the bread to toast the other side. The one at the hospital could cook four pieces at a time. This one looked like it worked the same way, though two pieces at a time. Not that it mattered since she had no bread.

You will have to buy some. You will go into a store and ask the person behind the counter for what you want. Harold had said it wasn't far. Yes, she had the money to pay for food, in her purse.

Closing the window, Caroline gave a closer examination of the furniture in her room- her bed, a dresser and nightstand, across the room, a wooden table flanked by two chairs. There was a small refrigerator and alongside the window, a tiny-white painted cupboard.

She opened the doors. Inside, standing upright inside a crockery mug were two forks, two knives and two spoons. On the lower shelf were two cups and saucers, two bowls, two plates— two of everything, like Noah's Ark.

Maybe she would have a visitor. Mrs. Bannister said she didn't mind her tenants having visitors as long as they were out by eleven o'clock. Maybe Martha could come for a visit some time.

No, they wouldn't allow that. They wouldn't let someone out who had killed a person, would they?

Not even if they had a very good reason.

Yesterday she'd worn her pretty blue suit, but today she would put on the raincoat she'd hung in the closet, the one she'd always worn when she went out in the yard in wet weather. It was olive green and baggy on her, but it would keep her dry if it rained again. And it might, from the look of the sky.

The piano man, as she'd come to think of him, (though that might not have been him) had worn a raincoat. A tan raincoat that fit his tall, slender body nicely. She imagined a tailor fitting him for the coat like they did in the movies.

As she buttoned the coat over her brown slacks and white sweater, she tried to remember where she'd gotten the coat. Probably someone donated it, as they often donated clothes, as they had her suit, and she got it because it fit her best. But she couldn't be sure. She'd had it for a long time.

She took the twenty dollar bills from her purse and counted them again, felt their crispness between her fingers, their promise of security. Four bills now, since she'd paid the cab driver, plus a five and some change. Slipping them back into her wallet, she left the room, locking the door after her.

She put the key back in her new blue bag and zipped it closed. The purse didn't really go with her coat. She might have been locked up a long time but she knew blue didn't really go with olive green. But it was the only purse she had.

As she stood outside her door, her heart began to thud in her ears and her breathing quickly became shallow. She wanted to run back inside the room and lock herself in. She swallowed hard, her hand moving to her throat.

No, you can't do that. Slow, deep breaths, the way Nurse Addison showed you. That works for you. What are you, an animal, trading one den for another? Cowering, afraid of shadows? No, she wouldn't be afraid. She wouldn't.

Only then did she realize her back was pressed against the wall, and she made herself move away from it, take a forward step. Letting out a long, shaky breath, she inched toward the stairway.

The stairs stretched down and down, impossible to reach the bottom, like looking through the wrong end of a telescope. Like stairs in a nightmare.

She froze there at the top, unable to lower one foot onto the step, her breath trapped in her throat.

Why did the hallway seem so much darker than yesterday when the landlady was with her? The realization of the door across the hall, behind which the murdered actress had lived not so long ago, crept over her on spider legs. Unable to resist its pull, her gaze involuntarily went there. She looked quickly away. Considered her dilemma. You can't stand here all day.

Even as it appeared she might, she became aware of the faint smell of pine oil, which reminded her of the cleaning solution they used to clean the floors at the hospital, and this bit of familiarity allowed her to grip the railing and set one foot out over the step which seemed a long reach, suspend it there.

Step down. Just put your foot down on the step. It is not as far away as it looks to you.

Suddenly, above her—a footfall. And another. Step…step…step …behind her.

Coming closer.

She lowered her trembling foot, feeling as if she was about to step out of an airplane into emptiness. Not daring to look behind her, catapulted by sheer terror, Caroline flew down the stairs. She hit the foyer just as Mrs. Bannister came out of her flat, dressed for outdoors in a black coat, and small forest-green hat with a little feather in front, and holding a closed, black umbrella. She turned to look at Caroline, one eyebrow raised in surprise.

"Hello, dear. My, you're all out of breath. I would have thought it was Harold bounding down those stairs if I didn't know he was away at work. You want to be careful running on those stairs; the tenants don't always wipe their feet and they can be slippery when wet. You could take a nasty spill and we wouldn't want the two of us hobbling around, now would we?" She chuckled.

"No, I will. I mean, I won't run...I just...I'm sorry..." Caroline jerked her head around at a footfall behind her.

Mrs. Bannister looked past Caroline's shoulder and smiled. "Good day, Mr. Mason. Taking your constitutional, are you?"

"Something like that, Mrs. Bannister." He smiled at Caroline and held the door for both of them. A pleasant man in a raincoat, more rumpled than hers, like Columbo's. Unlike the detective, one of his sleeves was empty and folded back. No one to fear. How foolish she was.

"Terrible thing about that nice Miss Winters," the landlady was saying, as she preceded Caroline through the door and out into the cool, gray day. "We're not safe in our beds anymore." To Caroline, she said, "I told you about it, dear. She used to live across the hall from you. She was an actress. Small parts, but she had big dreams. That's the second murder in a few weeks, Mr. Mason. The first one was a nurse, wasn't she? Walkin' home from her shift when he grabbed her, poor thing. Oh, by the by, this is your downstairs neighbor, Miss Hill. Just moved in."

He nodded and smiled at Caroline, a man of average size, receding hairline, clearly having no idea he'd frightened her.

"I believe you're right, Mrs. Bannister. Yes, I do remember Miss Winters very well. Lovely girl. Tragic. Of course they don't know yet that the two murders are connected. Anyway, I do hope they find whoever did this terrible thing."

They were standing on the sidewalk now, Caroline with her hands folded in front of her, like a child on the first day of school. When she became aware of it, she dropped her hands discretely to her sides.

"We can only pray." The landlady shook her head in dismay. "Her poor body found in an alley, not a block from here."

After a few more words were exchanged between the two, Mr. Mason bid them both good day and went on his way, a thoughtful expression on his face.

When he was out of earshot, the landlady said, "Poor man came back from Vietnam with an arm missing, and found his wife living with someone else. He's been here ever since, four years now. So where you are headed in such a big hurry this morning?"

"I need to buy food."

Everyone in the building knows about me, Caroline thought. They know where I've been. Did she know about them taking my baby? Did she know everything?

They were walking now, Mrs. Bannister with her fast, awkward gait, Caroline keeping pace with her. Though she was wearing a sweater under her coat, the cold damp air reached inside.

Everything looked so big. The street, the buildings, the gray sky, no fences or boundaries. She felt small and vulnerable, and was glad to be walking alongside her landlady and not by herself. I just need some time, she thought, mentally parroting Nurse Addison's own words to her: "Everything will seem big and strange at first."

She remembered feeling the same way when she was a little girl lying in the grass and gazing up into the vast blueness. After a few minutes, she would get that panicky feeling in her stomach, like she had now, as if she might just get swallowed up in all that blueness, and she would scramble to her feet.

"I think the rain has stopped for the day, but I brought the umbrella just in case. Better to be safe than sorry. By the way," she said, turning to smile at Caroline. "I just bought myself a bigger television set, so I've got one to put in your room, if you want it. Do you enjoy TV?"

"Oh, I do, yes. I like watching television. Thank you."

"Great. It's just a fourteen-inch, a Philco, but it's color and works fine. Did you sleep well your first night here?"

"Yes," she lied. The lie came easy.

Should she have told her the truth, that she'd felt afraid lying alone in the strange bed, listening to unfamiliar sounds outside her window, other noises throughout the building.

She let the lie stay. She didn't want the landlady to think her troublesome.

Mrs. Bannister was chatting away as they walked, divulging personal information about another of her tenants, happily and without malice. She was a nice and generous lady, just didn't keep secrets very well.

Caroline saw the yellow police tape even before she saw the small group of people gathered on the sidewalk, near the alley. A police cruiser was parked at an angle on the street, the door flung open. She could hear a squawking voice coming from the car radio, although there was no one to hear except passersby like herself and Mrs. Bannister.

A little ways past the cruiser, a small red car was being towed away.

"Most of the mob is thinned out now," the landlady said, slowing her step as they neared the alley. "You should have seen them yesterday—packed in like sardines, they were, craning their necks like starved giraffes." This comment was made as she herself peered into the alley, a deep dark well, even in daylight, between the two buildings.

"The cops had to force the crowd back," the landlady said, picking up her pace again as they passed on by the alley. "Wanting to get a look at that poor dead girl. Can you imagine?"

Yes, she could imagine. "We passed here yesterday in the taxi," Caroline said. "The driver told me what happened. I didn't know then that the woman who was killed used to live in your building." *Didn't know she had dark hair and blue eyes.*

"No, how could you? But that was a while ago and it's got nothing to do with you or my building. But I admit it's pretty unnerving. Well, here's where you'll be working come next Monday. Frank's. You wanna go in for a bite to eat?"

Caroline looked up at the red and white awning that bore the name FRANK'S in gothic scroll. The restaurant looked warm and inviting, but though she was hungry and the smell of good food and coffee wafted out to her, a new panic gripped her.

Monday. I'll be ready Monday.

"No, thank you, Mrs. Bannister." She moved on past the restaurant. "I'd just like to get some bread and tea and then I'll go home. Maybe I could watch some TV later."

The landlady laughed, and said, "Sure, I'll get Harold to carry it up. Speaking of Harold, there he is now. He's off for lunch. I'll give him the key to your room and he can take that TV upstairs and it'll be all set up when we get back."

"That's okay. He can just leave it outside the door."

She was looking across the street where Harold Bannister was unlocking his bike from the post in front of the bakery, and didn't see the displeasure on the landlady's face at her suggestion that her nephew leave the TV in the hallway.

Harold gave them a half-wave, then dropped his head as if embarrassed at seeing them here, so close to his workplace. He was dressed in a black hooded shirt, jeans and sneakers. Others were coming out of the place where he worked. Three girls, arm in arm, laughing together. She looked up at the dark green and gold sign on the faded red brick building that spelled out BIG BAKERY.

He was about to jump on his bike and Caroline saw that Mrs. Bannister was about to wave him over. "No, please, I don't want anyone else to have my key."

The woman's mouth tightened and the warmth went out of her eyes, like a light suddenly switched off.

"I have the key to your room, dear. I own the house."

"I know, but…"

"Harold is my nephew and he's a fine boy. What reason would you have not to trust him? I doubt you have anything so valuable he would want to steal it."

She'd offended her. She hadn't meant to. Hadn't meant to make her angry.

EIGHT

Out on the sidewalk, most of the onlookers had moved on, but the damage had been done, making a thorough investigation of the crime area difficult. Shoeprints over shoeprints, rubberneckers wanting to get a look, at the same time afraid of what they might see.

Yesterday, they had cordoned off the area with crime tape, then waited around until the body was zipped into a body bag and driven off to the morgue before leaving. No sirens, no speed, no reason for urgency.

He emerged from the alley, pretty certain she didn't die here. But before Detective Thomas O'Neal could get to the cruiser, a familiar looking glamour-puss blond from the local TV station shoved a microphone in his face.

"I'm hearing there's a similar pattern between how this girl met her fate and the nurse who was murdered in late August. Can you comment, Detective O'Neal?"

He paused long enough tell her he didn't know who her sources were, but that they were being premature, speculating. The investigation was hardly underway. "When I have more details to offer the public, I'll release them." Until then, he had no further comment. He pushed past her, as pleasantly as he could manage, ignoring the next question she threw at him. "Was she sexually assaulted, Detective?"

***

There is always a chill in the morgue, and that faint smell of death and formaldehyde permeating the air, that most cops never got used to. Detective O'Neal was no exception.

The alley had reeked of urine. O'Neal knew bums and drunks coming out of the bar down the street used it as a public toilet, evidenced by the dark yellow stains he saw running down the side of the building. She deserved a better resting place.

Even this was an improvement.

Her dark hair had fallen to one side of the slab she lay on. A clot of blood had dried at the corner of her mouth. Her face was bruised and swollen, eyes near shut, slits of dead blue showing.

Just as she'd looked back in that alley. Except she'd been fully dressed then, in a green paisley blouse and black slacks that looked expensive to Detective Tom O'Neal. Her white wool jacket was smeared with blood. She'd worn black stiletto sandals with those thin straps that flatter a woman's leg. Not that she'd needed any help. Beautiful woman when she was alive. Damn shame.

Her blouse had been buttoned unevenly, signaling to the detective that someone else had dressed her, probably after she was dead. Her hair was matted with blood, lifeless blue eyes staring blankly up at the strip of azure sky visible above the alley where she lay. There were blood spots in her eyes, evidence of strangulation, borne out by the bruises on her neck, no doubt made by the killer's thumbs.

St. Simeon was a quiet town, and Detective O'Neal liked it that way. Murder, especially one as brutal as this one, was rare here. Most crimes consisted of drunken driving and the occasional domestic. A couple of years ago there'd been a knifing at Dreagan's bar, but that was it.

"I'd say she was there maybe...five, six hours," Henry Beal, the medical examiner said in answer to his question. "We had partial rigor when we brought her in," he answered. He mimed covering the girl's face with the sheet, eyebrow raised in a question, and Tom nodded in the affirmative. Was relieved when he couldn't see her face any longer, only the telling shape beneath the sheet.

Henry Beal was a slight man with thick glasses, thinning brown hair. He was also a black belt in Karate, and had the deep voice of a radio announcer, which, each time he spoke, never failed to surprise Tom.

They'd searched the alley for clues, came up empty. A few

cigarette butts were bagged, but the alley was off a public street and they could belong to anyone. Her purse lay beside her, black, oversized, no money, but credit cards still in the wallet, along with her ID and a small black notebook.

On the first page of the notebook, at the top of the page, she'd neatly written her name, Lorraine Winters, and her address and phone number, which she'd presumably crossed out later and put her new address and phone number underneath. The pages following had the names and phones numbers of acting agents, friends. His partner, Detective Glen Aiken was back at the station, already going through that list with a fine-tooth comb, making phone calls, setting up interviews

They'd check out both addresses. One was on Peel, a quiet street. He thought he knew it, a rooming house, a few scraggly elms in front. The new address was a little more uptown, maybe something a little nicer, more fitting for a budding actress.

The M.E. had returned the body to its stainless steel locker, was peeling off his latex gloves. Tom thanked him for his help and left, eager to breathe in some fresh air.

NINE

Caroline knew she had insulted someone Mrs. Bannister loved dearly, but she didn't know what to say to make everything okay again. Could think of no words to dissolve the anger on the woman's face.

They continued walking in silence. Caroline felt like a child unfairly chastised for some wrongdoing. For she knew she had done nothing wrong. Knew she was within her rights as a tenant. Nurse Addison had spent a lot of time talking to her those last few days, forewarning her, telling her what to expect.

"He's a good boy, Caroline."

"I know, Mrs. Bannister. I'm sorry." She really didn't know. She didn't know him at all.

"You're not still worried because Lorraine Winters once lived across the hall from you, are you?"

"No." It gave her a strange feeling thinking of the woman who lived there, and she was sad about what happened to her. But it didn't frighten her.

It was not the first time violent death had touched Caroline. She remembered a roommate at the hospital, a young girl who slashed her wrists with a shard of broken glass. Caroline had just come back from lunch and found her on the floor, tears still drying on her ashen cheeks. There'd been blood on the sheets, the walls and the floor. Even after they cleaned it up, some of the stains were still visible.

Caroline knew it could just as easily have been her lying there. For as much as she didn't want to die, she hadn't known how to live. She had tried hard to crawl out of that deep hole, again and again, but the sides were slick and treacherous and she would slide back down into its depths, and darkness would once more claim her. She would not have made it out without Dr. Rosen's help. Or without Nurse Addison's friendship.

I don't want to go back to that awful place in my mind, ever. I want to stay strong.

Anyway, this was not about self-inflicted death. It was about murder.

"Don't look so worried, dear," her landlady said beside her. "I think you're being a little paranoid, but never mind. We'll wait till you're back home and then Harold can bring TV up then, if that'll make you feel better."

"Thank you. I like Harold," she said quickly, grasping onto this olive leaf offered her. "He's very nice. And he's kind." But she didn't change her mind about him going into her room when she wasn't there.

"People can turn on a dime," Martha used to say. "Only God can really know what's in someone's heart."

"Yes, he is," the landlady said. "But you're right. You pay your rent, you're entitled to your privacy."

It was exactly what Nurse Addison had told her.

She suddenly felt proud of herself that she hadn't gone against her own rules just to please someone, that she had stuck up for herself. But at the same time, she didn't want to lose favor with her landlady. She'd call Nurse Addison and ask her what she thought about it. She'd seen a pay phone next to a dry cleaning shop, not far from the restaurant where she would be going to work.

Would she be annoyed if I called her at the hospital? She didn't say it was okay to call but that was only because she believed I was ready to live life on my own and make my own decisions. Wasn't it?

She glanced at the landlady and saw the stiffness still there in her face as they walked along the sidewalk, Mrs. Bannister limping heavily beside her. She had promised her the TV, and they were shopping together like friends. But Caroline felt alone.

You were always alone. It's not so different now. Dr. Rosen and Nurse Addison have their own lives, their own families. You were just their patient. Nothing more. They were nice, but you couldn't take advantage of people just because they were kind to you.

Anyway, Nurse Addison might not even be there now. The hospital was closing down and soon no one would be there, no one to answer the phones. And finally not even any phones, no furniture, just an abandoned building, filled with echoes of lost souls.

What will happen to Martha?

The landlady turned and smiled at her, but it was a stingy smile. She's different now.

"Let's go in here, Caroline, I need some stockings."

The name *Natalie's Boutique* was etched in lavender on a sign hanging above the door. A little bell rang as they stepped inside.

A pretty woman with hair like cotton candy was draping lovely silk print scarves on hooks on what looked like a hall tree, by the counter. She smiled brightly at them, a smile that lifted Caroline's spirits. The shop was warm and cheery, and smelled nice.

TEN

The vision of the woman imprinted on his mind, he was trembling when he returned to home. Her gentle lovely face, dark hair, and blue eyes. It was her. She was the one. He knew it as soon as he saw her. Not like the others at all. They were mistakes.

Buddy, which was his secret name given him by his spirit father, crossed the linoleum floor and stood before the full-length closet mirror, studying his reflection in the glass, searching his eyes for some flicker of recognition.

Gradually, the room faded from view, and he was back in his old room, the room of his boyhood. As the years swept backward through the corridor of time, he now saw only a young boy in the glass, the boy he had been. A timid, needy boy, anxious, never knowing what would happen next, a ready flinch on his face. He was blond, small for his age.

Always eager to please his mother, and now and then he had succeeded. But she couldn't be trusted or counted on. Sometimes she'd be nice to him and he would dare to hope. But then she would disappear into a bottle of Vodka or a new lover and he would be nothing again. Only an irritant, someone in her way. She had a quick hand and he felt the sting of it often. He would try to stay out of range, and sometimes he managed it. But not always.

It wasn't just me she punished. Millie, too. Millie was only three years old. He could still hear her panicked screams coming from the bathroom, hear his mother's voice... "damn you, your little bitch, I told you if you wet the bed again... didn't I tell you? Didn't I...DIDN'T I...?"

"...No, please, mommy, no..." Millie want get out of tub..." more screams, struggle, the water splashing, awful sounds as some body part struck against the tub...her head, a small foot...

Buddy clapped his hands over his ears.

When at last he took them away the house was silent.

He never saw Millie again. Millie, who had followed him about the house, smiling sweetly, blond curls bobbing as she ran to hug his leg, looking adoringly up at her big brother. She had loved him, and he her. His mother had taken away that love. Had crushed it. Crushed him.

And then for a second time.

He went through a series of uncles his mother ordered him to 'be nice to'. A couple of them beat the hell out of him; one or two ignored him. And one raped him. He was eight years old at the time. The man threw him face-down on the bed, his big rough hand pressing down on the back of his head, pushing his face into the blue and white striped mattress. Its sour taste and smell was still in his mouth and nose and throat. He could smell it now, taste it, like filthy socks jammed into his mouth. His small body felt like it was being torn apart, and he screamed out in pain, but the man just drove his face deeper into the mattress, smothering his cries. Not that anyone would have heard him; his mother was passed out in the other bedroom. When he was sure he was going to die from the pain, for want of breath, the man gave a guttural groan, then got up off him and told him if he ever told anyone, he'd come back and kill both him and his mother.

He buried the bloody sheet and his small stained shorts in the backyard so no one would ever know his shame.

And then one day Uncle Earl entered his life—big, gruff, fun Uncle Earl Parker who played the guitar and sang country songs, ruffled his hair, and said with a grin, "Hey, Buddy, how you doin'?"

He made Buddy ham and eggs and sat across from and asked about school and what he thought about things. Leave the kid alone, he'd say, when his mother was about to backhand him.

He said I was a good kid. He loved me. He cared. I know he did.

Buddy thought he had died and gone to Heaven when Earl lived with them. But it was not to last.

"She sent him away," he told the boy in the mirror. She took away love.

He would get it back though. He had always dreamed of having a father who loved him, and Earl Parker gave reality to the dream. His mother would stop drinking and she and Earl would get married. They would be a real family. A normal family.

For a brief time, he had felt safe and protected.

The dream was shattered when one day he arrived home from school to find Earl and his guitar, gone, the closet emptied of his clothes. His mother said he just took off, but Buddy knew better. Hs mother had sent him away. He hated her.

He waited and waited for Earl to come back to him, but he never did. Buddy checked the mailbox every day for a letter, but none ever came. He suspected that his mother tore them up and burned the pieces, or maybe flushed them down the toilet.

But none of that mattered now. Everything would be the way he had always dreamed. He would find Earl very soon. He knew Earl would welcome him with open arms, would be so glad to see him again. Buddy never knew his biological father, but he didn't care about him. Earl was his real father, his father in spirit. That was what was important.

Gradually, the face of the boy in the glass darkened, and akin to a photo aging, the features broadened, the smooth skin coarsening until it morphed into the man the boy had become, who looked back at him. Something forever changed behind the eyes. Even Buddy could see that.

He turned from the mirror. He didn't like looking at himself for long.

He hadn't meant to kill that girl. Not at first. It was her own fault. He had only wanted to talk to her.

The phone was ringing. Fully present now, the dead woman another mistake he'd erased, he picked up the receiver. It was his boss calling; he had to go in to work.

ELEVEN

It was lovely to sit on the sofa and watch her own television, (not have to worry about someone changing channels in the middle of a program she was watching) and sipping tea she had made herself, from a real china cup. Even if the cup did have a chip at its rim. She bit off a corner of toast she had made in the toaster, spread with Kraft strawberry jam.

Pleasant to sit here warm and cozy in her new soft, yellow pile robe she had purchased when she was out shopping with Mrs. Bannister. While the landlady purchased her stockings, Caroline had spotted the robe on a rack, only $14.99 on sale. Even the color made her feel warm, like being wrapped in sunshine. She had been hesitant to spend the money but the landlady, who had stopped being mad at her by then, (or at least it seemed so) told her she deserved something new and special to celebrate her new life. On a whim, maybe because she was so relieved the landlady wasn't mad at her anymore, she bought it, and also bought two pretty blue cushions for the sofa.

Cozy in her robe, she brought the thin, china cup to her lips, avoiding the chipped side. The commercial for Tide Laundry soap ended, and the game show came back on. At the same moment, there was a knock at the door and her first thought was that she had shouted out the answers of some of the questions and disturbed a neighbor. She'd all but decided she hadn't when a male voice called through the door: "Miss Hill? This is the police. We'd like to talk to you, please, ma'am."

She stood at once, rattling the cup in its saucer, near spilling her tea. She set them carefully down on the coffee table.

The police? What would the police want with her? Her back turned to the handsome game show host, she wondered what had she done to bring the police to her door? Then she recalled the landlady's pursed mouth, the anger in her eyes as they walked along the sidewalk. Maybe Mrs. Bannister had only pretended to be friendly with her again. Did she call the hospital to complain as soon as we got home? Am I being sent to live somewhere else?

Absently, Caroline stood there in the middle of the floor finishing off the toast, chewing fitfully, as if it might be her last meal in this room. Swallowing the lump of toast, she finally crossed the room and opened the door a crack. "Yes," she said, eyeing the two policemen who stood in her doorway.

They were in suits and topcoats, one with graying hair and shrewd eyes. Square-jawed, just beginning to slacken. But still a nice looking man. The younger of the two was stocky and shorter with a bushy gingery-colored mustache, like a man in a cartoon. He looked like he might be someone's nice brother. She'd always thought it would be lovely to have a brother. Someone there for you, to take up your battles if you needed him to. To be in your corner. The Gingery man seemed that sort of person. But you couldn't always tell about people.

"May we come in, Miss Hill?" the older man said.

Since they didn't have uniforms on, how could she know for sure that they were policemen?

"Could I see some identification, please," she said in her new confident voice. She had heard people say this on TV programs.

They politely showed her their badges, not just flashing them like they did on those cops' shows, but holding them out long enough for her to examine their photos and read their names.

I'm Detective Tom O'Neal," the older policeman said. "This is my partner, Detective Aiken. We'd just like to ask you a few questions, Ma'am. Could we come inside, please?"

At Bayshore, people just came into your room if they wanted to and left the same way. No one ever asked her permission. Not for anything. But this was her own room, she reminded herself. Paid for with her own money. So she didn't need to let them in if she chose not to. Just like she hadn't needed to let Harold in.

"No, thank you," she said.

Detective O'Neal said nothing, just looked surprised. The

gingery man stifled a grin at this partner, and Caroline wondered what she had said that was funny. Was he laughing at her? The blood rose hot to her cheeks.

"I would prefer that you didn't come into my room if that's all right."

She saw the exchange of looks between them, fleeting. But she had grown adept over the years at catching nuances of people's expressions and could tell the two policemen weren't used to being told what they could and could not do.

She was relieved when the gray-haired policeman, who seemed the leader of the two, shrugged good-naturedly and said that that was fine with him. Either of them could have said 'No, it isn't all right,' and she thought she might have opened the door wider to let them in. She sensed they knew that, too, but decided to give her her way.

"Thank you," she said. It couldn't be about her, they would have come inside, taken her away in handcuffs if they had wanted to.

"No problem," the gingery man said. "We don't mean to upset you, Ma'am, but a woman who used to live in this building was murdered on Saturday night. We realize she wasn't living here at the time of the murder, but we're talking to everyone in the building. We wondered if you might have known her."

"Her name was Lorraine Winters," Detective O'Neal said. His eyes had softened. They were light brown, the color of the tea she'd been drinking when they knocked on her door. It wasn't about her. She had done nothing wrong. She wasn't being sent away.

"No, I didn't. I just moved here. But I know about her. We passed the alley where—he put her." The woman had been killed elsewhere, dumped there, said the newsman on TV.

"She lived there," she said, pointing at the dark maroon door across the hall. "Right there."

They glanced at the door, nodded.

"We?" Detective Aiken said. "You said we. You and someone else walked past the alley?"

"Mrs. Bannister and I. I saw the yellow tape, and the police cars. There were people on the sidewalk. A red car was being towed away. That was hers, wasn't it? You should talk to Mrs. Bannister. She knew her. She was her landlady. Just like she's mine. Mr. Mason knew her too. He lives upstairs."

She remembered looking in the alley, imagining the dead girl in there. It had made her think of her roommate who had slit her wrists. But she'd made that decision for herself. Though it wasn't her fault, how much worse it must be to have someone else take your life away. Lorraine Winters had been an actress and had had dreams for herself.

"We will," Detective O'Neal said, and Caroline knew then that they had already spoken with the landlady, and she had told them about her. Told them she used to be a mental patient. That would make Caroline a suspicious character. But Mrs. Bannister had done right to tell them about her tenants' history. They were trying to find a murderer, after all.

"We were shopping for things," she said, the words suddenly too loud, tumbling from her as if of their own volition. She softened her tone. "Groceries, stockings …other things. I bought this robe." Her voice trailed off. Why had she told them that? She sounded crazy. Even at the thought, she involuntarily ran a hand down the front of the soft material, unaware that she had, and smiled like a child. And felt a terrible helplessness. It was just that it was the first thing she'd worn in years that someone else hadn't worn first, and she loved it.

After a brief silence, the gingery man said in a brotherly voice, "It's very pretty with your dark hair. Looks comfy and warm as can be."

"Yes, it is." She was behaving inappropriately. In an effort to steer the conversation away from herself, she said, "The lady who was killed was an actress, wasn't she? I don't believe I ever saw her on TV. No one's moved in yet, but I think I heard someone in there."

"Oh?" Detective O'Neal raised an eyebrow. "When was that?"

"I don't know." He wasn't thinking of her yellow robe anymore. Or her dark hair. "Yesterday, maybe. Do you think you'll catch the bad man who killed her?"

"How do you know it was a man, Miss Hill?" Detective Aiken asked.

"It's almost always a man, isn't it? Maybe her boyfriend. I saw a TV show once where the boyfriend did it, except he poisoned her. But not all at once. It took a long time for her to die."

Neither policeman said anything, but she saw in their eyes that the actress didn't die right away either, and knowing made her feel sad. "Another woman was murdered too. A nurse. It might be a serial killer. Do you think it was?"

"That's what we're trying to find out, Miss," Detective O'Neal said. Then he thanked her for her help and handed her a card. "If you think of anything that might be useful, give us a call."

Back inside her room, the door locked behind her, she sat back down on the sofa. Her tea was cold. The credits were rolling on her game show over the applause of the audience. Restless and anxious, she got up again, paced. What could she possibly tell them? She set the card on the dresser. She didn't know the woman. Had only just moved here. And yet she felt she had already said too much. She had prattled on like a magpie? She wrung her hands. Why was she like this? Why couldn't she act like a normal person?

The question pulled her gaze to the trunk that sat on the floor by the sofa, still locked.

Detective Aiken stopped on the stairs to jot down some notes in his notebook, and O'Neal halted his own step to wait for him. Not one to rely on memory, his partner was a copious note taker. Not just facts, statements, but his impressions, thoughts. Reminders.

When they reached the bottom of the stairs, the landlady was waiting for them.

"I told you she wouldn't know anything. How could she? She just moved in on Monday. You two probably scared the wits out of her."

Ignoring her comments, Detective O'Neal asked to see inside Lorraine Winter's old room.

"I don't see the point; she hasn't lived here in weeks. But okay."

"Anyone in there?" Detective Aiken asked, as they followed

the labored, uneven step of the landlady up the stairs. "We can let ourselves in no problem," Glen said, behind her, concern in his voice.

"No, I'm fine, Detective. Still under my own steam. Such as it is." The keys dangled from her left hand, the other clutching the banister. "What are you looking for anyway?"

"Not sure. Anyone been in there lately?"

"Sure. The cleaner. Also hired a fellow from the homeless shelter come paint and lay some tile. Did a nice job, too. Got the place rented to an older lady."

As they passed Caroline's door," she said, "I suppose she told you she heard someone in there."

Caroline had heard them coming back upstairs, and now hearing the trace of irritation in the landlady's voice, she backed away from the door.

***

Driving back to the station. Detective Aiken got stuck behind a green Honda Civic, and now moved at a snail's pace because the woman driver had spotted a cop's car behind her. At the first opportunity, he took a left down a side street, so she could breathe again and they could get back to the station sometime today.

"Hope that Hill woman is wrong about it being a serial killer," Glen said beside him.

"Yeah, me, too. She was just repeating what she heard, of course. But the public buys it. Still, two murders don't necessarily add up to a serial killer."

Two in our jurisdiction, he corrected himself mentally. The nurse's body was also found in an alley, one wider with grassy patches, near an elementary school. It was around midnight when the girl's mother reported her missing, and the following morning some kids on their way to school spotted her in there. Freaked them out, no surprise there. The nurse had been walking, on her way home. No car. She'd died where he'd dragged her. No one saw anything. Late at night, quiet street. Different circumstances.

They'd questioned everyone close to her, the boyfriend being at the top of the list. He had an ironclad alibi. So far, nothing.

Serial killer?

He didn't really want to go there. Such cases were almost impossible to solve; the guy could go on for years and remain invisible. Just an ordinary looking man, someone's neighbor. 'He was always so nice,' the neighbor would invariably say ten years from now, 'If you needed anything, he'd be right there.' Or he could be a transient, staying a month or two in one place, moving on.

"What did you think of Caroline Hill?" Detective Aiken asked. "Think she knew anything?"

"No. Like her landlady said, why would she? But we needed to talk to her anyway. Eliminate any possibility. You never know. Winters could have visited someone at Bayshore Mental Hospital. Someone who had a connection to the killer. Maybe the killer himself. Though they'd gone through the list of recently released patients and no one grabbed his attention.

"Pretty woman," he said of Caroline Hill. "A little vague."

"I didn't see vague," Glen said. "Anxious, maybe. Wary. Who could blame her?"

***

Caroline sat on the sofa with her hands folded in her lap, fretting about the landlady being mad at her again.

In a little while she heard someone overhead playing the piano. Awkward, hesitant notes. Not the piano player. And she remembered that he gave lessons. She thought it would be lovely to be able to play the piano.

At a knock on the door, she jumped up from the sofa

"Caroline, could I talk to you please."

The landlady.

TWELVE

On Monday morning, Caroline rose two hours early for work, took a quick bath in the big apple-green painted claw-foot tub at the end of the hall, and dressed in a navy skirt and white blouse. In spite of her nerves, resulting from both fear and excitement, she managed to get down a cup of tea and a slice of toast.

It was a fifteen-minute walk to work and she used the time to work on her nerves. The day was sunny and bright, which also helped. She'd do fine. It was just a dishwashing job and she knew how to do that, for Heaven's sake. Her step became almost light as she drew nearer her new place of employment.

Yet, at the door, she had to take a couple of deep breaths and let them out slowly, before she could bring herself to open the door and walk into the warmth and cheery sounds of the restaurant. Enticing smells filled her senses—eggs, bacon, and toast, blending in with the aroma of rich coffee. Unlike before, when she'd stood outside the door with Mrs. Bannister, Caroline wasn't hungry, only anxious.

The place was a hive of conversation, laughter, the clattering of cutlery. In the background, Helen Ready sang *I am Woman*.

Caroline straightened her shoulders, and looking neither left nor right, made her way down the aisle past occupied blue-leather upholstered booths toward the swinging doors that she'd been told led into the kitchen. Just as she got there, the doors flung open and Caroline had to jump out of the way to avoid two waitresses coming through, balancing orders on their upturned palms. Caroline mumbled her apologies. The red-haired one with the ponytail grinned at her, said 'no problem'.

On entering the kitchen, she could feel the heat from the grill on the other side of the windowed partition. Heard the sizzle of things frying.

Was she late? Glancing at the big round clock on the wall, she saw that she still had ten minutes before she was to start, and breathed a sigh of relief. It wouldn't be good to be late on her first day.

She could see people working behind the partition. Two men, one with his back to her, the other a older black man in a cook's hat, a shade whiter than his hair, and an older woman with a flushed face and wearing a blue and white head scarf. This was Ethel Crookshank who, she would learn, had been there since Frank's opened, over a decade ago. Ethel would become a friend to Caroline.

Now, giving Caroline a wave, Ethel came out from behind the partition and introduced her to the others. "This is Caroline Hill," she said.

Ethel had a nice smile and soft, greenish gray eyes, crinkled at the corners.

The introductions were brief, a few people calling out to her, "Welcome, Caroline," no time for more. The black man, who Ethel introduced at Ron, gave her a wink and flashed a gold tooth as he set out steaming plates of food onto the stainless steel counter. Someone tossed her an apron and pointed her to the dishwasher.

If she'd felt anxious before, now she was stricken with panic. At the hospital, she'd washed dishes manually. She had liked immersing her hands in the hot, sudsy water, washing and drying and putting away. She knew how to do that. Knew where everything went.

As she stood there staring at the contraption, the red-haired waitress burst through the swinging doors calling out for an order of pancakes with bacon.

"Don't look so scared, honey," a male voice said beside Caroline. "You'll do okay. I'm Mike Handratty, assistant cook."

He'd had his back to her when Ethel introduced her, and was the only one she hadn't met. He held out his hand to her and Caroline tentatively put out her own, which was immediately swallowed up in his damp, hot grasp. She tried to smile but her face felt stiff. "I'm Caroline Hill," she said.

"Yeah, we heard. Well, Caroline Hill," he said, moving toward the dishwasher, giving it a little tap on the side, "You have to let it know who's boss. Just like a woman. Ha ha."

He finally let her hand go, and she resisted the urge to wipe it on her apron.

She knew the 'just like a woman' comment was a joke and although she didn't see the humor in it, the stiff smile remained.

Caroline took in his light brown, tight curly hair, his quick movements as he showed her how to use the dishwasher. He pointed to the shelves where she was to stack the thick, cream-colored plates and cups and saucers when they were clean. The knives, forks and spoons went in the special plastic racks in the drawers, the same as at the hospital, except those at the hospital were blue, while these were a tan color.

Caroline followed his directions exactly, scraping the bits of food from the dirty dishes on the bus trays into the garbage can, then stacking them carefully into the machine, standing the plates up in their proper slots, the cups and saucers in theirs. She poured in the measured amount of liquid soap, shut the door and pressed the button he had indicated. At once, water rushed into the machine and she couldn't suppress a smile of relief at her success.

The man named Mike Handratty laughed, and Caroline heard the mocking sound in the laugh, but she said nothing. "See?" he said. "You'll soon be an old pro at this, Carrie. It ain't exactly rocket science, honey."

She didn't like him calling her honey, or Carrie, which was not her name, but again she said nothing. When he turned to walk away, he gave her backside a slap and she whirled around, startled, feeling the burn through her skirt. But he was already crossing the floor to the big freezer against the pale yellow wall, paying her no further attention. Seconds later he disappeared behind the partition.

Caroline turned back to the dirty dishes, scraping more bits of food from them into the garbage can, her face still hot. She had not liked him touching her, but told herself he was just being friendly, a jokester kind of person.

Sometimes the ward-attendants would give you a hug or call you honey, as if you were a small child, and she didn't mind mostly. They were just being nice. Which was much better then when they weren't. But he had not made her feel child-like. No, that would not describe the feeling he gave her.

And no one had ever called her Carrie before either. Carrie was not her name. She was sure it was a very fine name, but it was not hers. Her name was Caroline, handed down to her from her maternal grandmother who died when Caroline was five, and it was like a light went out in her small world when she did.

Much had been taken from Caroline in her life. In the hospital, there was little that belonged to you. They were locked away, or other patients stole them from you when your back was turned, and insisted the thing was theirs. But you always had a right to your own name.

Not that she wasn't grateful for the man's help. He had been nice to her and made her first morning at work easier.

Late in the day, the crowd had thinned to one or two customers and Ethel Crookshank brought Caroline out a plate of steaming food and told her to sit in the last booth, closest to the kitchen.

"Hot chicken sandwich and a glass of milk," she smiled, setting it on the table. "You look like you could use a few morsels. You did well for your first day, Caroline. Dig in. I don't think you had any lunch, did you?"

"That's okay. I wasn't hungry."

"Well, ya gotta eat. You've been here since nine o'clock. I'd be dead. Go ahead. Enjoy."

And she did enjoy it, down to the last gravy-soaked french fry and green pea. "Thank you," she said, cutting through the bread and chicken with her fork and knife.

Nurse Addison was right; the food was delicious and though she was very hungry she tried not to eat it too fast like some of the patients at the hospital did, just stuffing everything into their mouths like starving pigs. It wasn't their fault though.

Caroline was still feeling the surprise of the landlady knocking on her door to say, not that she was mad at her for telling the detectives she'd heard noises in there, but that she was sorry for not letting her know someone had been working in there. The landlady was nice. She was her friend.

Ethel brought her a piece of apple pie and slid into the booth, facing her. "Think you'll be happy with us, Caroline?"

"I'm already happy. Thank you." She picked up her fork and started in on the pie.

Ethel grinned. "Part of your earnings. God knows we'll never get rich working here, but at least we won't go hungry." She patted her tummy and grinned. Then her face grew thoughtful. "Listen, don't let that Mike give you no problem, Caroline. You give him what for if he bothers you, okay?"

"Okay," she replied softly, then set her forkful of pie down because she couldn't swallow past the lump in her throat. She blinked back hot tears and dropped her gaze, and hated herself for being so stupid.

"I've left you a couple of fresh uniforms at the cash," Ethel said, as if she didn't notice her tears. "They're in a plastic bag. I think they'll fit okay. You're no bigger 'n a minute. It'll be your responsibility to keep them laundered. Shame to get grease on that nice skirt." Then Ethel gave Caroline's arm a slight pat, and slid out of the booth. "Night, now, honey. Take care on the way home. See you in the morning."

The owner, Frank, was at the cashier's counter; he was saying goodnight to Ethel, who was on her way out the door, wrapping a scarf around her neck. She said something to him, and he turned and gave Caroline a nod and a grin. She'd had little contact with him so far; he was a big, stern-looking man but with a Santa Claus belly and a few wisps of gray hair combed over his baldness. He seemed nice.

She worked till seven-thirty. When she left, every dish was clean and in its place on the shelf, and the stainless steel counters and dishwasher gleamed.

Out in the restaurant, a waitress who was filling salt and pepper-shakers, sugar-bowls and napkin-holders, called back to her. "Time to call it a day, kiddo. I'm headin' out. You don't want to get locked in here by yourself." She laughed.

Through the big front windows, Caroline could see that it was already starting to get dark out.

THIRTEEN

Caroline's job was going well, and really wasn't all that different than what she had been doing at the hospital. She had mastered the dishwasher. Everyone was kind to her here at Frank's restaurant, and she was already feeling very much at home.

The only fly in the ointment was Mike Handratty, who sometimes made lewd comments in her ear that made her cheeks grow hot, while he was always very careful to say them softly enough so that no one else could hear. But he hadn't done enough to persuade her to confront him. Though he continued to call her Carrie, or sweetheart or honey, he hadn't put his hands on her again. So she just kept telling herself he meant nothing by it, and tried to ignore him. She liked her job and didn't want to make trouble.

She liked her room, too. Loved that it was her room. It welcomed her as if she had always lived here, wrapping itself around her like her cozy yellow robe.

Since her shopping outing with Mrs. Bannister, she'd bought a pretty antique white lace tablecloth for the table, and a framed picture of a farmhouse by a stream and hung it on the wall. Gazing at the scene always brought her a sense of peace, as if she might have lived there in another lifetime. Some people believed we've been here before, lived other lives, and no one could say for sure it wasn't so, could they?

Occasionally, Caroline would pass another tenant in the hallway or on the stairs and they would say hello to one another, and smile. The lady across the hall was petite and white-haired, always with a hello. She never did run into the piano man though, and had not heard his piano for several nights now. She missed his music. And then Mrs. Bannister told her his mother was ill and he'd gone to stay with her for a few days. She was pleased to know he hadn't gone for good.

She was sleeping better lately, even without the pills. Although now and then she would wake in the night, and imagine she was still at Bayshore. Then, she would slip out of bed, put on her robe and open her door to look out into the silent dim hallway to be sure being here in her own room that she paid for with her own money, wasn't really just a dream. Then she would come back inside, locking the door after her, satisfied that she was indeed a free woman. Everyone once in a while she felt like a child set loose at a circus, clutching a handful of tickets to all the rides.

Not that she was very adventurous. Her circle of travel extended to walking back and forth to work, stopping at shops along the way, especially Goldman's bookstore, and the grocery store that carried all she needed to sustain herself, and kept her within three blocks of her building. On her days off she would sit on a bench in the park and read, the birds and the murmur of the water fountain in the background.

Every now and then when she came home with a bag of groceries, Mrs. Bannister would meet her at the door and tell her she was paying a higher price for her purchases than she would if she shopped at Creighton's Mall downtown, but that would mean she would have to take a bus to get there. Which she planned to do. Soon.

If occasionally, as she walked along the sidewalk, she sensed someone watching her, she mostly ignored it and told herself it was just her imagination, that she was still becoming accustomed to being on the outside that was all it was. Because always, when she turned around, there would be no one there.

FOURTEEN

Detective Tom O'Neal was at his desk going through murder files from the last ten years. There were very few, none unsolved, but for these last two. Which didn't mean a lot because the killer could have been transient, passing through, something he and Glen had already talked about. But his gut told him the killer was still in St. Simeon, maybe already stalking his next victim.

Two women, beaten, raped and strangled. Both with blue eyes and dark hair. Coincidence? Seemed unlikely. Young, attractive women who he was guessing had simply had the misfortune to cross the killer's path. Were they substitutes for someone who'd betrayed him, or at least as he perceived it? A girlfriend? A mother?

He was, of course, speculating. But you had to start somewhere. They were pulling in all known sex offenders in the area, but the interviews had turned up no one of interest. He slid another crime photo of the victim out of the folder, looked at it for a long time.

Why would the killer put himself at risk, he wondered, by dragging Lorraine Winters' body into an alley in the early morning hours? Someone could easily have spotted him. City workers, someone working the night shift, jogging in the park. It was obvious that he drove her there because he needed a ride back from wherever he'd killed her. But why take her with him? Or at least leave her in the car? The trunk would have been the obvious place.

He'd run it by his partner.

"Symbolic maybe?" Aiken said. "Telling the world she's an Alley cat. A whore."

"You're assuming he's that clever."

Lorraine Winters, the latest victim had been at Delveccio's with a girlfriend from work earlier that night. A kind of celebration of Winters' good news.

"She got a call from an agent and she was getting ready to head for L.A. for a screen test," Deborah Miller, the honey-blond said, trying to hold back the tears. Despite the swollen eyes and red nose, she was an attractive young woman, a girl-next-door type. "She was planning to move there," she told him.

He asked her if anyone had offered to buy them a drink, but no one had. They spoke to none of the male patrons, only to each other. "She was so excited about the screen test. We both were. That's all we talked about. Lorraine was gorgeous, but she also had major talent. She could sing and dance as well as act, a triple threat. She played the lead in all our school plays and musicals. Being an actress was her dream, and she was hungry to make it a reality. She was always sending out photos and resumes. I knew it was just a matter of time."

They were sitting in his office. She began to cry again, and O'Neal slid the box of tissues sitting on the desk, toward her. He waited until she got herself together, then he asked her if she recalled anyone in the bar that night who looked at all suspicious. "I need you to think carefully. Someone sitting alone, maybe."

"No. No one. At least I didn't notice."

"Anyone hanging around the parking lot when you left?"

"Not that I saw. We hugged good-bye and I wished her luck." She looked about to crumble again, but didn't. Staring off into space, she said, "I can't believe she's gone."

He asked about boyfriends, anyone she might be leaving behind on her rise to stardom. Someone who might have felt resentful at being cast aside. But there was no one, she said, her friend was totally devoted to her career. Casual dates now and again but that was it. No one special.

That didn't mean it worked both ways, though, did it? he thought now, closing the folder. Maybe one of those 'casual' dates took things seriously. Felt spurned when he found out she was leaving town. Leaving him. But hate her enough to kill her? Well, someone did, that was damn sure.

"Please find whoever did this to my friend, Detective,"

Deborah Miller had said before she left the office. "And put him where he can never hurt anyone else."

He promised he would.

The department had released the victim's body to her family for burial. The autopsy was completed, all pertinent information recorded. She died of strangulation.

FIFTEEN

It seemed the whole town of St. Simeon turned out at Eternity Gardens for Lorraine Winters' funeral. She was their rising star, filled with promise, her life cut down before she could make good on that promise. To her family of course, their loss was beyond measure.

The victim's two younger sisters stood on either side of their mother, supporting her so that her legs wouldn't crumble beneath her. The sound of her pain was hard for Tom to hear. Her husband stood behind her, a slender man with glasses, strain evident on his lined, ashen face, a hand on his wife's shoulder. Detective O'Neal saw through the girls and their mother, how Lorraine Winters would have looked in life. And wanted more than anything to keep his promise to them, and to Deborah Miller, Winters' friend since childhood. To all of them. To catch this monster before he killed again.

There'd been a light, cold rain overnight and the smell of wet grass and earth mingled with the sweet flower fragrance. The skies were gray, low. But it wasn't supposed to rain again, at least not for the next few days.

He scanned the faces in the crowd, trying to hone in on the one mourner who wasn't a mourner at all, but a spectator, one who had come to revel in the fallout of his handiwork. He wouldn't be the first killer to show up at the gravesite of his victim. It apparently gave them an extra rush to see the devastation they'd caused. A sick power trip. But no one caught Tom's attention.

And then his eye fell upon Deborah Miller, standing with a young man who had his arm around her. She was weeping softly. They stood just behind Mrs. Winters who was silent now, pale and gray as her husband, as her daughters, each in their turn, went forward and placed a rose upon the casket.

He looked away, could see his partner up on the hill near a giant oak, discreetly photographing the solemn gathering from every angle. They would go through the photos later, on their own. Then they would show them to the family, hoping one would stand out from the rest. Good luck. He knew damn well it wasn't going to be that easy. This wasn't a movie, to be wrapped up neatly and tied with a bow at the end of two hours. But he could always hope. A break wasn't impossible.

When next he glanced in Glen's direction, the camera was hanging idly about his neck, as he took notes, like the director of a play. Fitting in a perverse way. Anything significant? Glen was sharp. Had he spotted something out of place? Someone? Was the perp here? Enjoying the proceedings? Tom focused in more tightly on the male mourners. Men alone. Not that that would prove anything.

Maybe that guy in the brown leather jacket? Yeah, something familiar about him. Tom felt a rush go through him. Tall. Dark blond hair, longish.

The minister finished his prayer and closed the book, kissed it… a ritual. Maybe more. A light gust of wind blew a thatch of gray hair across his scalp and he finger-combed it down, nodded to two men in dark suits standing at the gravesite.

Seconds later, a shovel of dirt hit the coffin with an ominous rattle, causing something to break inside Mrs. Winters', her anguished sobs carried to him, lay heavy on his own chest. He heard himself sigh. At last, the funeral was over and people were wandering back to their cars in small groups, or by fours and twos.

Keeping the guy in the brown leather jacket in his sights, he followed him to a dark maroon sedan, memorized the license plate number. He reminded him a little of William Hurt, in the early years. Intense type. And then, as the guy eased his car out behind the train of cars, he remembered where he'd seen him. He was one of the tenants they'd interviewed at the rooming house on Peel, where only weeks ago Lorraine Winters had lived.

SIXTEEN

Harold had taken to bringing Caroline day old cakes and what she didn't eat, she secretly shared with the squirrels in the park, her favorite place to sit and read. Goldman's bookstore was a good place too. Mr. Goldman, with his neat gray beard and kindly smile, encouraged his customers to sit and read by providing chintz-covered chairs, three of them, at the far end of the store.

"Welcome, welcome," he greeted her that first day she entered his establishment. "Lots of books here, take your time. You look like a young lady with a real appreciation for books. Amazing, isn't it? The words of generations of writers long gone preserved for our enlightenment and enjoyment. When we read their books, they are alive again, through us. If you need help, you tell me."

Mr. Goldman liked to talk about his books and about those who wrote them, and Caroline liked listening to him. The sight and smell of so many books, both old and new, was almost overwhelming, and Caroline felt like the proverbial kid in the candy store.

She ran her fingers down the spines of many of the books and breathed in their new book smells. She liked the old books too, trapping the years between their yellowing, musty pages, many of which were dog-eared. Goldman's bookstore reminded her of St. Simeon Library which she frequented as a girl. She would sit at the big, round table near the window with the sun streaming in, and read, often books her father would not have approved of had he known. She would use the excuse of having to research a paper for school, and it had served her well. Her pleasure in the books, though, was always stained with guilt. But despite that, the library was her haven, a place where she could live vicariously through characters in a book, and travel to far-off lands on a magic carpet of words.

After some deliberation, she chose a hardcover copy of Harper Lee's To Kill a Mockingbird, and at Mr. Goldman's urging, sat in a chair at the back and read the first few chapters. Then, clutching the book to her, she took it home to finish it, to feel that it was really hers. She had read To Kill a Mockingbird in school, she remembered, and the class had had to write a report. She had loved the book. Now she had her very own copy.

SEVENTEEN

Nurse Addison was right; it was lovely to sit in the park and read. But it was getting colder now, especially in the early mornings. The walk to work sent her through the restaurant door shivering, fingers tingling with cold. Which was why on this Friday night after work, she'd decided to spend some of her savings on a winter coat, hat and gloves. And with only a little prodding from the landlady. "You look half-frozen, Caroline," she'd said. "You need to get yourself some warmer clothes—something other than that blue jacket."

There actually was a coat in the window that had caught Caroline's fancy. A double-breasted navy pea coat.

Natalie's Boutique was only a short distance from Frank's, and as she opened the door the little bell above her head made its sweet sound, silvery and tinkling.

The saleslady, Natalie Breen, with her carefully made-up face and pale smooth hair swept up high on her head, recognized her at once. Caroline had learned she was the owner. Today she was wearing a bronze, tailored suit and silky ruffled blouse underneath. She beamed a smile at Caroline, making her feel welcome, as the little bell had.

Caroline ended up purchasing the navy peacoat she had admired in, along with white knitted scarf and gloves and a knit tam with navy trim and tassel. She also bought low-heeled, comfortable shoes. Though the shop wasn't large, Mrs. Breen carried a little of everything in stock.

As she left wearing her purchases, her own jacket and shoes shoved in a bag, the little bell above her head made its sweet sound. A happy sound that belied the dark twist of fate her patronage of the little shop would set in motion.

***

Caroline knocked on the landlady's door. It was rent day and she had the cheque in her hand.

Mrs. Bannister opened the door, gave her a surprised look and stepped back. "My, my, you look just like that Mary Tyler Moore on the television. You oughta go out on the sidewalk there and throw your new hat in the air. On the other hand, I don't see you as a girl who would do that," she chuckled, as if the very idea were preposterous. "Might do you some good if you did, dear. You're much too serious. Anyway, you look lovely. And a hell of a lot warmer."

"Yes, I am warm. Thank you."

Mrs. Bannister laughed and Caroline only sensed why; it had something to do with how she expressed herself. Seeing what must have been confusion on Caroline's face, Greta Bannister quickly apologized for laughing. "It's just that dead pan look you sometimes get, Caroline. You're such an innocent. Come have tea, even if you don't need warming up. I could use someone to talk to. Harold's working late."

One of the cats had had kittens, little gray balls of fluff with blue eyes and pink noses, and Greta took her into the den to show them off. Picking up the tiniest one, she handed it Caroline. It felt like a tiny cloud cupped in her hands, and she held it to her cheek. Greta told her she could have one if she liked. "Just as soon as they're-weaned from their momma."

Caroline, stroking the kitten, was momentarily ecstatic at the offer. The joy dissolved almost at once. "No, no thank you." She handed it back, practically pushing it at Greta.

The landlady shrugged and gently placed the kitten back in the box with the other three. "Well, there's no rush. Maybe you'll change your mind."

They had tea while she wrote her out a receipt, and soon Caroline went up to her room.

***

Caroline stood before the mirror above the dresser in her room and stared at herself, in her new outfit, backing up to see as much of herself as she could.

She looked nothing like Mary Tyler Moore, the perky actress whose show she rarely missed if she could help it. Even at the hospital, no one ever jumped up to change channels with Mary was on, like they did during other shows.

But she liked looking at herself in her new coat, and the hat and gloves. The storekeeper had said the outfit was made for her. Though she didn't mention Mary Tyler Moore.

She stood a moment longer, then impulsively snatched the hat from her head and threw it into the air. She tried to catch it but it fell on the floor because she'd been trying to watch herself in the mirror when she did it. Though she was alone, she felt her cheeks grow warm with embarrassment. Then she giggled.

Bending to pick up her hat, her eye was drawn to the old trunk, sitting on the floor against the wall, mostly ignored, like the proverbial elephant in the room. More vividly seen in some far corner of her memory, in a far different setting.

It had been in her parents' bedroom, next to the bed for as long as she could remember. The trunk was in her mother's family for a very long time, passed down through generations, brought over from England by her great grandparents in the early 1800s. Strange that she recalled that story when she had forgotten so much else.

Her mother kept a salmon pink runner draped over the trunk, a vase of silk daisies on top. No dust collected on them for her mother was a very good housekeeper. Whether she liked it or not, the trunk was now hers. She might as well see what was in it.

She hung her coat in the closet, sat down on the sofa and gazed at the relic for a few minutes. Then, sighing heavily, she reached into her bag for the key. Don't think. Just do it.

She fit the key into the old rusting lock and turned it. There was a click and the lock fell open, and her heart gave an odd skip. She removed the lock. Almost in the same instant, upstairs, he began playing the piano. She looked up, both startled and pleased. She had not heard him up there for days now. His mother must be better, she thought.

The policemen were back again yesterday, knocking on doors, talking to tenants. She heard them pass by her door, go upstairs. She had nothing more to tell them. Did he? Had he known the actress when she lived across the hall? He would, wouldn't he? Mr. Mason had.

It was a classical piece he was playing, like a lullaby. Soft. Beautiful. Fingers up and down the keys, a gentle waterfall. Building. Almost as if he knew about the trunk and was providing music for the occasion.

What foolish thoughts she had. Fanciful. Her life was of no importance to anyone but herself.

But she was glad he was back. She liked listening to him play the piano.

She took a breath and lifted the trunk lid and had a sense of raising the lid of a coffin. In a way, she supposed she was. The perfume of ancient rose petals and musk rose up to her, filling her senses, bringing a flood of memories with it. She was like Pandora, opening the box and letting loose all that was chaos and misery into the world.

Except only she would be affected by what was in this trunk. Only her world would be touched.

EIGHTEEN

Detective O'Neal was at home in his den, drinking coffee and going through the murder file for the first victim, Rosalind Gibbs, making comparisons with the Lorraine Winters' case, trying to find something besides their physical likenesses, that would connect them. There was nothing. One an aspiring actress, the other a nurse. A caregiver and a performer. Couldn't be more different, at least in career choices.

Rosalind Gibbs was only two blocks from her home when she was grabbed. She had a live-in boyfriend, who'd been questioned a number of times and released. Name of Brian Redding, clean-cut kid, worked at Neilson's brewery. Tom thought another visit might be in order. After scanning the notes, he saw nothing that would constitute an ironclad alibi for the night of his girlfriend's murder. Redding said he was at a hockey game on the night in question, but they hadn't double-checked his story. If he recalled, the guy had a ticket stub, but you could get that off the sidewalk. Sometimes the smallest thing can be the key to unraveling a case.

Like with the David Berkowitz case, so-called Son of Sam, the psycho who stalked kids in parked cars and blew them away with his .44 Bulldog; it was a traffic ticket that did him in, and unquestionably saved more innocent kids from being slaughtered. Christ, it could have been his own two. The thought sent an icy bath through him. Life was a crapshoot.

He glanced up as Jake, his black lab let out a whine, his body jerking. He was curled up in front of the fireplace, dreaming again. After their run on the beach, he wiped out. They both did. Jake was shot in a domestic case a couple of years ago, a drunk fool with a gun, and he brought Jake straight here from the vet's. They were best friends. A friend he could talk to or not talk to, depending on how he felt. As for Jake, he was generally content if they were in the same room together. As good as new physically, Jake had a round scar on his left thigh where the bullet had penetrated. A bare spot where fur would never grow, like scar tissue over a wounded heart.

A sudden gust of wind rattled the big window that overlooked the ocean. He could hear the Atlantic crashing against the rocks below. He bought this place after the divorce, a five room bungalow he'd spent two summers winterizing, and was as content here as he was likely to get. But he did like the privacy, walking on the beach with his dog. Still, he missed being part of his kids' lives, both teenagers now. Missed being part of a family.

He closed the files, slipped them into his briefcase. He grabbed his coat, rattled the car keys, bringing Jake immediately to his feet.

"A drive?"

Jake answered with a single, joyful bark, tail thumping the floor.

As they drove in the direction of town, Tom ran other possible 'persons of interest' through his mind. There were a couple that warranted keeping an eye on. The piano player, for example, in the Peel Street building. Jeffrey Denton. When Tom questioned him about being at the funeral, he said, 'She was my downstairs neighbor for two years. I was paying my respects.' He also insisted he was visiting his mother on the night she was killed. Maybe. Another 'not exactly solid' alibi.

There was another note of interest: Several days after the murder, a cab driver came forward, reported seeing a runner in the park in the early morning, just a short time before Lorraine Winters' body was discovered. Just a guy in a hooded jacket. Average height, weight. Hadn't thought anything of it at the time.

The department put out a call for the man to come forward on the off chance that he saw something while on his run. Something he might have considered insignificant at the time, or that hadn't even registered with him.

But no one answered the call. True, he might just have been an ordinary jogger the cabby drove past that morning, who simply chose not to get involved. But Tom O'Neal had a feeling it just might have been her killer.

As he drove, he went back to thinking about his old life while his furry passenger enjoyed the sights they passed on the way to Brian Redding's place.

He was still thinking about his kids, and how he missed them. Oh, they talked on the phone from time to time, but they were usually on their way to somewhere, and when they weren't, it wasn't the same.

Not that he blamed his ex. It wasn't Mary's fault. She'd always complained he was married to the job, and she had a point. He knew she was unhappy but he kept promising himself, and her, that it was just a few years till he retired, and he'd have more time for vacations and so on after that. But she couldn't wait. Or didn't believe me, and maybe she was right not to.

The divorce papers shouldn't have come as a shock to him, yet they did. Like a fist to the gut. He held out hope for a long time that they'd get back together, until one night he showed up on the doorstep and she told him she was seeing someone else, and he'd seen sorrow on her lovely face. Maybe even pity. She had loved him once. He would always love her. If not quite in the same way. At any rate, she married the guy. A dentist. Someone who could give her the nice normal life Tom hadn't been able to.

The radio sputtered and crackled and Detective Glen Aiken's voice was loud and clear into the confines of the cruiser, ending his pity party.

"Got another one, Tom," his partner said. "Body found by a hiker at the edge of the woods, out near Crater Lake."

The road was clear both ways, and Tom made a squealing U-turn. Redding would have to wait.

NINETEEN

All their worldly goods are in this trunk, Caroline thought. The total accumulation of two lives lived. All of it, plus two thousand dollars, had come to her, their child. Compensation. She had hated them both.

Why don't you just close the lid? Everything in here will only be painful reminders of what happened. But Doctor Rosen said she had to find a way to forgive them if she ever hoped to be truly free. "Even though there may not be bars on the windows where you're going, Caroline, they'll still be across your heart." She knew he was right, but she didn't know if she could forgive them.

They had tried to reach out to her on those Sundays that they came to visit, but she had withdrawn herself from them, gone far away in her mind. They were strangers to her.

Though not entirely, she thought with a twinge of guilt. She could recall the woman sitting in hard-backed chair wearing her little black hat, weeping behind the veil, wiping tears away. They had meant nothing to her. Once, she had lashed out at her mother, telling her she was sick of her tears, and could still see the shock on her face, as if she had struck her. She'd taken a perverse pleasure in that. Felt good about it.

As for her father, he might have been any man who'd walked in off the street, she was so remote from him. Apparently, then, she had had her revenge even if her actions had not been deliberate, and she wasn't sure that at some level, they hadn't been. Had she meant to be so cruel? As they had been to her?

But that was the thing, wasn't it? They hadn't thought of it as cruelty; it was all for her own good.

The salmon-colored runner, edged at either end with silky fringes, lay folded atop the other items in the trunk. She picked it up and and it slid both weightless and weighty through her fingers, the fringes tickling her wrist, as if tiny spiders walked across it. She let it fall beside her on the bed.

Next, was her father's Bible with its black cover and well-turned pages. She held the weight of it in her hands. Every night, they would sit in the parlour and he would read aloud from a passage he'd chosen earlier in the day, his handsome face animated and commanding, like Charlton Heston in The Ten Commandments, while she and her mother sat quiet as mice. His captive audience. His congregation.

She used to imagine that God looked like her father. To the child she was, God and her father were interchangeable. She'd been taught that God was love. As a teenager, she would come to know his wrath.

'You won't be seeing that boy again,' he had bellowed, standing over her in the kitchen that day. 'If you try, I will lock you in your room and nail the windows shut. I'll tie you to a chair if you force me to.'

She saw his flushed face in her mind, the spittle forming at the corners of his mouth, his face dark with rage.

She had disgraced them. Demeaned them and herself in the eyes of God and society. 'We will not accept a bastard child into his family.' Scripture rolled off his tongue: 'A bastard child shall not enter into the congregation of the Lord...' She would go away to bear this spawn of Satan, and give it to a Christian family to raise. 'Perhaps if you throw yourself on his mercy, God will forgive you your whoring ways.'

All through his rant, her mother had sat silent and weepy at the table, her hands twisting a tissue into contortions in her lap, of no help. Caroline had felt only contempt for her.

'I am not a whore,' she had cried. 'Please...William and I love each other. We want to get married.'

I hated her far more than I hated him, Caroline thought now. I hated her for her weakness. But she had loved them both too.

Over the next days, as promised, she was locked in her small, windowless room, allowed out only to go to the bathroom. Downstairs, the phone rang and rang, and she knew it was William calling. She rattled her doorknob and begged them to let her talk to him, but her pleas went unheard. She was wild with her need of him, to feel his love, his arms around her, comforting, telling her that everything would be okay. But it was not to be. Once, she heard voices downstairs, one an angry rumble that belonged to her father. The other softer. William's. He was trying to reason with her father. She held a thread of hope, until she heard the door close.

Then, on one impossibly golden summer's day, they drove her to another province where they committed her to a home for unwed mothers. She never heard from William again.

Now, standing over the trunk, tears pricked her eyelids. She batted them away, returned the Bible to the trunk and closed the lid. She would do no more of this tonight.

TWENTY

The murdered woman was identified as forty-eight year old Pearl Grannan. Like the other two victims, she'd been beaten and strangled. The smell of pine was strong here, cut with an underlying odor of death.

"I saw a flash of purple in the bushes," the man said, clearly distraught at finding a dead woman in his path. "I moved in for a closer look, and that's when I realized it was a person lying there. I ran back to the house and called 911. Brought the wife back with me in case I was seeing things."

The purple turned out to be her polyester slacks. "Beat hell out of her, the crazy bastard," the man said. "Blood in her hair."

Red hair, O'Neal noted.

"Poor woman," his wife said, her voice trembly, her own face under her knitted blue and white stocking hat, drained of color. "It's that killer, isn't it? No one's safe. Why can't you people catch him and lock him up before anyone else is murdered?"

"Now, now, Elsie, they're doing their best," the man said, and patted her shoulder.

"Your husband's right, we are, Ma'am," Detective Aiken said. "And we'll get him. Just a matter of time." Looking around, he noticed just a few yards from where they stood, fresh tire tracks. They'd get a cast. Maybe this was the break they were hoping for.

A missing person's report had been filed that morning by the victim's husband, a Lawrence Grannan, who went by Larry. The officer who took the report said the husband had been beside him with worry about his wife.

Her I.D. was in her purse, leaving no doubt that she was the missing woman. As his partner had, Glen noted the red hair. Maybe darker than its natural shade, which might have been close to his own, but red just the same, borne out by the eyebrows.

No cop enjoyed delivering bad news to loved ones. While you didn't know, hope lived.

TWENTY-ONE

The trunk called to Caroline in the night. She switched on the lamp, slipped into her robe, and resigned herself to answering.

Picking up a family album, she opened it to a photo of her father as a young man, a half-smile, boyish, wearing a soft felt hat. The photos were held in with corner brackets. He looked smaller in the photo than in her memory of him. Not so fierce as she remembered. Yet he had been fierce and without mercy. All for the good of my soul.

Much of her rage was gone now though, like a lanced abscess, talked and cried out in endless sessions in Doctor Rosen's office. It was still there, only quieter now. Almost an echo of itself. An old wound that still seeped blood.

She turned to the next page in the album. Looked into the faces of the two people in the black and white photograph. How could you? How could you give your own granddaughter away to strangers? There was no answer of course. None that would satisfy.

Her parents looked not so much happily married as settled somehow. They were a perfect match. She submissive, he with a need to reign supreme in his own home.

In fairness to her mother, she could see that her father was quite nice looking, and certainly charming. They'd often entertained their church friends at home. He was well thought of in his circle. He sold insurance for a living, so had the power of persuasion.

A sudden sense memory let her feel the weight of his hand on her head, its gentleness, the love that came through his touch. *No. He was never nice to you.* She closed the book with a snap. She must have dreamed that memory, she told herself. A false memory, they called it at the hospital. Yes, that was it. He was horrid. He ruined my life.

And then she heard Dr. Rosen's voice, calm and reasoning. 'People are more than just one thing, Caroline. We are like prisms, reflecting different sides of our nature, each depending on the slant of light.'

The piano man had begun to play again, and she lifted her eyes to the ceiling as the notes spilled over her, like a soothing balm. Something lighter now, chasing the dark memories back into their corners, something familiar she couldn't name. She knew little about classical music, but enjoyed hearing him play. His music spoke to her, in a different way from Billie Holiday's, but as meaningful.

He must not be able to sleep, either.

She imagined him sitting at his keyboard, from the back of course, since she had not yet seen his face. Only his dark blond hair curling at the collar of his shirt. She sat on the bed, holding the fringed runner in her hands, letting the play of silk run through her fingers like water, letting it and the music still her mind and lull her senses.

Too soon, the playing stopped. But Caroline still couldn't sleep, so she turned on the TV with the volume down low, and learned another woman had been murdered.

TWENTY-TWO

The man who opened the door to Detectives Tom O'Leary and Glen Aiken, was bleary-eyed, unshaven, looked like he hadn't slept in days. Larry Grannan was of average build, with thinning hair, a slight paunch. He drove truck for a living. By his expression, he knew they had found her, and that she wasn't coming home, not ever.

"May we come inside?" Tom asked gently.

He nodded and moved away from the door.

He preceded them into the living room, a clean, modestly furnished room. Browns and beiges, a few plants. He moved like a very tired old man.

"You've found her." A statement, not a question.

"I'm afraid so. I'm very sorry." Tom briefly outlined the circumstances in which they'd found her. "Her purse was with her," Tom said. "Her ID, but we'll still need you to make a positive identification."

He nodded, then sagged down on the sofa. "Pearl was everything to me. We've been together since we were kids. I don't want to live without her."

Larry Grannan had already told the officer who filed the missing person's report, that she'd gone shopping and never returned. Now he repeated it. "I phoned all her friends," he repeated. "Drove around looking for her. Then I phoned you guys. Pearl didn't drive, always used the bus system."

"Is there anyone we can call to be with you, sir. Do you have grown children?" Glen asked.

"We got one daughter, but she lives at the other end of the country. Oh, God, I need to call Adele before she hears it on the news. No, no, there's no one."

They left him there, weeping, and saw themselves out.

Tom was sliding into the driver's seat and noticed Glen eyeing the blue Ford truck parked in the driveway. He was checking out the tire treads. Tom thought again of the victim's red hair. Older than the others, too.

TWENTY-THREE

It was Sunday, just past noon, sunny with blue skies, a lovely autumn day. Dressed in her new outfit, armed with a bag of peanuts for the squirrels and her new book, Caroline left for the park. There wouldn't be too many more days when she could sit in the park, and she planned to take advantage of this one.

The hallway was empty. From behind one of the doors, a TV was playing, and she recognized the voice of Pastor Jacob Warren, Sunday Morning Church of the Air. Some of the patients at the hospital had watched the program faithfully, but Caroline had had enough of preaching, thank you very much.

Without pause, no longer feeling as if she were about to step out of an airplane, she walked downstairs like any normal person, and out into the bright day, a little chillier than it looked from her window, and felt a gladness inside herself. She knew she had come far since her release. Doctor Rosen would be proud of her.

Stepping onto the sidewalk, she saw Mr. Mason, her upstairs neighbor, heading in her direction, clutching a newspaper. Seeing her, he tipped his tweed cap, wished her a good day and went into the building.

She had met most of the tenants. It was strange that she had not yet seen the face of the piano man. He was a mystery in a way.

Mr. Mason wasn't the sort who would play the piano, she thought idly, as she went on up the street toward the park. More like a man who might build a ship in a bottle. Or collect stamps. Or add up numbers, something in him satisfied to see them add up, which made sense considering Mrs. Bannister had told her he was an accountant.

She was sorry that his wife had taken their children and left him. She wondered if Mr. Mason had been mean to his wife like

Martha Blizzard's husband had been to her? Though she saw no meanness in Mr. Mason's face, nothing dark there to make a woman fearful, but you never knew about people.

Think of pleasant things, she told herself.

She envisioned her favorite bench, shiny green in the sunlight, the cooing doves, the bluejays and chickadees, with the lovely fountain babbling in the background. She hoped no one had taken her bench.

Hurrying along the sidewalk, her fingers were already anticipating turning the pages of her new copy of Great Expectations by Charles Dickens.

Though she had no interest in attending church, there was something about the sound of the church bells that struck a deep chord within her. Almost as though they rang just for her.

The church bells meant nothing to Buddy. He was aware only of the young woman who had just come out of her building. Caroline. Such a lovely old-fashioned name.

He'd been standing in the alley across from her building, and now let her get a safe distance away, so she wouldn't spot him. Adjusting the brown knit touque over his longish hair and flipping his coat collar up, he followed her, taking care to appear nonchalant, keeping a sure, easy stride. A man on his way to somewhere.

It was not the first time he had followed her. Once, he even walked right past her in the park, but she was so into her book she didn't even look up. Like he was invisible. He didn't like feeling invisible except when it suited his purpose.

But it was just a matter of time until he would have her full attention. In the end, she would be glad of his persistence, his patience.

More than anything, he wanted this to be true. But if she disappointed him, as the others had, then she would die, too. But that wasn't going to happen; he had chosen well this time. His heart filled with joy at the thought of what this meant. There was no mistake. His heart swelled with the rightness of it.

He had seen the softness of her face as she beckoned the squirrels to her, scattering food for them, smiling her sweet, serene smile. Goodness flowed from her. He knew her destiny was intertwined with his.

Still, he wanted to be very sure this time. No more mistakes. Not that he felt any regret at killing those women. They were nothing to him. He felt more remorse killing the buzzing, filthy flies in his mother's kitchen.

She was at the corner now, crossing on a green light. He picked up his pace until he was close enough to see the little tassel on her hat swaying to her rhythm, hear the soft fall of her shoes on the pavement.

Yes, he thought again, she was perfect.

Night Corridor
Page 91

TWENTY-FOUR

Lynne Addison had abandoned her husband Joe the last few days to stay with her mother and try to figure out what to do. At the moment, she was standing at the refrigerator with the door open, checking out the packages in the frozen section.

"Mom, what you like for supper? How about a baked piece of haddock? I'll put a couple of potatoes in the oven first. Sound good?"

Her mom was standing at the window, looking out at what exactly, Lynne didn't know. And then she turned from the window, looked at her with those faraway eyes.

"What about your dad, dear? Is there enough fish for Walter? He's very fond of haddock."

Turning away, Lynne pretended to check the freezer while her heart broke into a few more pieces. Her father was dead six years now. Heart attack on his way upstairs to bed. Just collapsed on the stairs. He was seventy-two, four years older than mom. Every time she told her mother he was gone, she would start crying again, just as if it was the first time she'd heard the terrible news. Lynne sighed. "He's working late, mom." She took out the fish. Two pieces.

For the most part, mom lived in the present. But then she would drift back. When she returned to the present as if waking from a long sleep. She would say, "Dad's gone, isn't he?" But there would be the confusion, a hesitation in her speech as she tried to remember when or how it had happened.

"Thank you, Lynne," she said now. "I'm so lucky to have such a wonderful daughter. But don't you have to…"

Her voice trailed away and she frowned in that way she had, deep, intense, and Lynne saw her mental struggle. She's unsure if

I'm married, or working or still in school, home for lunch. She probably doesn't remember Joe right now, though they'd become great friends over the years.

But she always remembers me. As soon as she saw me at the door today, she said, "Lynne, dear, I'm so glad you're here." Lynne feared the day she would look at her as if she were a stranger.

But today she knows me. She knows something is happening to her mind, and is terrified. That was the worst part; her knowing, feeling helpless and afraid. Unable to change the course she was on. Her mother had been so strong, so in control of things. She was Lynne's rock, growing up, always there for her. Now Lynne wanted to be there for her mother.

Lynne set the two pieces of white fileted fish on the counter and turned to look at her mother, now sitting at the kitchen table, contemplating her hands that lay in her lap, the fish forgotten. Perhaps even daddy. But then she saw she was twisting her gold wedding band round and round on her finger

Lynne looked at her mother with helplessness and sadness. Yet on the surface she looked the same, an attractive older woman, tall, statuesque, her white hair arranged in soft waves. Every Thursday she had it done at the beauty shop just down the street. Lynne had always felt proud when people told her she looked like her mother. It was only her mother's eyes that were sometimes vague or fearful.

Caroline Hill's eyes used to look like that when she first came on the ward. Once they took her off the drugs, her eyes cleared, and her mind became more lucid. Of course Caroline didn't have a brain disease like her mother. And she was barely more than a girl, not only chronologically but emotionally. But according to reports, she was doing well, and Lynne was glad to know her concerns hadn't been justified.

She washed the potatoes in the sink, feeling the icy water on her hands, cold as the knowledge that there was no good solution for her mother. It will get worse and it's bad now. I can't leave her alone anymore. But the last time Lynne suggested she sell the house and come live with her and Joe, her mom was adamant that she would not be leaving her home, the only home she had known since she was eighteen years old, and married Walter Raines. She'd been furious (and frightened) at the mere suggestion. In that moment, Lynne was the enemy.

But it's dangerous for her living alone here, Lynne thought, as she ran cold water over the fish, dried each of the filets with a paper towel and rolled them in the bread crumbs, sprinkled with dill. Another woman was found murdered. Older than the other two. A deviation in the killer's pattern.

Anyone could be next.

She wondered if Caroline knew that one of the murdered women had once lived in her building. Yes of course she would know that. The murders were the talk of the town. And Caroline was a working woman now, out in that world. She was also very bright.

Thoughts of her former patient gave her a twinge of guilt. I must call on Caroline, she told herself with resolve, as she set the potatoes on a rack and slid it into the oven. She would go see her. Soon.

"How about we go into the living room, Mom, and watch the afternoon movie. They're running an old Jerry Lewis flick." She was tired of thinking about death and dying—the many kinds of dying. Jerry was medicine for the soul.

TWENTY-FIVE

"Hi, Caroline."

She was sitting on her favorite park bench, engrossed in a scene between Pip, Mrs. Haversham, and the lovely Estella when the voice broke through to her. She looked up to see Harold Bannister grinning down at her. He was removing his knitted cap, stuffing it into his pocket, as if he had just entered a room and came upon a grand lady. Harold was always so nice and respectful.

"Hi, Harold." She looked around, and not seeing his bike, which he always rode, said, "You don't have your bike with you."

"Someone cut the lock and took it from in front of the bakery. Left a whole bunch of other new bikes and took mine."

She thought he seemed more puzzled than angry. "That's awful. Maybe the thief thought no one would come after him if he took an older one."

He shrugged his shoulders. He was wearing new jacket, one she hadn't seen before. Dark green, quilted and shiny.

"Yeah, I guess," he said. "Uh, okay if I sit down?"

Behind Harold, a small blond boy tossed a rock into the fountain, where it made a light splash. A startled pigeon took flight, descending seconds later onto the branch of a chestnut tree, causing its leaves to shiver.

"If you're…uh…really into your book," Harold stammered, "I don't want to bother…"

She closed the book reluctantly. "No, it's okay. Sure. Please sit down." She shifted over to give him room. Usually, she sat in the middle of the bench to discourage strangers from sitting beside her. "That's a nice coat. Looks warm."

"Yeah, it is. You look nice, too." His hand whispered down the front of his nylon jacket. "But you always look nice. Aunt Greta gave this to me for my birthday." He sat down. "It's got a detachable hood but I don't need it yet."

"Oh, it's really lovely. Happy birthday. How old are you? I'm sorry," she said at once. "I guess that's not a question a person should ask of someone."

She was getting better at not blurting things out, at thinking before she spoke, but sometimes she forgot. Harold had settled in beside her. He smelled of the baked cookies he often bought her. Cinnamon, she thought.

"I don't mind," he said. "I'm twenty-four."

"You look younger. I thought you were eighteen or nineteen."

"It's the zits," he said.

She didn't think so. "You don't have many. Just that one on your chin, and it's not too bad."

He laughed at that, and she did too. Not exactly sure why. Harold had a nice laugh. She had never thought of Harold as being nice looking, but in that moment he was. Not that he was ugly or anything. In fact, she had thought he looked like a poet the first time she saw him.

"I know how old you are," he said, smiling, proud that he knew. "You're twenty-six."

It surprised her that he knew her age, but then she supposed his aunt would have told him.

Harold asked her where she lived before she went into the mental hospital, and the question made her pause. Then, "With my parents. But that was a long time ago. They're dead now. Did you always live with your aunt?"

A squirrel began chattering from a nearby tree and Caroline took the bag of peanuts from her bag and tossed a peanut on the ground; the red squirrel with its big fluffy tail came warily down the tree, black eyes glittering, ventured close enough to snatch up the peanut and scurry back up. But not very far. Making a raspy, scolding noise. Hurry up! Feed me.

She smiled and tossed another as Harold said, "I've been with my Aunt Greta since I was twelve, after my parents divorced. I have a learning disability and I think that made my dad feel ashamed. He never said, but I could tell. Anyway, I bounced back and forth between them for awhile. Then I moved in with Aunt Greta, and I stayed. She's great, but I'd like to get my own place someday. You're more independent than I am."

"No, I'm not."

"Sure you are. You have your own place, upstairs."

"Oh, well. The hospital arranged it for me. I could never have rented a room on my own."

She asked him about his job. About how long he'd been there. Three years, he told her. "I pour the mixed batters from the vats into the bake pans, and I clean up and stuff. I guess I told you about that."

"Yes. It sounds interesting."

He shrugged. "I won't be pouring the batter much longer. It's all going to auto…automated. A big machine will do it."

He said he might go to the community college and learn a trade. "I think I could learn something new if I liked it."

"Sure you could. I learned to work the electric dishwasher at Frank's," she said. "You could learn anything you wanted to. I think you're very smart, Harold."

He looked pleased at that and smiled his shy smile at her. "Maybe you would like to go to a movie or something—sometime. I don't have a car but we could take the bus downtown. Maybe next Saturday…"

"No, thank you." The words were not out of her mouth when she wished she could snatch them back. Once more, she had spoken too quickly, too bluntly. Harold looked as if she had slapped him. She felt her heart sink in disappointment at herself. But she did not want to go to a movie with Harold.

She had liked going to the movies once, though they were forbidden to her. She and William had sneaked off to see Rosemary's Baby, and he had put his arm around her at the scary parts. She hadn't wanted to move in case he took it away. She could feel its weight even now across her shoulders, the excitement of his nearness. She recalled the smell of popcorn, the shifting of feet in the warm darkness. A movie about the devil's spawn, her father would have said. Which indeed it was.

She had not thought of that in years. Doctor Rosen had

promised her the memories would return, like snatches of dreams, he said, as she settled into her new life.

She knew it sounded crazy to say you were afraid to be in a movie theatre, so she said nothing, just sat there feeling bad inside herself that she had hurt Harold's feelings, who was already on his feet, his face pink, the zit on his chin glowing. Trying to look like her rejection didn't bother him, he tugged his knit hat over his head and looked around him, at everything but her. "I'll let you get back to your book. I guess I'll... see you around."

After he was gone, she opened her book again, but she couldn't concentrate on the story because she couldn't stop seeing the hurt on Harold's face. She sighed and let the book rest on her lap.

And it was at that moment she became aware of someone watching her.

TWENTY-SIX

A gust of wind came and lifted the pages of the book in her lap, and blew her hair around her tam and into her eyes. She finger-combed the hair away.

Searched the now deserted park, past the fountain, the trees, the swings, but saw no one.

She closed the book and slipped it into her bag and stood up, stiff from sitting so long, her backside numb. Glancing at her watch, she saw that it was nearly five o'clock, which surprised her. She hadn't realized she'd been here so long.

Shaking the last of the peanuts onto the ground, she scrunched the bag up in her hand and tossed it into a nearby trash bin. A heavy purple black cloud passed over the sun and another gust of wind chased ripples across the water in the fountain and rattled the leaves in the trees.

As she headed for the park's exit, she glanced to her right and noticed a man standing on the far side of the park, looking in her direction. She couldn't be sure if he was looking at her because he was wearing dark glasses, and his hat was pulled low on his forehead. Yet every instinct in her told her he was, and that behind those glasses lived cold, hard eyes.

Even from here she sensed something familiar about him, in the way his stood, in the menacing thrust of shoulders. Apprehension crept over her and she looked quickly away. Hitching her bag up higher on her shoulder, she walked on, her hurried step making her new shoes click eerily on the paved pathway.

The wind came up again and she had to clamp a hand over her hat to keep it from flying off. Cold burrowed down the neck of her new coat, and she buttoned the top button and drew up the collar, wishing she had worn her new scarf. Yet the deepest chill that had burrowed into her bone marrow had nothing at all to do with weather, but came from the eyes hidden behind those glasses that, even now, seemed to follow her.

By the time she reached her building, she was gasping for breath and sweaty inside her coat. She rummaged in her bag for her key with fingers that felt like thumbs, at last finding it. Sliding the key into the lock, she glanced over her shoulder, saw only an elderly lady rushing along the sidewalk, her black poodle on a leash, leaves skittering after the little dog.

Not until she was inside her room with the door locked, did she let out a long, shaky breath and sag down on the sofa.

The man wasn't watching you. It was only his dark glasses that made you think that. But she wasn't convinced.

She hung up her coat, wandered to the window and was surprised to see Harold standing down on the sidewalk, looking up at the window. Seeing her, he immediately dropped his head and disappeared inside the building.

She had thought Harold left the park before she did. Had he been following her?

TWENTY-SEVEN

It was not the first time in these past weeks that Caroline had sensed she was being followed, but she told herself it was just her imagination, triggered by knowing a killer was on the loose. Last night, after seeing Harold standing on the sidewalk looking up at her window, she wasn't so sure. It had made her suspicious of him.

Putting on the teakettle to make a cup of tea to calm herself, she caught a glimpse of her pale, frightened face in the shiny chrome, and that frightened her even more. She'd better get herself together, or they'd be sending her away again. Harold was mad at her because she wouldn't to the movies with him, but he wouldn't hurt her. Harold was her friend. And that's how she thought of him. A friend.

When she arrived at work that morning, Ethel told her one of the waitresses called in sick, and that they were shorthanded. She would have to fill in. She gave her an order book and tossed her a clean uniform and apron. White, with burgundy trim. "Change into this, Caroline. Just smile your sweet smile and be yourself, and you'll do great. C'mon, now, don't look like I just asked you to jump off a cliff."

"But I can't, Ethel. I don't know how…"

"Of course you can. What's to know? You take the order and come back here and yell it out. I'm here, if you have any problem. But you won't. It'll be good for you, honey. You've come a lot farther than you realize since you started working here."

Ethel found her a pair of white nurse's shoes a waitress had left behind when she quit. They looked near new. "There'll be a lot more comfy on your feet if they fit."

They did. Perfectly. Like they'd been waiting for her. She was both excited and terrified at the prospect of going out there.

"I figured they'd fit," Ethel said. "You got dainty feet. The shoes are yours, then. They don't fit anyone else around here."

For the first half hour, Caroline was a nervous wreck, getting her orders confused, once tripping and spilling a full cup of coffee on the floor. But after awhile she settled down and actually surprised herself by enjoying waiting tables. Ethel was giving her the confidence she needed to do this. Each time she went through the swinging doors into the kitchen and called out a new order just the way she'd heard other waitresses calling out theirs. Ethel would wink and smile at her, and give her order special attention.

Aside from the pleasure of serving customers, being out in the restaurant got her away from Mike, who was becoming more and more uncomfortable to be around. Everything he said and did seemed deliberate, a taunt, mocking her.

Once when he called her Carrie, she explained as pleasantly as she could that her name was Caroline, after her grandmother. She hoped he might understand, but the look he gave her was hardly apologetic. Turning away, he made a comment she didn't catch, but knew it wasn't anything nice.

Surely she had a right to be called by her proper name, didn't she? Why would that make him angry?

And why was she making so much of it?

She must learn to ignore him. Let him call her Carrie, if he wanted to. What did it matter? It's not as if it was a bad name. Maybe if he thought she didn't care, he'd stop. But she knew this was just wishful thinking. He wouldn't stop. Just like he wouldn't stop brushing against her every chance he got, or accidentally touching her breast when he reached for a plate on the shelf. Had Ethel noticed? Was that part of the reason she was out here waiting tables this morning?

She wasn't complaining. The customers were all nice to her, and if they noticed she was a little hesitant or awkward, no one said anything. Maybe because so many were caught up in talking about the recent murder. You couldn't escape it.

"Hope you don't have to walk home after work, darlin'," one heavy-set woman with a dimpled smile said to her, as Caroline handed her the menu. "Not with that madman running around loose."

She took the menu from Caroline's hand and scanned the specials. "Of course that actress he strangled had her own car, didn't she, and it didn't save her." One crimson fingernail tapped the plastic-covered menu. "I'll have the extra-thin pancakes with maple syrup and sausages, and a glass of orange juice." She flashed her deep dimples. "And a coffee now, dear. Extra cream on the side."

TWENTY-EIGHT

Caroline took the bus home, glad to be off her feet, and warm. Ethel said she'd be back washing dishes tomorrow, but as soon as there was an opening she'd put her out in the restaurant full time.

She changed into her yellow robe and curled up on the sofa, feet tucked under her. She surveyed her surroundings, always pleased at the coziness of her little room. At the homey touches she'd added since moving in. She looked up at the wall, where she'd hung a few family pictures she unpacked from the trunk. One a black and white photo of her grandparents, taken in front of their old house. It gave her a sense of connection having their pictures where she could see them. She'd also hung a photo of her parents, herself between them at around three years old. They each held one of her small hands, and she was smiling into the camera, at whoever held it. A child who felt loved. And she had loved them back.

"Your father made a bad judgment in forcing you to give your child away," Doctor Rosen had said. "I believe he came to regret his decision. Had you been of a different nature, who knows? It might have been the right one."

She flicked on the TV. The newscaster was talking about the murders. Women were afraid, he said, and cautioned those who lived alone to keep their doors locked. At first they were warning only young women, but now they were telling everyone to be careful, to always be aware of their surroundings. "If you have to go out at night, don't go alone."

Locksmiths were doing a thriving business, he said. Dog adoptions from shelters were at an all time high. Baseball bats stood in corners, knives hidden under pillows. Who would be next?

People wondered.

Caroline wondered too. She wouldn't be going back to the park, that was sure, not until they caught the killer. She no longer felt safe there. Mrs. Bannister said she was being silly, it was perfectly safe in the daytime, but Caroline remembered the man in the park, and wasn't so sure. Not that it mattered now with the days growing colder.

She couldn't get the man in the park out of her mind. Had he really been watching her? If he was, and she was more and more convinced that he was, did he know where she lived?

Mrs. Bannister tried to convince her that no one but the tenants could gain access to this building, but Caroline knew if someone really wanted to get in, they would find a way.

"You could just come in with someone else, say you lost your key, or forgot it in your room," she told the landlady. "You could pretend you were delivering flowers to someone in the building. Or visiting someone. Or selling magazines." These were some of the things the customers and other waitresses were saying about their own residences and their words had given Caroline shivers.

TWENTY-NINE

It would have surprised Caroline to know how much her words had upset the landlady. Greta could recall another monster that preyed on women living alone. She was just a girl when the Boston Strangler had terrified an entire city, but she would never forget that awful time. Albert DeSalvo murdered those women in their flats. He obviously used some ruse to get inside their homes, something of the sort Caroline had suggested. How else could you explain why all these women willingly opened their doors to him. But this killer didn't murder women in their homes, did he? she reminded herself.

Who's to stay he won't start? Certainly not the cops. They haven't a clue.

She moved from the window, and went out to the kitchen where she was thawing hamburger for supper. Cheeseburgers were a particular favorite of Harold's. She'd make them just the way he liked them, sliced tomato and dill pickle. Maybe it would cheer him up. Poor Harold, he was so smitten with Caroline. At his aunt's suggestion, he'd asked her to a movie but she turned him down and Greta felt bad about that. She shouldn't have made the suggestion. Poor Harold didn't need another rejection. She was a meddling old woman and should have minded her own business.

THIRTY

"No time for daydreaming, Carrie, me lass," Mike said, grabbing some plates off the shelf. He lowered his voice, said in her ear, "What's the problem, got your period. Gotta get the lead out of that cute little ass. Dishes are piling up."

Her face flamed at his insulting words, tears prickling behind her eyelids. She was never behind on her dishes, and wasn't now. While he was criticizing her work, he was also letting her know he would call her by any name he chose, say anything to her he wanted, and there was nothing she could do about it.

Was he right? Was she just another version of her mother? Weak, unable to stand up for herself.

'Act strong,' Dr. Rosen said. 'And you will be.'

Gathering all her nerve, she turned and faced him squarely. "If you insult me again, I shall call you Michelle—like a girl." It was the best she could do.

His eyes shot open with surprise that she would dare to answer him back, and then they darkened with fury as he muttered, just loud enough for her to hear, "Freakin' mental case."

From then on, her problems with Mike grew even beyond what they had been, and she wished with all that was in her that she had not challenged him. He launched an all-out campaign to make her life as miserable as he could. Once helpful and friendly, or so she had perceived him, now he was her tormentor, and there was no letting up. Every chance he got, he touched her, coming close enough so that she could smell the hair gel he used, and his sweat. He whispered ugly things in her ear that she tried not to hear, comments that made her feel small and dirty and ashamed. And he always made sure no one else saw or heard him. His words followed her home, and replayed in her mind even as she sat alone in her little room, which had itself lost its charm for her, turning as shabby as she felt inside.

She began to sleep poorly, even with her little white pill, her hard-won confidence crumbling like so much sand. Her nerves were frayed and she was always on the verge of tears. As much as she had enjoyed her job before, now she dreaded going into work. She fought getting out of bed, wanting only to pull the covers over her head and retreat into a womb of darkness, where nothing could hurt her.

Mrs. Bannister stopped her on her way out the door one morning and asked her if anything was wrong, but she lied and said no, thinking no one would believe her about Mike. They would say she was paranoid. If she told anyone at work about him, she would be stamped a troublemaker and sent away. But to where?

No. The known was preferable to the unknown, so she didn't complain about Mike Handratty.

But she also knew she didn't want to crawl back inside herself again, though it was already happening. She could feel herself slipping, and it frightened her more than Mike did. She had to fight against it. I won't go back there, she vowed to the pale woman in the mirror, as she got ready for another day at work. I won't disappear from the world again. She'd have to fight him.

She hadn't expected the fight to come so soon. It was shortly after the breakfast rush and Caroline was sliding the clean knives into the butcher's block when she felt a hot breath on the back of her neck and an increasingly familiar hand squeeze her left buttock. At his touch, something snapped in her and she spun around, completely forgetting that she was still clutching a large butcher's knife in her hand, not noticing the way it flashed evilly under the flourescent light.

"Keep your hands off me," she heard herself say loudly. "Leave me alone."

Seeing him back away from her, eyes wide, surprised her even more than her own outburst. But she wasn't finished yet. Her resentment had built up to such fever pitch over these past weeks, now it spilled over like a burst dam.

"Don't you touch me again, don't you speak to me."

A dark flush crawled up Mike's neck and face and the kitchen fell silent. All eyes were on them. Caroline felt the heat rise to her own cheeks. She was shaking inside.

"I never touched you, you crazy bitch. You gonna stab me now, you nut case." His eyes darted around at the silent faces, searching out allies. "I never touched her. I ain't workin' with her anymore. That's it. She didn't even know how to operate the goddamn dishwasher when she came here; I had to show her how. Look at her; she's a basket case."

It was only then that Caroline became aware of the knife in her hand, and dropped it as if it was on fire, letting it clatter to the floor. Her eyes spilling with over with tears, she grabbed her coat off the rack and ran out of the restaurant.

She ran half a block before she slowed her step. Not knowing where else to go, and not wanting to go home and chance running into the landlady, Caroline slipped into Mr. Goldman's bookstore. He gave a surprised smile at seeing her, then frowned, and she realized she was crying in earnest now. Embarrassed, she wiped her eyes with the sleeves of her coat, like a child. Mr. Goldman turned away, pretending not to notice as Caroline made her way through the shelves of books, to the back of the store. Once there, she simply stood not knowing what to do next.

Suddenly, Mr. Goldman was there, beside her. "You're off early today. Sit, sit, my dear," the elderly man said. "I have a wonderful book for you. A little present for my good customer." He handed her the book; it had a maroon cover with the title written in silver, but she could make it out. *Stone Angel* by Margaret Laurence. "It'll make you appreciate your youth."

He was trying wanted to make her feel better, Caroline thought. There were good people in the world. Mr. Goldman was one of them. She had known it instinctively; it was why she had come here.

"Would you like to talk about what happened?" he said now. "I'm told I'm a good listener."

It was all the encouragement she needed. It all spilled out of her. To Mr. Goldman, a stranger, yet not a stranger. "No one ever saw him do anything," she said. "So it's just my word against his. And I'm the one who was holding a knife, though I certainly wouldn't have used it on him. But no one will believe that. I'm the one who was in the mental hospital."

"But you weren't in there for killing anyone, were you?"

"No. No." Her answer came with something between a laugh and a sob.

They both turned as the door opened and a customer entered the shop.

"Well then. There you are." He smiled at her. "You sit awhile, read your book. Everything will be fine, my dear. Have a little faith."

He left her alone and went to wait on the customer. She sat for a few minutes, turning pages in the book, then rose and left the store, relieved that Mr. Goldman was still busy with his customer. She had to admit, she felt better having told Mr. Goldman about Mike, even if it didn't change anything.

THIRTY-ONE

It had begun to snow while she was inside the bookstore, heavy fat flakes that fell straight down, quickly turning the streets white. Nothing to do now but go back to her room. She would buy a newspaper on the way and check the want ads. But she would need a reference?

She must have looked like such a crazy woman to everyone, standing there with that knife in her hand. Who would hire her now? She forgot about the newspaper. At least she still had a little money in the bank, so she wouldn't starve and she could pay her rent for a while. Unless she was arrested for threatening someone with a deadly weapon.

She arrived at her building just as Ethel Crookshank pulled up alongside her. in a battered red Volkswagon. "Are you okay, Caroline?" she asked, getting out of the car.

"Ethel. Yes, I—I guess so. I'm sorry I caused so much trouble. I..."

"You didn't cause the trouble, dear. I know what's been going on. You were merely standing up for yourself. And about time, too. Don't you worry. I talked to Frank and Mike's services will no longer be required. Frank wants you to come back. You're a good little worker, Caroline. Everyone likes you. We're also putting you out in the restaurant full time. We've got a new dishwasher starting tomorrow."

She felt both stunned and overwhelmed with gratitude and this unexpected kindness. At the same time, she didn't want to be responsible for someone getting fired.

"But Mike didn't really hurt me, he..."

"Stop that. Of course he did. It hurts a lot to be constantly embarrassed and humiliated. And it was obviously having an effect on you. Anyway, you're not the first young woman he's gone after. Just so you know."

"I'm really sorry. I…"

"Stop apologizing, Caroline. But keep an eye out for him. Mike doesn't like to be crossed."

THIRTY-TWO

In mid December, people's minds turned happily from murder to Christmas. Phone calls to the department had trickled to a stop. All leads in the case had gone nowhere. Detective Tom O'Neal was in his office, going to the files yet again. Fine-tooth combing. Looking for a clue they might have missed.

Parents of both victims called often, and Tom had nothing new to tell them, which depressed him. Lorraine Winters' mother's voice was familiar enough that he now recognized it when she said hello, detective. Rosalind Gibbs' mother didn't call as often, mainly because she didn't expect to find closure. Or maybe there couldn't be any anyway, because no matter what happened, her daughter, who had wanted to be a nurse since she was a little girl, wasn't coming back. People grieved differently. It was obvious though that she didn't believe Rosalind's boyfriend was guilty. Actually, neither did he nor Glen. His alibi checked out and he was devastated by his loss. So much for Tom's promises to find the killer and bring him to justice. And the more time that passed, the less likely that was that that would happen.

Jeffrey Denton was still in his radar, however. He had no prior convictions, but that could just mean he never got caught at anything. They were keeping an eye on him.

Pearl Grannan's murder was another story. They were waiting for a match of the tires and tracks, and it was a good bet they'd be filing charges against her husband for first degree murder. It appeared from the evidence, and his own strange behavior, that Fred Grannan had used the recent killings to try to cover his own crime against his wife. After Fred Grannan killed her in a fit of rage, he'd transported her body in the trunk of his van, dumping it where it was found by the hiker. With the help of luminol, the trunk revealed more than traces of her blood, though Grannan had obviously tried to clean it up.

But Denton might be good for the other two. He knew Winters, even went to her funeral. Other than teaching kids piano, he was pretty much a loner, white, mid-thirties, fitting the profile of many serial killers. Which could mean Caroline Hill was in danger, living downstairs from him.

"Never knew a musician who was a murderer," his partner said, rationalizing that musicians released their frustrations and tensions, through their music. Tom reminded him that Charles Manson was pretty damn good on the guitar. Wrote a lot of his own stuff, in fact.

Tom's office door was partly open and he could see one of the secretaries hanging a sparkling blue star on the wall, taping branches of cedar on either side. The smell wafted in to him.

Everyone needed a break, and Christmas provided it. No one wanted to think about a murderer running loose at this time of year; they wanted to think of decorating, cooking, school pageants, shopping.

Even though plagued with darker thoughts because his job demanded it, Tom was no exception. He wondered about what to get his kids this Christmas. Money would probably be most welcomed. He didn't see them often enough to know what they might like. Mary had always looked after Christmas. Maybe that was part of the problem, why he was alone at Christmas. Well, no sense crying over what he couldn't change. He hoped she was happy with the dentist. No, he didn't. Yeah, a part of him really did. Mary deserved to be happy.

Like most people in St. Simeon, he too needed to turn his face to the light. But rather than sugarplums and fairies, to Tom, that meant he needed to hear and see the ocean. The ocean made you feel small and insignificant in the scheme of things. He needed to run on the beach with his dog, and let all the ugliness of the world wash out to sea. Even if it did wash back in and roll over you as soon as you took your eyes away.

THIRTY-THREE

This would be Caroline's first Christmas celebrated in her own little corner of the world.

She was on her way home from work, admiring the bright decorations in storefront windows, the twinkling lights and garlands of red and green. With the lights reflecting on the snowy sidewalk, and Carols piped out into the street, window-shoppers were enticed inside.

She let herself be enticed into Natalie's Boutique where she purchased a periwinkle blue wool scarf for Ethel, and was treated by the shopkeeper to a glass of hot, cinnamon-flavored cider. She'd already bought Mrs. Bannister's gift, a fat cookie-jar with the lid the likeness of a cat face.

Caroline thought of her friends at the hospital. For a moment, she missed singing the Christmas Carols with them while Mrs. Green thundered away on the out-of-tune piano.

Not that she would really want to be back there. She was enjoying her job as a waitress. Every day was a little easier. What with all the shoppers out in full force, they'd been very busy at the restaurant lately, and would probably get busier as it grew closer to Christmas. Harold was talking to her again, but he was shyer now, and there were no more cookies left outside her door.

She smiled at the Salvation Army Santa on the corner ringing his bell, and stuffed a bill into his pot. Turned suddenly, as she felt someone close behind her, her heart constricting at the perceived threat of a hand on her shoulder.

Only busy shoppers scurrying in either direction.

"Something wrong, Miss?" the Santa asked.

No, nothing."

She wished him happy holidays, and tried to recapture her sense of good cheer.

It was snowing again when Caroline headed home, struggling with her packages and the small fir tree she'd bought from a teenage boy selling trees in front of the hardware store. The smell of it so close to her face, brought to mind other Christmases, not those at Bayshore, but Christmases from her childhood. How could she have forgotten? Carols playing on the old stereo. Her father trimming the tree, while her mother served them eggnog with sprinkles of nutmeg on top. Yes, the birth of the baby Jesus was well celebrated in her home.

As she neared her building, she saw the blond man going up the stairs. The piano player. Tall and slender, he was wearing a camel hair coat with the collar up, a white wool scarf draped about his neck. His fair hair was speckled with snow. She took him all in in an instant.

Seeing her, he smiled and came back down the steps. "Hello. Miss Hill, isn't it? Please, let me help you with that."

He had such a lovely voice. Deep and resonant. She wondered if he sang as well as played the piano. "Thank you," Caroline said, as he took the tree from her arms. She brushed the needles from her coat, which gave her a moment to contain herself. He was very handsome. It was the first time she had seen him up close, but she knew who he was from his dress, the way he moved. "You're the piano player," she said.

He shook the snow from the tree before taking it inside the foyer, and she liked how thoughtful he was. "Guilty as charged. I'm Jeffrey Denton. Hope my playing doesn't disturb you. I use the headphones when I think of it. That way, only I can hear it."

She preceded him up the stairs. Outside her door, he stood the tree against the door and removed his gloves, and extended a hand. "Jeffrey Denton. Nice to meet you finally, Miss…"

"…Caroline Hill," she said. His hand was warm from being inside the glove, and the warmth traveled through her. "I'm happy to meet you. I… I like it very much when you play. I'm always sorry when you stop."

"Well, then, I have your permission to forego the earphones."

"Yes, you do." He had seemed so serious, but now she saw the playful grin and knew he was teasing her. She looked to the tree for refuge. "It's just a little tree," she said. "But I wanted my room to feel Christmassy."

"It's a lovely tree. I've seen you from my window, Caroline. I guess considering we both live in this building, it was inevitable that we meet. I'm sorry it took so long."

"Yes. Well, thank you very much for your help. I'd better..."

"I...uh, I'd like to get you know you better. Maybe you'll consider having a Christmas drink with me. Some wine and music. I hope you won't think me too bold. I..."

"Yes, please. I would like that. When?"

The instant the words were out, she knew by the raising of his eyebrow that she had answered too quickly, too eagerly and felt the color flood her cheeks. Hearing him play on those late nights, she came to feel as if she knew him, but she didn't really. He was a stranger to her. What must he think?

Yet, as far as she could tell, he seemed pleased that she had accepted his invitation, even relieved, and she realized he'd thought she might refuse him. As she'd refused Harold. Harold, who she still saw now and now, talked to, but who was always quick to scurry off. She had hurt him, and she was sorry about that. But Harold felt more like a younger brother than someone she would date. Jeffery Denton, on the other hand, was making her feel things she hadn't felt since William. You should be afraid, Caroline. *You should run like the wind away from him.*

"Christmas Eve, if you don't have other plans," he said, burying his hands in his pockets, tilting his head so that a lick of dark blond hair fell over his brow.

"No. I have no plans. That would be nice. A glass of wine to toast Christmas." Her father had approved of wine during the holidays, and had poured a little into her glass that last Christmas at home. Even Jesus drank wine.

"And each other," Jeffrey smiled. "We'll toast each other. I'll knock on your door about eight, then. I'm looking forward to it, Caroline."

She walked about her room smiling to herself, feeling all fluttery inside. She had a date for Christmas Eve. Imagine. She wondered if he would try to kiss her. She imagined his mouth on hers, and felt a surge of excitement mixed with shyness. Even disbelief. He was so nice-looking, and smelled good too. Of the outdoors and of shaving lotion. She studied herself in the mirror. Tried to see herself as Jeffrey Denton might see her. Blue eyes, smoky lashes, dark shiny hair. A nice mouth, full lips. Soft for kissing?

What should she wear? She had nothing suitable in her closet. Most of the stuff hanging on hangers were second-hand and didn't fit right. The truth was, she wanted to buy something new for this special occasion. She'd go back to Natalie's Boutique, and ask for her help in choosing the perfect dress. It's my money, after all, no one can tell me what to do with it.

She felt like a young girl again. She had missed so much of her life. Now she wanted to seize it with both hands. She must be careful, though. As Nurse Addison had said, people will take advantage of you if you let them. But the words were like a vaccination that didn't take, and Caroline was already counting the minutes until Christmas Eve.

THIRTY-FOUR

Darkness came early now, and it was snapping cold when Caroline dropped in at Natalie's Boutique after work. The little bell above the door tinkled its welcome and the warmth of the shop coupled with the smell of hot cider and cinnamon, added its own special welcome. Bing Crosby's White Christmas played on the sound system.

Caroline was admiring the little tree in the corner, bright and sparkling with decorations, when the woman with the big platinum hair came out from behind a rack of clothes, a smile on her face. "Nice to see you again. Merry Christmas."

"Merry Christmas to you," Caroline said. "It's very cold outside."

"It sure is. Well, if you've just come in to get warm, enjoy. Feel free to look around. Have a cup of cider there. If there's anything you need help with…"

"Oh, I do," she said quickly, not wanting her to go back behind the rack of clothes.

"Oh. Well, I'm here to serve." Her dark eyes sparkled and Caroline thought how happy she must be in her work.

"What are you looking for? Dress? Pants maybe to match your new pea jacket?"

"A dress. A special Christmas dress, but not too fancy."

"Ahh. You're having company? Is it a dinner?"

"I'm going on a date with a piano player. His name is Jeffrey Denton and he's very talented. We're going to toast Christmas." Was she saying too much?

But the woman's smile only broadened with pleasure and enthusiasm. "Well, then he'll probably take you out to a little piano bar, I'm guessing, if he's a piano player. Jeffrey Denton—I've heard the name. Anyway, you're absolutely right. You don't want fancy, but something elegant. To set off your classy good looks. I'm Natalie, by the way. Natalie Breen. I own this place."

"Hi, Natalie. I'm Caroline Hill."

"Nice to meet you, Caroline." She gave her another once over, then said, as if she were sharing a happy secret, "I think I've got just the dress for you."

Caroline followed her to a rack of more expensive looking dresses at the back of the store. Without hesitation, she reached in and brought one the one she had in mind. It was black with a crew neck and three-quarter length sleeves. "What do you think?"

Caroline tried it on in the dressing room and looking at herself in the mirror, felt almost as pretty as a movie star. She looked so different than she did in her waitress uniform.

When she came out, she clapped her hands. "I knew it," Natalie Breen said. She stood back to get the full effect. "It's perfect on you, Caroline. And I'm not just saying that to sell it. Every woman should have some version of the little black dress and this has got to be yours." With a slight frown, she came forward and straightened a sleeve, smiled again, reminding Caroline just then of Nurse Addision.

The phone on the counter rang and the proprietor excused herself to answer it. The song on the sound system slid into Elvis' *I'll Be Home For Christmas*. Caroline turned this way and that, in the full-length mirror, smiling shyly at her reflection.

***

Buddy was watching her through the storefront window, keeping his head down mostly so as not to catch her eye. The vision of her in the black dress made his throat swell and his eyes tear. She was so lovely. It was hard to be patient, but he must be. He could not go to her until New Year's Eve.

He had seen it in a dream a few nights ago. Fireworks exploding in the sky. Horns blowing in celebration. It would be new beginning for both of them.

That was my daughter on the phone," the woman said,

returning. "She and my grandson are visiting over Christmas. Well, now. Where were we?" Her eyes were warm and admiring. "My goodness, Caroline, you don't have an ounce of fat on you, you lucky girl. But you need something with a little heel to bring it all together. Not too high. I know just the thing."

Seconds later she returned with a pair of beautiful black suede boots, sat Caroline down on a chair and knelt and fit them on her. "They're perfect," the woman said, smiling up at her. "How do they feel?"

She stood and walked a few steps. "Like slippers."

"Quality always tells. Now what about accessories? Jewellery?"

"I have a pair of gold drop earrings that belonged to my mother, in the shape of teardrops. I think they would look nice with this dress. Do you think so?"

The earrings had been in the trunk, along with a few other pieces of jewelry. She had finally gone through everything in there. Had found Christmas ornaments she'd hung on her own small tree. Ornaments she remembered. Also a rhinestone belt and earrings she didn't remember seeing before and couldn't imagine her mother wearing. She wasn't much for glamour. Not that Caroline recalled anyway. Perhaps there was a time when she was different.

Thought Caroline did remember her wearing those gold earrings in church. She could see them now, gleaming against her dark hair in the light coming through the high arched window where they sat.

"I do think they would go well," Natalie Breen said. "I do indeed. It's hard to go wrong with gold."

Aside from finding the earrings in the trunk, Caroline had also found a pack of yellowing love letters her father had written from Korea. Her parents had had a life apart from her, one she knew nothing about. A private life. Why then, hadn't they been able to understand about her and William?

It doesn't matter, Caroline. It doesn't matter anymore.

The shop owner was down on one knee, checking the hem of the dress, then standing and fussing with the sleeves, smoothing them, and Caroline thought again of Nurse Addison, wondered what she would think to find her here buying an outfit to wear on a date.

Would she think me a fool imagining that a sophisticated, talented man like Jeffrey Denton would find me interesting? That he would want to spend time with me? No. Nurse Addison would never think that. What was wrong with her? Hadn't the nurse told her she was smart? That she could even go back to school if she wanted to? Become whatever she wanted to be. Nurse Addison was her friend.

"Yes, gold hoop-earrings would be lovely," Natalie Breen was saying. "Teardrops, huh. You know, I think I might even have a brooch that would work."

She left her to reach into the store window, where various pieces of bright jewellery, colorful scarves and purses were on display. She returned with the brooch, pinned it on the dress, by the shoulder.

"There. What do you think?"

Caroline turned to look at herself in the mirror.

***

In spite of the bitter cold, a few shoppers were still out, rushing about, buying gifts for friends and family. Buddy shivered in the hooded jacket, feeling alone and apart as he had since a child. But all that would end soon. There would be good Christmases then.

Christmases like that the one the year Earl Parker was staying with them, Earl, with his cheerful grin and happy-go-lucky ways. He had bought Buddy presents, among them an erector set, a G.I. Joe and a superman puzzle. Buddy and Earl were at the kitchen table putting it together. His mother had bought them mugs of hot chocolate with miniature marshmallows on top. I was happy then.

But she took it all away. She took love away.

He would have it back.

Caroline looked beautiful in the black dress. Was she buying it for their trip together? still watching her in through the storefront window. He imagined the time when they would all be together? Does she know my dream? Share it?

But maybe the dress is for someone else, a voice taunted. He had this awful sick feeling inside him that something wanted to destroy his plan, wanted to rip it apart like so much rotted fabric. The ugly voice in his head had set off a throbbing in his temple, confused him. Made him feel panicky. He wanted to take her tonight, but the voice in the dream said wait until the New Year. The voice was Earl's. That was when the time would be right, he had promised him.

Suddenly, the woman's white-blond head appeared like a full moon in the storefront window, and he stumbled backwards, nearly bumping into a passing pedestrian.

But she had already seen him and smiled, gave him a little wave. Probably thinks I'm a potential customer, considering a gift for my wife or girlfriend. I could be, he thought, as he watched the woman take a gold brooch out of the window.

He stepped to one side so that he could see the clerk fastening the pin onto Caroline's dress. She was looking at her reflection in the mirror, touching the gold pin with her fingertips. She likes it, he thought. But then he saw her check the price tag and hand it back to the clerk, shaking her head no.

It's too expensive for her, he thought, and a rush of giddiness coursed through him. He would please her with the brooch.

When the blond returned the pin to its place in the window, Buddy had already moved well back, out of view.

Not that it mattered.

THIRTY-FIVE

Carrying her lavender bags with the new purchases inside, Caroline hurried along the snow-covered sidewalk, cold even in the new coat after the welcoming warmth of Natalie's Boutique. As she walked, she could see her breath in the night air, like little puffs of white smoke. But her heart was filled with Christmas cheer, so she didn't really mind the cold. It was a pretty evening, the indigo sky scattered with stars. She could have waited for the bus, but she liked walking on such a nice night with the Christmas music in the background.

She had the strangest sensation, walking along with her packages, of having entered someone else's life, not her own. Not an ex-mate of a mental institution at all, but a normal young woman with fun plans for the holidays. She had a date with a very nice man who was also a talented musician, and she liked him very much.

She wondered where he would take her. A piano bar, Natalie had said. That would be nice. He hadn't said, exactly, only that he would knock on her door at eight o'clock and they would go somewhere and have a drink to toast the season.

She hoped he would like her new dress? The pin Natalie had taken out of the window was nice, but too much money, and also it was bigger than the earrings she planned to wear, although she hadn't wanted to say because she was being so helpful and nice. The gold earrings would be enough. She liked it that her mother had worn them, which made them more special. She had loved her mother, though she realized she hadn't really known her; the woman's real self had been locked away. Maybe she no longer knew who she was either by the time Caroline came along. But Caroline was glad for the earrings.

"Your new dress can be casual or dressy, Caroline, depending on accessories," Natalie had said. "That's the beauty of 'the little black dress'. And you can switch these boots for flats if you decide to have a little drink at his place after-or yours." She had grinned and winked at the implication and Caroline felt herself blushing. Even now thinking about it, despite the cold night, her face grew warm.

She had asked if she could include her in her mailing list, saying she liked to send her good customers special news of sales and special events, she said, and Caroline had no objections. It would be lovely to get mail addressed to her personally.

She had left the well-lit shops ten minutes ago, the Christmas music behind her now, a faint thin tune on the night air, soon fading altogether. Merely a memory, playing in her head. Though not yet eight o'clock, it was dark out. Other than her breathing and the crunch of her boots on the sidewalk, all was silent. *Silent Night.*

She loved Christmas.

Harold was getting a new bike, Mrs. Bannister had confided to her. He'd be happy about that, though he wouldn't be able to use it until spring. Caroline's Christmas gift to Harold was a model airplane he could put together, or hang it from the ceiling, the man in the shop told her, or just set it on shelf. His aunt had told her that Harold like putting models together. It relaxed him.

At the sound of footsteps behind her, all thoughts of Christmas and airplanes fled Caroline's mind and fear took their place. It struck her that she was walking alone on a dark street, something everyone, including the landlady and Ethel Crookshank had warned her against. She had known better herself. But for a little while, caught up in the joy of the season, she had forgotten about the murdered women, and about the man in the park, watching her.

She remembered now.

Afraid to turn around, heart thumping in her chest, she picked up her pace. She was very close to home, not far now. It's just another shopper on their way home, she told herself. Then: No, not a shopper.

To her horror, the footsteps behind quickened in keeping with hers. He was following her, quickly catching up to her. And she knew instinctively that it was a *he*. The killer?

She was about to break into a run when a strong hand gripped her arm. "Hey, what's your hurry, little girl?"

Caroline whirled around, startled, and at the same time almost relieved to see Mike Handratty standing there, leering at her. She tried to yank her arm from his grasp but he was too strong. "Let me go."

His coat was open, the shirt beneath it askew. You'd think he'd be freezing. She guessed the liquor was keeping him warm. He reeked of it.

Ethel had told her to keep an eye out for him, that 'Mike didn't like to be crossed', but enough time had passed that Caroline was able to put Mike Handratty, and what had occurred between between them, out of her mind. Clearly, it hadn't work both ways. He'd been just waiting his chance to get her alone. He must be very angry with her.

"Hello, Mike," she said, forcing a friendly tone into her voice. "How are you?"

He gave a harsh laugh and squeezed her arm tighter, hurting her. "How do you think I am, sweetheart? It's Christmas and because of you, I ain't got no freaking job."

"I'm really sorry. I didn't want that to happen. Please let go of my arm. You're hurting me."

Ignoring her, he said, "Didn't you? Well, what the hell. No big deal. I was sick of the place, anyway, I'll get another job."

He was on his way to drunk, slurring his words, but not quite there. She grabbed at the straw he offered. "Yes, yes you will. You're a very good cook and someone will hire you."

"Yeah. Ya think so." The grinned became something dirty, ugly then. "That ain't all I'm good at, Carrie, me love." His hand was still gripping her arm, refusing to let her go. "You know I like you, don't you, Carrie. I like that cute little ass of yours, those big blue eyes. You really turn me on, kiddo. Why don't we just let bygones be bygones and you and me get to know one another a little better."

He had backed her against the wall of a building, and the icy cold of the brick seeped through her coat. His body was pressed against hers and she could feel his arousal as he breathed his boozy breath into her face. A terrifying thought occurred to her; maybe Mike was the predator who raped and murdered those women. Panic and fear filled her and she managed to yank her arm from his grasp, but he quickly made a trap of his arms, setting his palms flat against the building's wall, encircling her. She could feel the edge of a brick digging into her back.

She realized he'd deliberately chosen this particular pool of darkness, in the stretch between two streetlights, waiting until she arrived at this spot, to accost her.

"Please, let me go. I have to go home now."

"Oh, I don't think so. You owe me, baby, and you're gonna pay up." His hand moved up under her coat and she tried to push it away. "Stop it. Please…"

"Is this man bothering you, Ma'am?" a friendly soft voice said out of the darkness. A whispery voice that froze Mike's hand near her breast. She sensed his surprise at the voice that came so sudden out of the blue. She herself felt only great relief. She couldn't see the stranger's face, which seemed to have some kind of hood drawn over it, concealing his features. He was merely a dark shape against the lighter night.

"Yes, yes, he is. Thank you."

Mike took his hand away and Caroline drew her coat tighter about her, fighting tears.

"Take off, Mac," Mike said. "I'm talkin' to my girlfriend here. We're just having a friendly disagreement. Right, Carrie." But she thought he sounded a little nervous, the bravado feigned.

"No. I'm not his girlfriend. He attacked me. I just want to go home."

"Go ahead, then," the whispery voice said. "You're safe now, Caroline. He won't be bothering you anymore."

The voice seemed to be trying to disguise itself in whispers. He had called her by name. Caroline. Who was he? Someone she knew?

Mike had released his hold on her and she intuited a trickling away of his earlier cockiness, replaced by the same fear he'd instilled in her not a moment ago. Not letting herself dwell on any of it, she escaped the scene where the two men stood on the sidewalk, her shopping bags slapping against her hip as she ran.

Behind her, the ominous, frightening sounds of body blows and grunts of pain were hard to listen to, so she blocked them from her mind and didn't stop running until she was inside her building, the door locked behind her.

Upstairs in her room, she stood gasping for breath, until the liquid thumping of her heart slowed to normal. Then she put her packages away. And tried not to think about what had just happened.

But her efforts at pretending that nothing happened really weren't working, and she spent a sleepless night reliving the frightening attack and wondering about the man came on the scene so suddenly, so unexpectedly. Who was he? How did he know her name?

***

Sometime in the small hours, she got up and examined her upper arm in the mirror. It was still sore where Mike had gripped it and she could see the bruises reflected in the glass, made by his cruel fingers. But she still didn't want to be the cause of him being badly hurt, or worse. All her good spirits had drained away, replaced by angst and fear throughout the night, and she was glad when morning dawned.

On her way to work, she passed the place where Mike had accosted her. A scene she'd fled minutes later, leaving him in the hands of her rescuer. There was no sign at all that anything ugly had happened here last night, as if the experience was no more than a bad dream.

That notion was quickly dispelled when she arrived at work to find everyone talking about Mike Handratty getting beat up last night. Ethel told her he was in the hospital. "He told the cops he was walking along minding his own business and these three guys came out of nowhere and jumped him," Ethel said. "He's in pretty rough shape, jaw wired together, broken nose. But he'll live, apparently, according to the news."

Caroline was sorry he was in the hospital, but glad that his injuries would heal and that he'd be okay. But she couldn't say she was sorry the stranger had come along when he did. No, she couldn't say that and be truthful about it.

"Scambled eggs, bacon," the cook, Ron Graham called out, setting Caroline's order on the counter. "Last I heard his wife divorced him and he moved in with his widowed mother, so no doubt she'll take care of him. I'm surprised someone didn't beat the crap out of Mike long ago." He gave Caroline a wink and her stomach flipped over. Did he know something? She turned away before he could see the question on her face, and sailed back through the doors with her order of bacon and eggs.

Why hadn't she told them the truth about what happened? That Mike attacked her on the way home and a man interceded on her behalf. One man, not three, as Mike had claimed. A stranger who appeared out of the darkness likes a guardian angel. A stranger who whispered her name. She might have ended up dead like those other women, for all she knew. Like Lorraine Winters who'd once lived right across the hall from her. Last night, she had thought it possible. But despite what he'd done, somehow, in the light of day, she didn't think Mike was the killer.

She should call the police. Then why didn't she? She knew why. Because she was afraid. Afraid they wouldn't believe her. Or maybe even blame her.

Caroline was finished her day and getting ready to leave when Ethel came up to her, drying her hands on a paper towel. "Mike's been cruisin' for a bruisin' for some time now, Caroline. It's got nothing to do with you. You musn't feel sorry for him." She tossed the paper towel in the garbage can.

"I don't. Why would I blame myself?" She busied herself putting on her winter boots. What was Ethel asking? Should I tell her what really happened?

When she stood up, Ethel was standing there looking curiously at her. "I didn't say you blamed yourself. As you say, why would you? I said you shouldn't feel sorry for him. You just look—so sad."

"I just, well—it's Christmas. I hope he'll be okay."

"He will. Yeah, I'm glad he's gonna live, too. You okay, Caroline?"

She could only nod. And then she was out the door.

THIRTY-SIX

When next Detectives Tom O'Neal and Glen Aiken called on Fred Grannan, they had a search warrant. As they were walking up the walkway, Tom saw the curtain move, then fall back into place. Grannan looked a sight worse than he had when they first saw him, haunted and he'd lost weight. There were bags under his eyes as if he hadn't slept in weeks.

"Why aren't you out there catching that killer that murdered, Pearl?" he demanded of them. "Why you hassling me?"

His demeanor had changed considerably now that he was feeling cornered. There was a wariness in his eyes, along with a certain cunning Tom hadn't observed on the first visit. He had no choice but to let them in but this time didn't ask them to sit down. All pretense at hospitality was gone. "I already told you everything I know. She went shopping and didn't come back. I tried to find her, phoned all her friends. That's it. I don't know what you think you'll find going through my stuff," he yelled as they made their way upstairs to the bedrooms. I've got nothing to hide."

That wasn't true, though. No, not by a long shot.

He had a feeling Fred Grannan just might be spending Christmas behind bars, and a number of Christmases after that.

As for him, he'd be taking his kids out for Chinese on Boxing Day, and he was looking forward to that. So he was trying his best to salvage a little of the spirit of Christmas within himself. Not easy to hang onto in this job.

THIRTY-SEVEN

It was Christmas Eve, seven minutes before closing time at Natalie's Boutique on this special eve, when the little bell above the door jangled lightly and a man entered. He pushed the hood of his jacket back off his head and clapped his hands together in their leather gloves. "Cold night."

Natalie Breen was returning several dresses a customer had tried on and not bought, back on their hangers.

"Sure is," she smiled. "Help yourself to the cider, it'll warm you up. I'll just be a minute."

"Take your time. I know what I want." Accepting the offer of cider, he poured a little from the crockery jug on the festively decorated table, into one of the clear plastic glasses provided. He had taken only a sip when she was at his side.

"Yes, sir. Merry Christmas. What can I do for you? You said you already know what you want?"

"I do. I'd like that gold pin in the window." He walked over and pointed it out. "That one. Sorry for the trouble, I realize you're about to close."

"No trouble at all," she said, still smiling, reaching in and taking the brooch out of the window. "I usually take the higher priced items out of the window before I close up anyway. This is one of my favorites. The teardrop. Fourteen Karat gold." She handed it to him. "Lovely piece of jewelry."

"Yes, it is. I've been admiring it."

"I know. I saw you outside looking in at it."

In a way, he was sorry she'd said that. He hadn't quite made up his mind about killing her. But now it was clear she had seen him. He didn't like hurting people for no reason. He wasn't a monster, as one newspaper reporter had dubbed him.

The price tag said $219.99. Not that it mattered; he wouldn't be paying for it. "Would you mind gift-wrapping it for me?" He gave her an easy grin. "I'm lucky no one grabbed it before me. By the way, there was a woman in here trying on a dress at the time I was admiring this. She was apparently considering it...?"

"Oh, that was Caroline. Caroline Hill. A very sweet young woman, lives not too far from here. Do you know her?"

"We've met," he said shortly. Anger made the vein pulse in his jaw. She had given Caroline's name so easily; he could have been anyone.

She saw something in his expression that hurried her along. "Oh, I'm sorry. I'm holding us both up," she said, taking his cue. "It's my pleasure to gift-wrap it for you. Mr.."

Not answering, he turned away from her, pretending to look over some angora gloves on a shelf. He could have been anyone, he thought again, like that jerk who was man-handling her when she was on her way home the other night. Lucky he'd been close by at the time, watching out for her.

It was wrong of this woman to give out her name. She should be more careful about protecting her customers' identities. She needed to be punished for her betrayal. He would see to it. No longer having any reluctance about what he was about to do, he looked at his watch. Leaving her wrapping the gift for Caroline, he wandered away. He knew he was overreacting to the situation, in a rage even he didn't understand, but he didn't care. The beast was rising within him.

As Natalie drew a small length of wrapping paper from its roll, she thought again of Caroline and how well this brooch would have gone with that black dress. But never mind, she mused, crimping the silver ribbon and winding it around the blue metallic paper. A sale was a sale, and she needed every nickel she brought in. Gloria would need her financial help for awhile, as well as her moral support. Divorce was tough to get through.

Not looking up, still fussing with the wrapping, she said cheerfully to the back of her customer's head: "Someone's going to be thrilled Christmas morning."

Getting no answer, her thoughts drifted away from her

customer to her grandson, David, who would soon turn four. Handsomest kid around. She'd bought him the red pedal car he'd asked Santa for, and could hardly wait to see his face when he opened the box. David was such a joy to her. She wished Jim was here to enjoy him, but her husband had died of a sudden heart attack six years ago, and never had the chance to know his grandson. But in her heart she knew he was looking down on all of them.

She couldn't have been happier that Gloria and David were spending Christmas with her, but secretly wished Eric was with them, that they weren't going through this painful divorce. She'd like to say she didn't like Eric, never had, but it wouldn't be true. He'd been like a son to her. How could he do this? His secretary for God's sake. How cliché. Well, it happens. Gloria will just have to get on with her life. She's still young and attractive with many good years ahead of her. Someone else would come into her life. But right now she was in pain and needed all her support. In the meantime, Natalie determined that the three of them would have a good Christmas. She'd finish up this sale and get on home.

"I'm Natalie Breen, owner of Natalie's Boutique," she said, holding her finger taut on the ribbon as she knotted it, then proceeding to fashion a perfect silver bow. "If you'll give me your name and address, I'd be happy to send you notices of spec..."

At the sound of the lock clicking into place, her head shot up, her words severed. A cold draft brushed her heart as if it already knew something her brain was too frightened to take in. The man was standing at the door, his back to her.

"What are you...?" Her voice caught in her throat as slowly he turned and smiled at her.

"You wanted my name?" His voice was low and friendly, deadly.

"No, uh, it's not necess..."

"Buddy," he said. "I'm Buddy."

THIRTY-EIGHT

When her mother didn't arrive home by eight o'clock, Gloria Breen-Clark called the store to see what was keeping her. The phone rang and rang but no one answered. Fifteen minutes later, she tried again thinking her mother might have been in the washroom when she called the first time, but there was still no answer. She was starting to worry now. Where could she be? Mom said she'd try to lock up a few minutes early so she could be home before David's bedtime.

"When's Nanna coming home, mommy?" David asked sleepily from the sofa, where Gloria had let him curl up to wait for her. "Is she coming home soon?"

"I'm sure she is, honey," Gloria answered, still staring at the phone, wondering what could be keeping her. She closed up at seven and it was only a ten minute drive. She should be here by now. She was pacing back and forth across her mother's cream-colored carpeting. She stopped and looked out the window, hoping to see the glow of headlights that would announce her arrival.

David had crawled up on the sofa earlier in front of the Christmas tree and had now fallen back to sleep. Poor David. He was trying so hard to stay awake for his Nanna. So much excitement. Right now, he looked pretty zonked out to her. Taking the multi-colored afghan off the back of the sofa, she covered him with it. Then proceeded to pace some more and gnaw on her already bitten-to-the-quick fingernails.

By eight-thirty she was in a full-blown panic and phoned the police to report her mother missing.

"Well, ma'am, if you say she closed up at seven on Christmas Eve, then I'd have to say you're jumping the gun a little." The officer at the other end of the line had a smile in his voice as he said, "It's only been an hour and a half since she locked up. She probably met some friends and went out for a little Christmas cheer. Or maybe she's doing some last minute shopping. Lots of stores are open till ten tonight."

"No, you don't understand. She wouldn't do that. I phoned her earlier and she said she was going to close up early so she could get home for David, my son. Her grandson. They're very close."

"So there you are. She's out buying something extra for David."

His patronizing tone brought a flare of frustration. She was just one more hysterical female he had to contend with in his job as an officer of the law. She tried again, forcing a calmness into her voice she didn't feel. "No, she knows we're waiting for her." She had a bad feeling in the pit of her stomach. "Officer, please, you have to listen…"

"Got another phone ringing," he cut in. "Sorry, ma'am. Look, if your mom's not home in an hour give us a call back, okay? Merry Christmas now, and to David too."

She opened her mouth to argue but he had already hung up.

"Was that Nanna?" David asked, his voice still thick with sleep.

"No, sweetie. Go to sleep. I'll wake you when Nanna gets here." Gazing at her son lying there curled up in his colorful cocoon, blond head peeking out, her heart ached, knowing how hard it was on David not having his daddy around. He adored Eric. *Please God, don't let anything happen to David's Nanna. To my mother.*

"Honey, I'm going to call Mrs. Abrams to come over and keep an eye on you for a little bit. Nanna's car might have broken down."

Mrs. Abrams was a widowed neighbor and a good friend of her mother's. She dialed the number and five minutes later Mrs. Abrams, a woman of ample girth and a cheery face was ringing the doorbell.

"I won't be long," Gloria told her, already into her coat and scarf. "An hour at most. I'm sorry for bothering you on Christmas Eve, but I'm worried. Her car might have broken down," she repeated for Mrs. Abrams, and prayed that's all it was.

"No problem at all, dear. I'm a little concerned myself. She sure wouldn't miss Christmas eve with her favorite boy if she had anything to say about it." Mrs. Abrams turned a smile in David's direction. He was awake again, and she tousled his hair playfully. "Bet you can't wait for Santa to get here, eh, David? Were you a good boy all year?"

"Hi, Mrs. Abrams," he said shyly. "I was good." Then, "Mom, is Nanna lost?"

"No, honey. Well, maybe."

The phone rang and Gloria snapped up the receiver. "Mom?"

"It's me, Gloria. Eric." The sound of her soon-to-be ex-husband's voice brought a rush of longing, of pain, of anger. Hearing it never failed to send a myriad of conflicting emotions through her. Most of all hurt, that after ten years of marriage he'd stopped loving her. Had found someone younger, prettier, and sexier. More interesting. Eric was a lawyer, Leslie his secretary. But for once, she was more focused on her mother's whereabouts than on her shattered marriage.

"Eric, Hi. Mom's not home yet. I thought it was her on the phone."

"Oh. Well…Gloria. I know it's past his bedtime but I, uh, wondered if I might talk to David, wish him a Merry Christmas. Uh, Merry Christmas to you too. And your mom. I have some gifts for David. I'll drop them off in the morning, if that's okay. Am I calling at a bad time? Is he asleep?" She heard the guilt in his voice, and thought with a flare of anger, Good, you bastard, you should feel guilty.

"Dad?" Behind her, David stood in his pajamas, barefoot, eyes wide with excitement.

"Yes, it's your dad, Sweetie." The anger died. "Of course it's okay, Eric. David's right here. One sec."

Leaving a happily distracted David talking on the phone to his father, she rushed out into the night to look for her mother, Mrs. Abrams' words ringing like a death knoll in her mind: 'She wouldn't miss Christmas Eve with her favorite boy if she had anything to say about it'.

If she had anything to say about it.

THIRTY-NINE

Caroline sipped from her second glass of red wine and smiled at the man who sat across from her. She had little experience with wine, but this one tasted very nice to her. Neither too sweet nor too dry, and tingled on her lips.

"Thank you for bringing me here. Natalie Breen said you might bring me to a piano bar."

"Natalie…?"

"She owns Natalie's Boutique. She's a very nice lady. I brought this dress there. Do you like it?"

"I do. Very much. You look amazing, Caroline." He smiled and sipped his wine.

"Thank you." She paused. "I shouldn't have asked that, should I? It was inappropriate. Are you laughing at me?"

His expression turned serious and he set the glass down, laid a hand over hers, his touch warm as the candle-flame reflected in his amber eyes.

"Please, don't ever think that, Caroline. I would never laugh at you. Never. I love your frankness, your honesty. There's nothing coy about you. So many women play games; you're just never sure what's true. Meeting you, well, it's the best Christmas present I could ask for."

When she opened the door to his light rap tonight, she'd been ready with her coat on, and then fretted she might seem too eager. He was late, but only by a few minutes. He had said she looked lovely. But he hadn't seen the dress yet. So maybe it was okay to ask.

The little bar was nice, softly lit, a chimneyed red candle on every table. A big Christmas tree glittering in the corner of the room. It was so cozy here.

The elderly piano player, with his cottony white hair and shiny blue dinner jacket was up on the dais, playing Christmas carols, one following the other, all her favorites. He had nodded at Jeffrey when they walked in. Jeffrey gave him a small salute and a smile. So they knew each other.

Sitting at their table, the flickering candle cast shadows over the planes of Jeffrey's face and she thought how handsome he looked in a soft blue sweater and gray slacks.

There were only a few other couples in the room. Most people would be at home with their families on Christmas Eve, but she was happy to be here with Jeffrey.

"Did you grow up in St. Simeon?" he asked her.

She told him she did, that they'd lived on Gleneton Street, near the bay. "What about you?" she asked, eager to turn the conversation away from herself. "Were you born here?"

Three women came in just then, middle-aged, nicely dressed in their holiday finery, smelling of expensive perfume and the cold night air. They sat at a table across from them, talking, laughing merrily. A waitress came and took their order. Martinis, she guessed from the shapes of the glasses, which she'd seen on one of the soaps, and the olives that floated near the bottoms.

"No, we moved here when I was twelve," Jeffrey said. "I'm an army brat. My dad was in the service and we moved around a lot. But you're deliberately changing the subject," he said, grinning in mock chastisement, and poured more of the wine into her glass, then into his own. "I know a little about your past, where you've been, so you mustn't feel uncomfortable about it."

"Oh. Mrs. Bannister."

"She's a good person, our landlady, but she does like to talk. Not that it matters. My mother suffers from depression. She's been on antidepressant pills ever since my dad died six years ago. Christmas is especially tough on her. I try to be there, as much as I can. It's why I was a little late tonight. I was on the phone with her."

She wished he didn't know about her being at Bayshore, but then supposed he'd have to know sooner or later. You couldn't keep something like that a secret, even without Mrs. Bannister. She was glad it hadn't changed his mind about her.

"Christmas wasn't always the best time of year at the hospital either," she confided. "Not for many of them. But let's not talk about that now."

"Of course. I'm sorry."

She fell silent for a moment, then looked into his eyes, solemn. "It's okay. I don't know how much Mrs. Bannister told you, but I've been in Bayshore for the last nine years. I wouldn't be very good at games."

It seemed important to get that out, to say the words aloud, and dispense with the matter, because it had crossed her mind that he might be amusing himself with her. She hoped that wasn't so.

The silence between them seemed to go on forever. Then he said, "She didn't say how long you were in the hospital. Nine years. Did you kill someone?"

He'd spoken in such earnestness, she had to smile. She told him what she had told Mr. Goldman. "No. I didn't kill anyone."

"Oh, good. Well, I'm not good at games either. I hope we'll be good friends, Caroline. Very good friends."

She stared into her wine as if looking into a crystal ball and hoping to see her future there. Her cheeks were flushed, whether from the way he was looking at her or from the effects of the wine, she wasn't sure. To break the tension of the moment, she asked him if he enjoyed teaching piano, and he talked about that for a few minutes, the mood lightening.

"The most rewarding thing is not necessarily that you've discovered the next Floyd Cramer," he said, warming to his subject, "but that your student has mastered some difficulty he or she has been struggling with. Taking pleasure in their own musical expression. Maybe just learning to play a piece all the way through and feeling good about it. That's the best."

She liked him. Liked the way he cared about his students." It's really nice here. I'm glad you asked me—to come out with you."

The piano player had slid into *Let it Snow, Let it Snow, Let it Snow*. A happy, bouncy tune that made her feel the same way inside.

"Me, too," he said. "I was afraid you might say no."

"I know. I could tell."

He laughed softly. "You are so refreshing, Caroline."

Again, she wondered if he was mocking her, but she refused to give in to such thoughts. She would let nothing ruin this Christmas Eve. Sitting in these elegant surroundings listening to Jeffrey talk, it was hard to reconcile herself with the woman who only a short time ago was an inmate in a lunatic asylum, with no thought of ever getting out. It seemed like a dream. One from which she hoped never to wake.

Her dreamy thoughts scattered with the wail of sirens outside, and as the chilling sound faded into the night she knew intuitively that something bad had happened.

FORTY

Detective O'Neal looked down at the battered, bloodied body of Natalie Breen, the store's owner, sprawled on the floor, a scarf wrapped around her neck, near embedded in the pale flesh. Her face was swollen and bruised, dried blood trailing from one nostril. Her open eyes had trapped the horror of the last few minutes of her life. What the hell was going on? This victim wasn't young, neither was she dark-haired or blue-eyed. There was no obvious sign of sexual assault either.

The place reeked of apple cider and cinnamon He was quite sure he'd never be able to stomach the stuff again. Lights were flashing, hardly signifying the birth of Jesus. Hardly that. They were camera flashes.

"She put up a hell of a fight," his partner said softly beside him, not wanting the victim's daughter to hear.

Tom glanced behind him at the woman huddled on a stool at the back of the store, trembling and crying softly. She'd been hysterical when they arrived on the scene and it took some time to bring her down. Some Christmas present, Tom thought.

"He used one of those scarves," Detective Aiken said, indicating the rack of print scarves by the door.

It was practically the only thing upright in the store. The place was destroyed. The jug of cider had spilled onto the wood floor, was threaded through with her blood. The hems and cuffs of coats and dresses were soaking in the obscene mess.

Photos had already been taken of one very clear shoe print, leading to the door that could only belong to the killer.

The victim's daughter was silent now and simply sat on the stool, huddled in her coat, staring at the floor. Blond and slender, she looked very fragile sitting there, crushed under the weight of shock and grief. She would never forget the sight of her mother lying on the floor, dead, brutalized. She wouldn't be able to close her eyes at night for a long time without that ungodly scene visiting her. Christmases would always be a reminder. The thought angered Tom.

He walked over to her. "Just a couple of questions," he said gently. "I'm sorry."

"It's okay." She dabbed at her eyes with a tissue. "Who would do this to her?" she asked him, or anyone who might have an answer. "She was such a good person, lovely to everyone. She was my best friend." She began to cry again, then abruptly regained control of her emotions, insisting they find the person who did this, make him pay for his crime.

"We're going to do our best to make sure that happens," Tom said. "Maybe you can help. Do you don't know of anyone who would want to hurt your mother?"

Whoever it was had been savage in his attack, out of control. In a rage. Why? Nothing was taken, as far as they could tell; there was money in the till and some fairly expensive items were still displayed in the window, including a pair of diamond stud earrings. Half a dozen suede and leather bags hung on one of the racks that somehow had remained upright in the violent assault.

She answered their questions with as much calm as she could manage. No, she knew no one who would want to hurt her mother. Tom then asked her to recount exactly what she saw or heard upon arriving. She added nothing he didn't already know.

"The door was partly open when I got here. Christmas music was playing. "I didn't see anyone around. The street was deserted."

It Came Upon a Midnight Clear was playing when they got here. Tom had turned the music off, but the unintended double-entendre wasn't lost on him.

"My son, David—he fell asleep on the sofa waiting for his Nanna to come home. David's four. He worships his grandmother. What will I tell him? It's Christmas Eve. Oh, God…mom…"

He had other questions, but they could wait. She needed to get home to her boy. "I'll drive you home," Tom said. "My partner will follow in your car. Is there anyone you'd like us to call?"

She shook her head sadly. "No. No one."

FORTY-ONE

Buddy stood in a pool of darkness across the street from Caroline's building, gazing up at her window. He could see the shiny bulbs on a Christmas tree through the lacy curtain. Her light was on.

He'd gone home and showered away the blood and sour sweat and combed his hair neatly. Feeling the weight of the small package in his inside jacket pocket, he suddenly felt shy as a Victorian suitor. He hadn't wanted to kill that woman tonight. It was just that he'd had such a bad a feeling that everything was getting away from him. And the blond woman had suddenly seemed to represent all that in his way. The depth of his fury had frightened even him and some of what he had done while in its throes he could barely remember.

But there were forces out to destroy their plans. He had to save Caroline. Save her from herself. Their very lives were at stake. But everything had to be timed perfectly. He would need a car, though. You couldn't get to Toronto without a car. He planned to steal one, and he knew which one, too. He'd ditch it when they got there.

He wished Caroline could know how he had protected her tonight. How he had punished the woman who would so readily expose her to strangers. His own mother had left him vulnerable to such strangers, unable to escape. Trapped like a rabbit in a snare. She had invited the beast into their lives, and it had devoured his soul.

Well, never mind that. Soon it would be as it was meant to be.

When he saw her light go out, he started across the street, the key clutched in his hand.

FORTY-TWO

Caroline removed her earrings, kissed them lightly the way she might have kissed her mother had she been here, then put them back in their small velvet case. You couldn't have your heart this full of happiness and still be mad at anybody. She took off her boots, slipped out of her dress and returned it to the closet. She would be wearing it again on New Year's Eve.

"Do you like to dance?" he had asked her.

She had told him she didn't know, but she thought she used to like it. He only smiled at the puzzling answer, said good; they would dance in the new year.

She didn't tell him that her father didn't believe in dancing, or that he'd said it was the devil's way to tempt young people into sins of the flesh. The only dancing she had ever done was in her room with the door shut and the music turned low. Music she was always quick to shut off at the sound of approaching footsteps.

She was standing at the closet door, caressing the soft fabric of new dress. She couldn't afford another new dress, but she wouldn't need to. The owner said just wearing different accessories would totally change the look of this one. Caroline knew exactly what she'd wear with the dress too; the rhinestone belt and dangly earrings that had been in the trunk. They'd be perfect for New Year's Eve. She wondered when her mother had worn them. And suddenly wished she was here so she could ask her.

Jeffrey had said they were going to a veteran's club his father had belonged to when he was alive. As his son, he'd inherited the privilege of membership. The place was near the bay not far from where she used to live. She told him the number of the house and he said he'd driven past it on a number of occasions. "I think it's up for sale," he said.

Later, as they stood at her door, his eyes lingered on her mouth and she knew he wanted to kiss her, and she was drawn to him like a heat magnet. But she made no move toward him. And without touching her, he had merely leaned forward and kissed her on the cheek. "Goodnight, Caroline. Sleep well."

Then he went on upstairs to his own room.

FORTY-THREE

Her cheek still tingling from the touch of his lips on her skin, she let herself into her room and closed and locked the door. Smiling dreamily. She'd forgotten that you could be this happy.

The wine had made her sleepy and she had thought she might fall asleep at once, but instead she lay awake admiring her little tree and thinking about Jeffrey Denton, spinning dreams she dared to imagine had a possibility of coming true.

The streetlight entered her room like a bright moon. A magical moon. Its light played over the backs of her hands that rested on the blanket, turning them an ethereal blue-white as she lay there reliving the evening, replaying Jeffrey's every word and gesture and expression.

Then, like a slow eclipse blocking the moon, other thoughts, other voices infiltrated her mind, diminished her smile and chased the glow of tonight away. She tried to deny them entry but to no avail. He kept you waiting tonight, the voice said, made you anxious, worried that he might not come at all. How do you know it wasn't a deliberate ploy? You don't know this man, really. Just because you heard him playing piano and spent a couple of hours in his company doesn't mean you know him. He had was late calling for her because he was talking to his mother on the phone, but how did she know that was true? She didn't.

She tried to shake off the rush of insecurity, of anxiety, told herself she was being silly. If he hadn't wanted to be with her he wouldn't have asked her out in the first place.

He might have changed his mind. It would have been awkward not to show up considering they both lived in the same building. Well, he certainly wouldn't have asked you out twice, would he? Yes, this finally made sense to her. This voice belonged to the part of her that wanted her to be happy. That wanted her to be able to trust her heart again.

In a way, life was easier living at Bayshore, which had served as a kind of cocoon, leaving her with no decisions to make. No responsibility. In a way, like crawling back into the womb. Then she thought of Ella's snoring beside her, the constant rhythmic squeak of the rocking chair, and those pretend knitting-needles that you could almost hear clicking madly as Ella's fingers busily knitted one, pearled two. No, she didn't miss that, nor did she want to return to it.

She had come to like the sound of rain outside her barless window, hearing the laughter of children playing down on the sidewalk. She liked talking to her customers, being treated like a whole person, someone strong and intact. Someone a man like Jeffrey Denton would find interesting.

With this pleasant thought, she closed her eyes and was soon asleep.

Sometime in the night, she woke up thinking she heard something. She sat up in the bed and listened.

The green glowing numbers on the clock on her night table said 3:01 a.m.

The room was in semi-darkness. She peered into deep shadows the glow from the streetlight did not reach. Everything seemed fine. Glints of Christmas bulbs pierced the darkness. Just a dream, she told herself, and snuggled down into the blankets again. She was about to go to sleep when she heard it another sound, a soft shuffling of feet outside her door.

She stared at the door. The narrow strip at the bottom, where light found its way from a low watt bulb in the hallway, had darkened, like ink spilled and spreading, blocking out the light.

Someone was standing outside her door. At first she was not really afraid, just startled and curious. But when the doorknob slowly turned, first one way and then the other, her simple surprise and puzzlement turned to fear and her heart galloped in her breast like a small hunted animal. She willed herself to remain calm. It was probably just a neighbor coming home late from a party, confused from having consumed a little too much Christmas cheer.

Maybe he was on the wrong floor. Obviously not the wrong building, since whoever it was out there, had to have a key to the outside door.

Finally she called out in a timid voice, "Who's there?" The doorknob grew immediately still and silent. But someone was out there. She pushed back the blankets and sat up, eased her feet onto the cool floor, reached for her robe at the foot of the bed.

She padded to the door, tying the robe as she went. Yes, whoever it was still out there; she could hear them breathing. Who was it? Jeffrey? Harold? Mrs. Bannister? Why didn't they answer? Why would anyone want to frighten her?

Maybe it was someone else. Maybe the killer. Hadn't she told Mrs. Bannister anyone could get in here if they really wanted to? She remembered the sirens she had heard tonight as she sat across from Jeffrey. The sinking feeling she had had at the bone-chilling wail, the fading of it into the night.

She told herself it had nothing to do with her.

She wanted to tell whoever it was to go away but her throat seemed to have closed up, robbing her of voice. Cautiously, she moved closer and pressed an ear to the door.

"Caroline," came the soft whisper from the other side, as though whoever it was had sensed her there. She jumped back with a lurching of her heart, hand at her throat. Again, the doorknob rattled softly in its casing while her heart thumped against her ribcage like a small faulty engine.

She stood hugging herself in the yellow robe that suddenly seemed to have lost all ability to warm her. The whispered voice might have belonged to a man or a woman; she couldn't be sure but she sensed a man.

Standing there, her fear was gradually replaced with anger and indignance. How dare they? This is my room. No one had a right to intrude on her privacy, to wake her in the middle of the night. No one. She made her voice firm, authoritative. "Who is it?" she called out.

Act strong and you will be strong, Dr. Rosen had told her.

"What do you want?" she called.

"Y O U..."

At once, a chill slipped through her as she thought of the man who rescued her from Mike Handratty. The man who had hid his face and whispered her name. She'd just come from shopping at Natalie's Boutique, had her packages with her. They'd slapped against her hip as she ran home.

Hearing soft footsteps descending the stairs, she hurried to the window, and saw a hooded figure fleeing into the night.

The whispered word YOU echoed in her mind. It had come through the door like the hiss of a serpent and coiled itself around her heart. Had she not been listening with every fibre of her being, she might not have heard him going downstairs at all. The strip of light was back beneath the door.

Even seeing the figure disappear into the night did not satisfy her that he was really gone. Maybe it was a trick, and he was back now. A good twenty minutes passed before she gathered the courage to open the door. She unlocked and opened the door a crack and looked out into the scantily lighted hallway. She was about to close it again when she noticed the tiny lavender bag hanging on her doorknob, the logo of Natalie's Boutique clearly visible on the side of the bag. Both puzzled and curious, she unhooked it from the knob and took it inside. Her name was printed on the tiny card, nothing else.

She undid the wrapping, and lifted the lid of the creamy velvet box. She was surprised to find inside the gold pin the storeowner had suggested to her.

Looking at it, you would have thought it would be a perfect match for the teardrop earrings, but it wasn't. It was too large for one thing, and the gold had a more yellow cast than her mother's earrings. But not wanting to seem unappreciative, Caroline had let the storekeeper think they were not in her budget. Which was true, but not the main reason she didn't get it.

Had Jeffrey bought it for her as a Christmas gift? But why would he? How would he even know she'd been looking at it? Coincidence? One thing was sure; she had no intention of keeping such an expensive gift. She would return it and hope he understood. If it was Jeffrey who had hung it there. The more she thought about it, the less it made sense. Why would he knock on her door at such an hour and then not identify himself? Then run out into the night. Why had he whispered? Because he didn't want to wake the neighbors? Yet that whispered voice had given her the creeps. Made her feel threatened. Anyway, why wouldn't he simply have given it to her when they were at the bar if he'd bought it for her?

But if he didn't leave this gift, then whose footsteps had she heard going down the stairs? What shadowy figure had she glimpsed running into the night?

Her thoughts went round like mice in a maze. She wished she had someone to talk to. Someone she could trust. But there was no more time to dwell on the mystery, she needed some sleep. She had to get up for work in a few hours.

FORTY-FOUR

Upon entering the restaurant the next morning, Christmas day, it was obvious the place was in a state of terrified excitement. She thought of the sirens last night, and the bad feeling returned.

"Isn't it awful about that poor woman," Ethel said, as soon as she walked into the kitchen.

"What woman, Ethel?" She hung her coat on the rack.

"Didn't you hear, Caroline? That woman who owns that nice store—Natalie's Boutique. I think you got my scarf there. It's lovely by the way and so thoughtful of you."

Caroline, barely able to answer, said she was glad she liked it. "No, I didn't hear anything," she breathed. Only the sirens. "What happened?"

"She was murdered last night. Horrible. Her daughter found her on the floor of her shop. The place was in shambles. Something like that to happen on Christmas Eve, so tragic?"

A numbness went through her. Yet while the news was shocking, it was not altogether a surprise. Something in her had known when she heard those sirens last night that something terrible had happened.

"The cops think it was the same man who killed those other women," Ethel continued, putting on a new pot of coffee, "but no one knows, really. Though, according to a friend of mine who should, she apparently wasn't sexually molested like the others. That's why I'm hearing anyway, but mostly it's all speculation. There hasn't been time to do an autopsy. The cops aren't saying much in the media."

Caroline didn't realize tears were streaming down her cheeks until Ethel said, "Did you know her, honey? I can see that you're upset. Not so surprising though, even if you didn't. There's a devil out there killing women. Enough to upset anyone."

"I shopped there a couple of times," Caroline said. "She was really nice. She told me her daughter and grandson were spending Christmas with her. She was so happy about that."

Caroline wanted to sit and weep but there was no time to dwell on this latest horror. She mopped at her eyes with some tissues, then got into a clean uniform, grabbed her checkbook and went out into the restaurant where the tables were already filling up. She found herself studying the male customers, those with nowhere else to go on Christmas, wondering if one of them might be him.

FORTY-FIVE

When Caroline got home from work, without even taking off her coat, she grabbed the little bag with the brooch inside and went upstairs to knock on Jeffrey's door. Her feet hurt and her mind was a whirl of uncertainties and fears. Thinking of Natalie Breen sent a fresh wave of sadness and anger over her. Why can't the police catch him? He must have left something of himself behind at the scene. Some clue.

She knocked on Jeffrey's door lightly, twice, harder the second time, but there was no answer. He wasn't home. As she was coming back downstairs, Mrs. Bannister called up to her. "Caroline, dear, you have visitor."

And then Nurse Addison was coming up the stairs to meet her, a wide smile on her face and Caroline could hardly believe her eyes. She looked so different out of her white uniform, dressed fashionably as a model in a long, brown coat with a rolled black velvet collar. Forgetting the bag she still held in her hand, Caroline rushed down the stairs, and threw her arms about her old friend and nurse, almost knocking her over in the process. "I'm so happy to see you, Nurse Addison," she cried. "Oh, what a wonderful Christmas present."

Lynne Addison grabbed the handrail and laughed softly, managing to hug her back with her other arm. "For me, too. And it's Lynne, Caroline. You don't have to call me Nurse Addison anymore. You and I are good friends. I left my husband and son engaged in a electronic hockey game," she laughed. "I doubt they'll even miss me. I really wanted to see you."

Mrs. Bannister stood at the foot of the stairs looking up with curiosity, smiling expectantly.

"This is my good friend, Lynne Addison," Caroline said.

"That's Mrs. Bannister." Then, not wanting to share her visitor further, Caroline ushered the nurse upstairs and into her room. She closed the door and it shut with a small snick, the sound of privacy. She left the bag on top of the bureau and hugged the nurse again, feeling as if she never wanted to let her go. She knew she'd missed her, but she didn't realize how much.

"You smell so good," Caroline said, finally releasing Lynne from her embrace.

"Thank you. New perfume for Christmas from my dear hubby, Joe. L'air Du Temps. I'm glad you like it. Me, too. It's nice to be able to wear perfume; I couldn't at the hospital. Some of the patients and staff were allergic."

Caroline listened enraptured as Lynne told her a little about her life. She learned her husband was a firefighter, retired now as she was. They'd been married for thirty-five years and had one married son and a granddaughter named Angel. How could I have forgotten her name? Lynne used to show us pictures and talk about her, like she was doing now.

"Angel's our pride and joy, of course. Joe's a pushover for her. But no one adores her more than her great-grandma, my mom. And it's mutual. They both light up at the sight of one another, but I don't know how much longer that will be true for my mother, Caroline. She has Alzheimer's'. We've moved her into our son, Kevin's old room. Thank God I'm home now so I can take care of her. But it's been difficult. Otherwise, I would have been to see you a lot sooner."

"I'm just glad you're here now. I've really missed you. I'm so sorry about your mother."

"Thanks. I try not to dwell on it. It doesn't help and it won't change anything. But enough about me. I want to hear all about you. You've been on my mind a lot, Caroline. I've worried about you ever since I put you in that taxi, though it's obvious I needn't have. You're doing great. Tell me everything. You're enjoying your job. I hear you're a waitress now."

"Yes. I was really nervous when they first put me out in the restaurant, but I like it now. People are nice, mostly."

"Yes, they are. But then you're easy to be nice to. Oh, by the way, Martha Blizzard has been released into her sister's care. She lives in Vancouver now. I knew you'd be happy to know that. You two were good friends."

So far away, Caroline thought. Not likely they would ever have that cup of tea together. But she was glad for Martha. Maybe she would write to her. She would always remember her kindness. What Caroline said next seemed to come out of nowhere. "I think of Elizabeth every day. Especially now, at Christmas."

"Your little girl."

"Yes. I know that wouldn't be her name now, but it's how I always think of her. She'd be nine now. I wonder what she looks like, what sort of present she might like for Christmas. I wish I could send her something."

A look of resolve came into Lynne's face. "I can't promise anything, but I'm going to make sure there's a note in the adoption file that you are anxious to hear from her. You never know, Caroline. When she's of age, she might want to find you too. We keep your current information on file. She looked around her. "This is really a very nice room, Caroline. And what a sweet tree."

"Thank you." Caroline knew this was Lynne's way of steering the conversation onto an easier path, and that was fine with her. "Some of those Christmas bulbs belonged to my parents. They were in the trunk."

Lynne said they were beautiful with their old fashioned hand-paintings. She also commented on the wallpaper with its tiny gold flowers, the white woodwork. "Everything so sparkling and tidy. But then you always were a great little worker."

"Let me take your coat, Nurse...Lynne." She touched the soft, velvety sleeve. "It's so beautiful."

After hanging the coat in the closet, Caroline put the tea on and set out a plate of the mixed Christmas cakes and cookies Harold had brought her. He wasn't mad at her anymore, and she was glad about that. He had really liked his model airplane, and Mrs. Bannister had washed out the cat cookie jar and filled it with cookies almost as soon as she unwrapped it. She kept smiling at the cat cover, saying the face looked exactly like Saucy's, one of her cats that was no longer in the world.

She was flitting around the room like Wendi in Peter Pan, putting on water for tea, setting out cups and saucers and plates, sore feet forgotten in the pure pleasure of her friend's company. She set her new cups and saucers out. "You're always looking after people, aren't you?" she said.

"Like you're doing now," she smiled. "I'm lucky to be able to do it, though, Caroline. My, what pretty cups and saucers."

"They're real bone china, too," she said proudly. "A Christmas gift from my landlady."

Painted with pink flowers and tiny green leaves, Caroline had seen them in Mrs. Bannister's china cabinet many times. She was touched that she had given it to her, and now pleased to set them out before her special guest.

Having poured their tea, Caroline finally sat herself down in the chair opposite Lynne. She slid the plate of Christmas goodies across to her. "Harold bought me these cakes; he works in the bakery."

"Harold?"

"The landlady's nephew. He lives downstairs with her."

Lynne took one of the chocolate chip and cherry cookies. "Mmm. My favorite. Now, tell me everything. I want details."

Caroline took her at her word and once she started talking, everything spilled out. Or almost everything. She told her about Mike Handratty and about the man who came to her rescue, and about how much she enjoyed going to the park, although it was too cold now. She told her about Mr. Goldman's asking her if she might like to work in a bookstore someday. She told her about Jeffrey Denton.

"He teaches piano and composes music. We went to a small lounge on Christmas Eve. A little piano bar and had wine and talked. He's very nice, Lynne. I had a lovely time."

This last came out involuntarily, in her blurting fashion, as if confessing to some indiscretion. She rushed to show her the new dress and boots, and her mother's earrings, and Lynne admired them, saying she was sure she had looked stunning in them.

Caroline had been even more starved for someone to talk to than she knew and she'd always been able to talk to Lynne. That hadn't changed. Lynne had listened intently the whole time Caroline talked, and now was looking both pleased for her, despite a certain wariness in her eyes. Being a mother hen again, Caroline smiled to herself.

"That's wonderful, Caroline. Really great." After a beat, she reached into her bag hanging over the back of the chair "Oh, you reminded me, I have something for you. I hope you like them. I guessed at the size."

They were blue leather gloves, matching the bag Lynne had given her when she left Bayshore. They fit perfectly, like a second skin. Soft and buttery, like the bag. "They're beautiful," she said, and held up her hands to better admire them in their new gloves. "Thank you so much. I don't have anything for you."

Lynne laughed. "Seeing you looking so terrific is enough of a present for me," she said. "I don't think you realize how well you've done, Caroline. It's really pretty amazing."

"It's because of you, and Dr. Rosen. You were always so nice to me. You always…"

"Like I said, you're easy to be nice to. But you're the one who deserves the credit. You're making it all on your own. You should be very proud of yourself."

They talked some more. Lynne told her that Olga Farmer had died. Passed away in her sleep. She was eighty-five."

"Not so tragic when you're eight-five, is it," Caroline said.

"No. There are worse things," she said, and Caroline knew she was thinking of her mother. She felt a heaviness come over her. Her own problems seemed so small in comparison.

"What's wrong, Caroline?"

She had to tell someone. Rising from the chair, she went to the bureau and got the small bag. She showed Lynne the brooch. "It's too expensive. I have to give it back."

"Your friend—Jeffrey gave you this?"

"I—I'm not sure. But someone left this outside my door in the night. Hung it on the doorknob. I don't know who else it could be."

She wanted to tell her about the man in the park, about her feeling of being stalked, but she didn't want her to worry. And about the figure she had seen running from the house last night.

Could it have been Jeffrey? But she didn't want to appear fragile in Lynne's eyes, or paranoid. She didn't want to seem like a patient anymore. They were friends now, Lynne had said.

"If it was your friend who left this hanging on your door," Lynne said slowly, as if working out some difficult problem in her mind, "then he must be very shy not to give this to you in person."

"No, not really. Maybe he just wanted to surprise me. Anyway, he's not home now. I think he might be with his mother. She's not well."

Lynne was frowning at the logo on the bag. "Natalie's Boutique. That's the woman who was murdered last night." She looked into Caroline's eyes. "Caroline, you have to take this to the police."

She nodded, knowing Lynne was right. "I will," she half-whispered, feeling a tremor of fear at Lynne's firm insistence, at the alarm she saw in her eyes. "I'll give it to the police."

"Good. How well do you know this—Jeffrey?"

"Not very. But he's a nice man. He wouldn't hurt anyone, I'm sure of it."

Lynne nodded and patted her hand, then rose from the table and crossed the room, her heels clicking lightly on the linoleum floor. Being the thoughtful person she was, she'd changed her boots at the door.

She was looking at the photos Caroline had hung on the wall, the ones she had taken from the album in the trunk, and framed.

"This is a picture of you with your mom and dad, isn't it?" Lynne asked over her shoulder.

"Yes."

"What a delightful looking little girl you were. You all look so happy here, Caroline. This one alongside it you'd be in—fourth, fifth grade here?"

"Fifth. It was taken in the summer."

"And is this your grandmother?"

She was referring to the picture in the small oval frame. "Yes. I was named for her. I think we were all happy then."

Returning to her chair, Lynne laughed and said was sorry she'd eaten most of the cookies and cakes.

"I'm really glad you liked them. You're my first visitor."

"Oh, Jeffrey hasn't been here?"

"No." She felt herself blushing. "Not yet."

Lynne looked thoughtful. Then she told her that Dr. Rosen had had a mild heart attack and was retiring with his wife to Florida. Caroline was stunned at the news. Dr. Rosen had seemed invincible to her, so strong, always there to help his patients, to listen. But she knew that no one was invincible. "I hope he'll be okay."

"I think he'll be fine now. It was a good wake-up call. He was overworked and his body let him know it. They'll enjoy Florida. All that lovely sunshine." She smiled. "Caroline, I want you to know how proud I am of you. I know it hasn't been easy."

"No. It hasn't. Sometimes I worry…"

"What? What do you worry about? You can talk to me, Caroline. You know that."

"Well, I really like Jeffrey. A lot. What if I start to like him too much, and it doesn't work out. How do I know what happened to me before…?"

"…Won't happen again? Well, anything's possible, I suppose. But that was a different time, different circumstances. You were just a girl. You're a woman now. You've faced a lot of obstacles and overcome them."

Her answer was comforting.

"On the other hand," she went on, "don't give your heart away too easily. But you're a strong woman, you've proven that. And we all take chances in life; there are no guarantees. No one knows that better than you. I think whatever happens, you'll be just fine. But if you need to talk, by all means give me a call. I mean that—night or day." To prove it, she wrote her name and number on a piece of paper and handed it to her.

Caroline was happy she'd gotten the phone installed. It rang only once since she got it and that was when Ethel called asking her to trade shifts with another waitress.

FORTY-SIX

Driving home, Lynne thought how much she had enjoyed her visit with her old patient, who wasn't anyone's patient anymore. And that was where the dilemma lay. I spoke to her as if she were a child, telling her give that brooch to the police. I had no right.

And yet Lynne was afraid for her. Caroline was a young, attractive woman who lived on her own. She was vulnerable. As smart as Caroline was, and as strong, which she had proved herself to be, she was not sophisticated in the ways of the world. Because of her years inside the walls of a mental institution, she possessed a child's naivety. Though not an innocence. She had been through too much for that.

I'm sure I managed to frighten her, Lynne thought, stopping for a light, and maybe that's to the good. But maybe I overreacted. The brooch might easily have come from a shy admirer. Whether from this Jeffrey Denton or the landlady's nephew, who knew? Someone else who lived in the building? Definitely from someone with a key to the front door, she thought, unaware that Caroline had had the same thought.

Why do I have a nagging feeling she was holding something back? She wondered.

**

It was early evening when Caroline, clutching the little lavender bag with the brooch inside, went back upstairs to knock on Jeffrey Denton's door. She had heard him go up awhile ago and now she could hear him inside, at the piano. The angry notes were coming fast and furious, louder than her thumping heart. He was clearly upset about something. Just let me get this over with, she told herself.

She didn't knock right away though, but stood in the doorway listening to him play with a fury that was disturbing. She thought of Lynne's words: "How well do you know this Jeffrey, Caroline?" Had she really said that? Even now Caroline found it hard to believe Lynne had sat across from her in her kitchen, talking to her, just like she used to at the hospital.

Her last words before heading out to her car had been, "You've come a long way. But you need to be careful. There's a maniac out there, and he's killing women. Especially women living alone.'

I can take care of myself, she thought, and squared her shoulders. The anger had drained from his playing which was softer now, so she knocked on the door. The music stopped at once and she heard his footsteps crossing the room. And then he was standing in the open doorway, seeming different in faded jeans and a white, open-necked sweatshirt, a thatch of hair fallen over his brow. There was a coldness in his eyes she'd not seen before, though it vanished at once upon seeing her. He looked surprised, but definitely not displeased. "Caroline. Hi."

"I tried your door this morning before I left for work, but you weren't home. Or maybe you were sleeping. You look upset, Jeffrey. Is anything wrong?" She could still hear the ring of the piano keys releasing their fury into the room, and out into the hallway. He definitely had no inclination to turn down the volume on this occasion.

"No, nothing. Please, come in."

She took in the room behind him, much like her own but for the wallpaper patterned with beige and brown stripes and a big electronic piano standing against the wall by the window. Sheet music and books were everywhere, some even stacked on the floor by the piano. The mad artist, she thought, and felt a small tremor slip through her.

He glanced over his shoulder and shrugged. "I agree. I'm not much of a housekeeper, I'm afraid. I spent the day at my mother's. Not a great time for her as I mentioned. But please, do come inside. I'll play something for you more in keeping with the season, if you like. Perhaps Silent Night?" He laughed. Inappropriately, Caroline thought. "Did you have a nice Christmas day?"

"I did," she said. "A friend came to visit." She had promised Lynne she would let the police know about the brooch, but she needed to first ask Jeffrey if he had brought it for her. "No, thank you. I Just wanted to..."

He opened the door wider. "Please." His voice, and his eyes, had warmed. His eyes were hazel, but held a glint of green in their depths, like mysterious pools.

Standing so close to him, she felt something deep within her pulling her to him, like a magnet. The way Mr. Rochester had described his feelings for Jane Eyre. 'It is as if I had a string somewhere under my left ribs, tightly and inextricably knotted to a similar string situated in you...'

She chastised herself for being such a romantic fool. Yet the force of her attraction to him couldn't be denied. Fighting it, she handed him the bag. "No thank you, it's late. I won't come in. I just came to return this, if in fact it was you who left it hanging on my doorknob. I appreciate your kindness. But I can't accept it. It's much too expensive."

He raised an eyebrow and tentatively took the bag from her hand. "Maybe I should see what we're talking about here." After a brief examination of the brooch, he said, "It's very nice, but not something I would have chosen for you. And I didn't." He handed it back. "I'm sorry. You say you found this hanging on your doorknob?"

Caroline's face was burning with embarrassment. "Yes I heard someone out in the hallway in the middle of the night."

The eyebrow went up again. "And you thought it was me?"

"Well, I thought... it might..."

"It's not my style to prowl outside the doors of unsuspecting young women, Caroline."

"I'm sorry. I feel stupid."

"There's no need. Unless you're seeing someone else, I suppose I'm the likely candidate." He cocked his head at her, and smiled. "It appears I have competition."

"No. You don't." She did not return the smile.

"I've—uh, seen the way our landlady's nephew looks at you with those hound dog eyes. I think he's got a crush on you. Could he...?"

"No. Harold bought me cakes and cookies. He wrapped the box in Christmas paper so he intended it as my gift. We're friends. That's all."

"Perhaps he's hoping for more. I can't fault him on his taste, even though I am a little jealous." He was teasing her. He wasn't jealous at all.

He was looking at the bag again. "Natalie's Boutique," he said.

A casual observation, no change of expression. No other comment. He didn't know then. Or pretended not to know.

"Yes. Natalie Breen. She owned the boutique where this was purchased. She was murdered last night."

"What?" he said, looking genuinely shocked at the news. Or else he was a very good actor.

FORTY-SEVEN

Photos of the tire tracks taken near the place where Pearl Grannan's body was dumped turned out to match those on Fred Grannan's Station Wagon. That, and Grannan's record of wife beating was enough to get them a search warrant. It paid off. Luminol showed numerous bloodstains on the carpet in the upstairs bedroom. Some of the beige color had been bleached from the carpet in the process of trying to remove them. A few spots he'd missed entirely.

At least they could cross Fred Grannan off the list as the possible serial killer, Detective Tom O'Neal thought, setting his plate in the sink and running hot water over it. Finding out he had a record of domestic assaults against his wife put a different light on the man. Painted a different picture of the marriage.

They'd even turned up a 911 tape of his wife's hysterical call a couple of years back saying her husband was threatening to kill her. According to a couple of friends and neighbors, seems she couldn't move without arousing Fred's suspicions. Her best friend from school said Pearl was terrified of Fred. Always walked softly around him. Tried to leave him a few times, but like a bad vaccination, it never took. The public would be spared the expense of a trial. A couple of hours at the station had brought a tearful confession, made amidst much sobbing and nose blowing. He'd accused her of seeing other men and they got into one of their fights. This one got out of control and Pearl ended up dead. Grannan panicked and seized on the idea of pinning her murder on the man police were looking for, for the other murders. A copycat killing. Read his Miranda rights, the silent, gray and contrite man was handcuffed and led off to his cell to await sentencing.

Maybe he *was* genuinely sorry. Who knew? But Fred's remorse or lack thereof was not Tom's problem. His problem was trying to find a serial killer, a man who it appeared was murdering women at random. The headline in the local paper did little to ease the fears of St. Simeon women. Their killer was still out there.

It was coming onto dusk when Tom plugged in the lights he'd hung on the porch railing. His contribution to Christmas. They twinkled merrily, throwing their blue and green and red lights on the snowy stretch of land in front of the house and made him smile. "Don't look too bad, eh, fella," he said to his friend who stood on the porch watching him, tail thumping the deck floor, grinning right along with him.

It had begun to snow, and was cold, which for some odd reason made him think of Caroline Hill and her fuzzy, yellow robe. Odder still, she called him a few minutes later. He went inside to answer. It gave him a weird feeling hearing her voice on the phone, but he wasn't really surprised. Not that he was a big believer in ESP, but he didn't discount it either. Someone had hung a gift bag with a gold brooch inside on her door on Christmas Eve, she told him. The bag came from Natalie's Boutique. "I work all day tomorrow, but if you'll come to my room anytime after six, I'll give it to you."

He thanked her for calling. Said he'd be there. Then stood with the phone in his hand, frowning.

FORTY-EIGHT

The following evening at twenty past six, Detective O'Neal was standing in Caroline Hill's room, looking at the brooch someone had left for her. Not that he expected it to reveal any clues, but a mystery fingerprint was always possible, maybe on the box or the bag. He would ask the victim's daughter to check out the day's receipts. With luck, Mrs. Breen kept a list of customers' names on file. He'd know quickly enough who had purchased it.

"I didn't buy it," Caroline Hill said, "if that's what you're thinking. "I'm not crazy." She was sitting on the sofa, picking at a fingernail. She hadn't answered her door in her yellow robe this time, however, but in a white sweater and navy slacks. Tiny pearl earrings. There was a new self-confidence about her, despite the nervousness.

"No one's suggesting you are, Miss Hill. But someone bought it. You must have an idea. I don't expect you still believe in Santa." The question was rhetorical and she didn't answer it.

"No, I have no idea who hung it on my doorknob. I asked who it was. He said YOU. Then he fled down the stairs and out of the building.

"Did you see him?"

"Just a glimpse. It was dark."

"But you didn't recognize him."

"No, she whispered." She'd had a few suspicions, but that's all they were.

"Or his voice."

"No."

"Are you seeing anyone who lives in the building?" He already knew she was, thanks to her landlady.

"I went out on Christmas Eve with Mr. Denton upstairs," she

said without hesitation. "He teaches piano. I've already asked him and he assured me it did not come from him. There's no one else I can think of. Well, there's just one… but I don't think…"

"You let me do the detective work, okay? Who?" He took out his pen and notebook.

She told him all about Mike Handratty, including his getting beaten up on the night he accosted her on the way home, not by a gang of three, as he'd told police, but by a man who came to her rescue.

The detective listened attentively, then he said, "Seems unlikely Mike Handratty would be leaving you Christmas presents after taking a pretty serious knocking about on your behalf." He remembered the incident; her version of what happened had a ring of truth. "What didn't you call the police and report the incident?"

"I know I should have called that night when I got home, but I was afraid. I didn't know what to do. Seeing as how I spent the last…anyway, I thought I might be blamed somehow. Called a troublemaker. Crazy. I might even lose my job."

"I can understand that. Well, I'm glad you're being forthcoming now. We'll check him out of course. Anything else?"

"There's Harold. Mrs. Bannister's nephew. I—uh, think he likes me. But he already gave me a Christmas present, a box of cakes and cookies, in Christmas wrapping. He wouldn't be buying a brooch too. Anyway, he doesn't make much money. He works at a The Big Bakery, across from the restaurant where I work. Frank's."

"I know it. Get a meal there from time to time. I'll have to take this brooch with me, Miss Hill."

"Yes, please. I don't want to look at it again. Mrs. Breen was a nice lady. I hope you catch her killer. He's the same one who killed those other women, isn't he?"

"We don't know that for sure, but it's possible."

And then she told him about feeling that someone had been stalking her for weeks now. When she was in the park, on her way home from work before she started taking the bus. "I never told anyone. I thought people would just think I was being paranoid. In fact, I wondered that myself."

O'Neal wondered too. At first, as she'd suspected, he

considered she might have purchased the brooch herself and called the police, looking for attention. It happened more than occasionally. And as she herself had pointed out, she was in a mental institution for a good part of her life. But in spite of that, or maybe because of it, he was starting to feel an admiration for Caroline Hill, though not altogether ready to give up on his earlier theory. As she talked, he merely listened and nodded, kept his cop's poker face, then slipped the Natalie's lavender bag into an evidence bag.

She didn't look so much scared as concerned, he thought. She also looked relieved to have gotten some stuff off her chest.

"You keep your doors locked, and be careful," he told her. "You might even want to keep a chair wedged under the knob. I don't want to frighten you needlessly, but anyone who ever lived here could have a key to the front door. They could have had an extra key made. Or failed to turn theirs in. I just don't want you to have a false sense of security here."

"Oh, I don't, not at all."

"Good. At the same time go about your life as usual, as much as you can. You have my card. If you feel threatened for whatever reason, don't hesitate to call. In the meantime, we'll send a cruiser around to keep an eye on things. I'll be in touch."

Since he was already in the building, he went upstairs and knocked on Jeffrey Denton's door. He wasn't at home. Or if he was, he wasn't he wasn't answering the door. The landlady, on the other hand, answered his knock at once and Tom suspected she'd been standing on the other side of the door waiting for him for come back downstairs. He asked to speak with Harold.

After the detective left Caroline's room and went downstairs, it seemed eerily silent. As if it were alive, and holding its breath…

She wedged a chair under the doorknob.

FORTY-NINE

At work the next day at work Caroline sought out Ethel in the kitchen and told her the truth about what happened that night with Mike Handratty. She didn't like having lied to her. And she didn't want to hold any more secrets; secrets were heavy. Ethel showed little surprise at the revelation.

"I thought it was something like that," she said. "It was written all over your face that something had happened when you came in that morning. You're not the best cover-upper, Caroline. Well, now we know how Mike ended up in the hospital. You were lucky that fella came along. Who knows what Mike might have done. Do you think it's Mike who's been following you?"

"I don't know, Ethel. I'm sure he blames me for what happened to him."

"I think that's fair to assume," Ethel agreed. "Not only did he lose his job, but got beat up in the bargain." A devilish grin passed over her lips. "It wouldn't occur to him that all of it happened because of his own actions. But that's Mike."

"I know. And yet somehow I don't really think it's him. Anyway, how would he get into the building? He'd need a key."

"Oh, that wouldn't stop him," Ethel said. "If he was determined enough, I'm sure he'd find a way."

Almost Caroline's own words to Mrs. Bannister.

"Don't sell Mike short, Caroline," Ethel said, wiping down the grill. "He's very sly. And quite the charmer when it suits him, as you well know. He could just slip in with one of the tenants, and then hide in a broom closet or something. Then again, it wouldn't surprise me if he never wanted to look on your face again. I don't see him as a particularly brave soul."

But then it still left the question of who left the brooch?

FIFTY

Buddy stood across the street from Frank's, watching the restaurant. He hiked up his coat collar. He was tired of lurking in shadows, cold and alone. But all that would end soon. He'd tracked down Earl in Toronto, singing in a small bar on Yonge Street. Buddy had practically jumped inside his skin when the guy on the phone told him. He had started to ask him what he wanted him for, but Buddy hung up, cutting him off.

It would be better even than that other Christmas Earl had been with him, a long time ago. And yet to Buddy, only yesterday.

Earl had probably been looking for him, too, he thought almost tearfully, blocking out the small voice in his head that reminded him that Earl knew very well where he lived all those years he was growing up. He hadn't even sent him a postcard. But Buddy wasn't listening. He believed Earl did write to him and that his mother destroyed the letters.

"Son-of-a-bitch is gone," his mother had told him when he got home from school that day, lighting up yet another cigarette, gray smoke curling up past her face. She was still in her faded blue robe, her frowsy dark hair messy, letting him know she just crawled out of bed. She smelled of booze, but she wasn't drunk. "Packed his crap and took off, just like that." She sucked in smoke and blew it at the ceiling. "Stole some cash out of my purse, too, the bastard."

Buddy had been so stunned at this news he momentarily forgot his fear of his mother. "When's he coming back?" he demanded.

"Don't you listen, you little shit? I said he packed his stuff and left. He ain't comin' back, and good riddance."

The scalding tears had poured down his face. He could feel them now, taste their salt, could almost hear the shattering of his heart. He screamed at her that it wasn't true. It couldn't be. "He didn't go for good, momma. Earl's coming back. He loves me, he wouldn't just go. You sent Earl away. You sent my daddy away. You sent my dadd..."

The force of her backhand across his mouth rattled his teeth and sent him flying across the room. Then her face was thrust into his own. "Earl ain't your daddy," she hissed at him, breathing that stale booze in his face. "You ain't got no daddy, you little bastard. Okay? You got that? Now get the hell out of here. Go find the son-of-a-bitch and see if he'll take you with him." She laughed, a dog's bark. "Wouldn't be no loss to me if he did. Probably took off for Toronto, his old stomping ground."

That nugget of information stuck in Danny's head. She'd been right about that and now he had found him after all these years. He'd tried before to find him before but never had any luck. This time he'd just called a bunch of bars listed in the phone book and someone finally told him he was at a place called Curly's. Buddy had come to the end of a long road. He would take Caroline with him to Toronto and they would be a family again. Like before. Only better. He wiped his tears of joy with his sleeve.

Caroline would be happy too. She would understand that this was her destiny. He would come for her New Year's Eve, at midnight.

She was different from the others, he told himself for the millionth time, as if he'd needed to convince himself that this was so. Not some common slut like his mother, like those other women he'd mistaken for special. He knew she'd felt the connection with him too; he'd sensed it deep within himself. He heard it in his head like a small click. Like finding the right series of numbers on a wall safe, hearing it open.

She would wear the brooch he'd given her, on their trip, pinned to the collar of her navy coat. She looked so pretty in that coat, with the little tam and scarf. So pure and sweet.

He smiled to himself and walked on up the street. Not long now.

FIFTY-ONE

When Lynne arrived home from Caroline's, her mother was sitting on the sofa in her camel-haired coat, clutching her purse in her lap, waiting to be taking back to her house.

"I'm so glad you're back, dear. I've enjoyed my visit, but I must go home now. Walter will be wondering where I am."

Before she could get up, Lynne sighed, set the bags on a chair and went to sit beside her. She looked into her eyes and saw the anxiousness there, the smile that wavered. When she tried to stand, Lynne put a hand on her arm. "Wait, mom. I've missed you. Let's talk a few minutes, okay?"

"Oh. All right, dear." At least she still knows me, Lynne thought and was grateful. For how long, as she'd told Caroline, no one knew. Not her doctor. No one. Only God.

It was a near disaster that finally prompted Lynne to bring her mother here and put the house on the market. Her mother had set about cooking a turkey dinner for her young family, the members of which had grown up years before and had children of their own. She had turned the oven up full-blast and the grease splattered on the walls of the oven, setting off a small fire. Luckily, a canvasser for some charity was ringing doorbells in the neighborhood at the time, had heard her mother's cries, smelled smoke and called the fire department.

It wasn't just that she'd set fire to the oven; that could happen to anyone. As a young bride, Lynne herself had once set a pot of grease on fire while trying to make doughnuts. Joe'd been summoned to more than one flare-up of similar origins. But with her mother's condition, it was just a matter of time before something more terrible occurred. She didn't want to think about what could have happened if that canvasser hadn't happened along.

Lynne would never forgive herself if anything had happened to her mother while she was trying to make up her mind about what to do. In the midst of Lynne's thoughts, her mother said, "Walter's dead, isn't he, dear?"

Lynne held back her tears and took her mother's hand. The bones felt fragile. Fragile as her mind had become. The hand that had brushed Lynne's hair, bandaged a scraped knee.

"Yes, mom. Daddy's gone."

"I forget sometimes."

"I know, mom. He's here in spirit though; he's still with us."

She helped her mother off with her hat and coat, unable to remember when she'd been so tired. She was hanging the coats in the closet, when she turned to see Joe standing in the archway, trying to look cheerful, as if everything was just the same as it had always been. Tall, solid Joe, hair thinning, mostly gray now, but always her loving husband right there beside her, wanting to make the bad things go away. Well he couldn't, but he sure as hell made things easier to bear. She didn't know what she'd do without him.

"Got tea on." He smiled at the two of them, his eyes questioning. "Everything good?"

"Good as gold," Lynne said, as she put an arm around her mother's shoulders and the three of them went out to the kitchen. Over tea and sandwiches, she told him about her visit with Caroline, including the matter of the mysterious gold brooch. "I told her she needed to take it to the police."

"Good advice. Do you think she will?"

"I think she would have already if she wasn't afraid they might not believe her. If she hadn't been at Bayshore. Yes, I do think she will, Joe. I'll phone her in a couple of days though. Just to make sure. I'll wish her a happy New Year. I think it will be too. I have a good feeling. More tea, mom?"

FIFTY-TWO

The pressure was on to find the killer, this latest murder having fuelled new fears in the community. Natalie Breen had been well known around town and well-liked. Her murder made every woman in town feel threatened. Not only did she not fit the physical description of the first two victims, but she also wasn't sexually assaulted or robbed, which was strange in itself. The brutal nature of the killing told Detective O'Neal there was something personal about it, yet Gloria, (which she had asked him to call her,) insisted her mother wasn't seeing anyone, and hadn't been.

"She never stopped feeling that she was still married to dad," she told him. "Even though he was gone from this earth. I like to think they're together now."

He was standing in her living room waiting for her to finish going through the receipts from December 31st. She remembered the brooch being in the window, had seen it earlier that day when she and David dropped into the store for lunch, picking up a Pizza on the way. Pineapple topping, her mom's favorite.

The room was large and comfortable, fancier than he was used to, with plush ash rose sofa and chair, white wall to wall carpeting, blond furniture. The woman had enjoyed the pleasant surroundings her hard work had afforded her.

"There's no receipt for it," she said from the small rolltop desk where she sat going through the receipts. "And yet it was gift-wrapped, you said."

"Beautifully, according to Caroline Hill."

Animated sounds issued from the den where David was watching cartoons. Tom wondered how he was handling all this. Neither of them would ever feel the same way about Christmas.

But maybe especially Gloria. David was young and kids had a way of bouncing back.

"Mom had an artistic bent," she said sadly, but with pride. "Well, then, whoever she wrapped it for must have killed her. What other explanation could there be? It wasn't cheap, but it wasn't the hope diamond either. Who would kill someone for a two-hundred dollar brooch?"

"People have been killed for a pair of sneakers, their jacket. A couple of bucks. But I don't think your mother died for the sake of a brooch. There's another reason. I just don't know what it is yet. But I will."

He was promising again. Something about her made him want to protect her. Not the same as just wanting to find a killer, which was his job. He wanted to be there for her, take care of her and David. He hadn't felt like this about a woman in years. Nuts, he'd just met her. It wasn't because she was beautiful, either, although he saw beauty in her. Her fair hair needed washing and her eyes were swollen from all the tears. And she'd lost weight even since he'd last seen her. Aside from that, he was too damned old for her. But that didn't stop him from feeling an urge to beat the hell out of her ex for hurting her, which made him about as mature as a high school kid.

"Can't you check the wrapping paper for prints?" she asked. "The killer's would be on it, wouldn't they?"

"Did that, but nothing. Only your mom's thumb print. He probably wore gloves."

She let out a weary sigh, said wistfully, "We ate the Pizza in the back room. You could hear if a customer came in, there's a little bell above the door. That was the last time I saw mom alive."

He could only nod.

"I could feel him when I was in the store, you know. I could feel his insanity. The terrible violence he unleashed on my mother hung like residue in the air." More tears leaked from her eyes and he resisted the compulsion to go to her and put his arms around her. "She must have been so terrified," she said. He saw her mentally pull herself together. "Would you like a cup of coffee, Detective O'Neal?"

He said he would. Against his better judgment he also said, "If I'm to call you Gloria, please call me Tom."

FIFTY-THREE

All New Years' Eve day, Caroline couldn't quiet the anxious feeling she had that Jeffrey might not show up tonight. The last time she saw him, he'd seemed irritated, and she hadn't heard from him since. Well, she'd just be ready for nine o'clock, which was the time he said he'd call for her and if he showed up, fine. If not, fine too. She knew it would hurt. She also knew she'd get over it.

Lynne called to wish her a Happy New Year, and Caroline guessed it was an excuse to see if she'd turned the brooch over to the police. She didn't mind. It was only because she was worried about her. A 'mother hen' she'd called herself. I don't think I need that anymore, Caroline thought. I just need her to be my friend.

She swept her hair back from her face, which looked kind of Audrey Hepburnish with the dangling rhinestone earrings. The rhinestone belt made the dress look totally different.

He knocked on her door at ten to nine and she almost ran to answer it. He looked very handsome in a shirt and tie, and topcoat. They took a cab to the club. His car was in the shop. In the cab, he said, "You really look stunning, Caroline. I can't take my eyes off you."

At his words, a warm glow of pleasure washed through her.

The big room was decorated festively, draped with blue and gold crepe paper, streamers and garlands. A big glittery sign on the back wall wished everyone HAPPY NEW YEAR!

The air in the room was charged with excitement. Caroline was relieved to see that only a couple of the women were wearing long dresses, and in fact, one woman, a redhead, wore jeans and a purple sequined top.

Jeffrey found a small table off by itself against the wall, then went to fill their plates with goodies from the buffet table, including two glasses of spiked punch from the punchbowl.

As they enjoyed the food and punch, Jeffrey told her about his father who had fought in the war. She, in turn, talked about her own father serving in Korea and thought about his passionate letters to her mother. It was nice here, she thought, though she preferred the small piano bar where they'd gone Christmas Eve. Gradually, it got too loud to hear each other.

As the band was tuning up for the next set, the redhead in the sequined top was up on her feet, whirling around the room, a glass in her hand. "Play *I Can't Stop Loving You*," she yelled, evoking a burst of laughter from the crowd. She responded by telling them what they could do with themselves.

"I'm sorry. Not exactly the Ritz, is it," he grinned sheepishly. "But the tickets were cheap. You wanna leave?"

"No. Not yet. I've heard worse language, believe me."

The band obliged the redhead and Jeffrey drew Caroline to her feet. "I'm not much of a dancer," she whispered in his ear, but he just smiled and pulled her closer and led her in a slow dance to the middle of the floor. She tried to keep a space between them, which made her steps awkward. He laughed lightly, a very fetching laugh. "Relax, Caroline," he murmured, and drew her ever closer. A small sigh escaped her as she gave in and let him guide her around the floor. She followed him easily. Too easily. She danced as if she had always danced or at least it felt that way. She was quite happy to dance the night away, in Jeffrey's arms.

Soon, however, the place became so crowded you couldn't walk onto the floor without bumping into someone, and the noise ended any chance of conversation. Perfumes mingled with perspiration and liquor. Anxiety began to creep over her and it was getting hard for her to breathe.

She withdrew from his embrace. "I need to get some air, Jeffrey."

"Sure." Looking concerned, he got their coats. Outside she leaned against the red brick building and breathed in the crisp winter's night air, let it calm her. She looked up at the dark blue velvet sky strewn with stars and an almost full moon.

"Are you okay?" he asked.

"Fine now. It's such a beautiful evening. I hope I haven't ruined it for you."

He laughed. "Hardly. You're right; it is a lovely night. Anyway, I'm just happy to be with you, wherever we are." He glanced at his watch. Eleven-thirty. Feel like walking?"

"Yes, please. I love to walk."

The street was tree-lined, their branches silvered with frost. As they walked, the noise from inside the club grew fainter, finally dying away. Overhead wires sang in the sharp night air.

For a time they walked silently, holding hands, collars turned up against the cold, their breaths visible in the cold air. "Will your friends think it odd your leaving before the midnight hour?" Caroline asked.

He laughed. "I didn't know a soul in there. My dad used to frequent the place; he had a lot of friends who did too, many gone now. Like I said, the tickets were reasonable. You don't make big bucks teaching kids how to play the piano. And I'm still waiting to be discovered as a composer. I'm a very poor catch, Caroline."

"No, you're not." She smiled. They were passing Gleneton, the street where she once lived and she averted her eyes. With her hand in his, for a moment she recalled walking alongside William, the way their hands had fit together, entwined. Then William receded to that far place in her memory, and she was back with Jeffrey again.

"I owe you an apology," he said unexpectedly.

"Oh?"

"When you knocked on my door Christmas night, I was in a bit of a mood. My mother had been crying most of the day, digging out old pictures of dad. I also knew I was a suspect in the murders. The detectives came back twice to interview me. Then they put a tail on me."

"Are you sure?"

"I'm sure. It's because Lorraine Winters used to live in the building and I went to her funeral. I knew the girl, for God's sake."

"Did you—go out with her?" She was sorry she'd asked the question as soon as it was out of her mouth, but he seemed to take no offense.

"We were neighbors. We passed the time of day when we met coming or going from the building. Nothing more. But she seemed like a lovely girl and I was very sorry about what happened to her."

She was surprised to see that they were standing in front of their building, as if she'd been in a kind of trance and just woken up.

"Listen," Jeffrey said. "Can you hear the horns?"

She listened. And suddenly fireworks exploded in the night sky, a spectacular starburst of electric blues. Then another...*boom*...*boom*...*boom*...one after the other, displaying a kaleidoscope of colors—gold, silver fuchsia, green, reds—a burst of flowers lighting the midnight sky. As she looked on with the wonderment of a child, she felt Jeffrey's arm go around her.

"The city holds these fireworks down by the docks every year," he said, just as another chorus of horns blew in celebration. He glanced at his watch, then at her. "Happy New Year, Caroline," he said, and took her into his arms and kissed her.

There on the deserted sidewalk, wrapped in the magic of the night, he kissed her long and tenderly, and finally with an urgency that matched her own. Without words, he unlocked the front door and he followed her upstairs, a hand at the small of her back.

Caroline was trying to think clearly, trying to rein in the passion flowing through her like hot lava. And then they were in her room and somehow their boots were off, and he was unbuttoning her coat, then his own, tossing them. One part of her wanted to surrender to her desire while a rational part of her was flashing red lights, warning her of a barrier ahead, and the very steep cliff beyond it.

His warm hands were gently cupping her face and he was kissing her again and again, his mouth searching and hungry. Murmuring her name, he guided her toward the sofa, kissing her throat as they moved, her eyes, and then they were on the sofa, her fingers wound in his hair as if with a will of their own; it was thick and silky. William's hair had had a lighter feel, like a child's hair. Everything is going too fast. This isn't right. No, no. He wanted to swallow her up. She would need him. She didn't want to need him.

"No, no, Jeffrey," she gasped, pushing him away, fighting them both.

He groaned at her resistance. "I want you, Caroline." His breath warm against her cheek, he murmured, "Please, I know you want me too."

"I do, but I'm not ready, Jeffrey. I'm sorry." She sat up and readjusted her clothes. She was shaking, her own breathing not quite under control.

The glaze of passion was still in his eyes, mixed with frustration. "No, no, it's okay. I didn't mean to pressure you." Running a hand through his mussed hair, he stood up. "I thought..." He picked up his coat from the floor and brushed it off.

Most of Caroline's coat had managed to find the end table. She hung it in the closet. "I'm sorry," she said, walking him to the door. "Would you like some coffee before you go?"

He grinned like she'd said something incredulous. "I'll take a rain check, okay?" He kissed her lightly on the corner of her mouth. "Sleep well."

She was silent. She had ruined everything. She was about to close the door when he asked, "Do you work tomorrow?"

"No," she said, puzzled. "I worked Christmas day so I have it off."

"Great. I'll take you to lunch? How's one o'clock."

"Fine." The dark feelings evaporated and she was happy again.

Down in the foyer, Buddy melted into the shadows, fists closing and unclosing, rage born of yet another betrayal pounding through his veins.

FIFTY-FOUR

Detective Tom O'Neal spent New Year's Eve with his dog, Jake. They'd had pizza earlier to mark the occasion. Tom had a couple of brews and now they were walking along the beach, a big white moon lighting their way along the stretch of sand, and reflecting silvery off the water. The night was cold but invigorating, helped to clear his head.

Looking toward town, he could see the bursts of fireworks blooming in the night sky, but he couldn't hear them, which made them almost dreamlike. The whooshing of the waves rushing at the shore near his feet accompanied his thoughts.

Earlier, he and Glen had poured over the facts of the case again. He was beginning to have his doubts Jeffrey Denton was their guy. He'd have to be a complete moron. Though he did fit the profile—early thirties, lived alone, close to his mother. But bad guys usually weren't that bright, despite popular belief. And Glen had told him he thought Denton picked up his tail. And why the hell would he savage Natalie Breen like he had, then hang that brooch on Caroline Hill's doorknob, knowing it would connect him to the killing? Didn't make sense. Nothing about this case did.

There could be other victims for all he knew. Missing women they'd figured were runaways, others no one reported missing. Prostitutes were prime targets for these predators. The guy could be a transient, moving from state to state. A salesman, a truck driver. He'd had the thoughts before and now they returned, running full circle in his mind.

Then there was the landlady's nephew who'd been hesitant to answer their questions, but maybe only because he had some challenges. Although Tom didn't discount that there might be more ominous reasons. Caroline had said he'd asked her out to a movie and that she'd turned him down. When Tom mentioned it, he'd hung his head, said that that was okay. She was still his friend. It was clear the landlady, very protective of her Harold, hadn't liked them questioning him.

They'd also interrogated Handratty who swore he never touched 'that crazy bitch'. Though they questioned him for four hours, they couldn't break him down and get to him admit what really happened to him that night, even when it was clear they all knew the truth, that only one man had put him in the hospital. When they started pushing him about the killings, he shut down altogether and demanded to be permitted to make a call to his lawyer. As it turned out, he'd actually called his mother, but now was lawyered up.

Other thoughts inserted themselves in the mix. Mainly of Gloria on her own in that house with David. Who knew where the bastard would strike next? You couldn't put a squad car on every house. And he couldn't play favorites.

A wave snuck up on him, rushing over his sneakers before he could jump out of its reach, sending a shock of cold seeping through the canvas.

Jake was running ahead of him, nosing under logs, checking stuff out, tail wagging happily. Every so often, he would turn and look in Tom's direction to reassure himself that everything was cool.

FIFTY-FIVE

Mrs. Bannister met Caroline at the bottom of the stairs next morning and invited her in for tea. "Aren't you looking spiffy. Day off?"

"Yes." Once Caroline decided to revisit the house she grew up in, a strange urgency had overtaken her and she was anxious to be on her way. "I'm taking the bus to Gleneton Street," she said, but Mrs. Bannister had already taken her hand and was drawing her inside her flat.

"I—I guess I can come in for a minute."

As she followed the landlady down the hallway, she found herself looking for the kitten Mrs. Bannister had offered her, but Mimi wasn't to be seen among the menagerie of felines who had taken up post on various pieces of furniture. Not that she had changed her mind.

Stepping into the kitchen, she was surprised to see Harold sitting at the table, eating Cheerios from a blue bowl. He explained he didn't have to go in till ten this morning, smiled at her and went back to eating. There was a Cheerio stuck to the corner of his mouth.

"What number, dear," Mrs. Bannister asked, as she poured their tea. "I know a woman lives over on Gleneton."

"Number 264. Near the Bay. You put that model airplane together yet?" she asked Harold.

"Yeah, you wanna see?" Before she could answer, Harold was gone. Sometimes he seemed like he was no more than ten or twelve. But she was happy he liked the gift she'd bought him.

As soon as he was out of earshot, the landlady eased herself into a chair. "The was a thoughtful gift, Caroline. You're a good girl, but I have to tell you I'm not happy about that police car cruising by at all hours, slowing down when they pass our building. The neighbors will think we're selling dope or something. They questioned poor Harold for over an hour. They were asking him about a gold brooch someone hung on your door. They thought it might have been him. Did you tell them that?"

So Mrs. Bannister hadn't asked her in because she wanted company. She was angry about the police talking to Harold. "I told them I thought it might be possible," she said truthfully.

"Why didn't you just ask him? Or me? Anyway, Harold doesn't have that kind of money if he did want to buy you something so extravagant. Did you consider that Mr. Denton might have left it? I've noticed you two are quite an item."

She was probably watching out her window and saw us kissing, Caroline thought. "Yes, I did ask. He says he didn't. I'm sorry about the police questioning Harold, Mrs. Bannister. I guess they have to talk to everyone who knows me, and who knew Lorraine Winters, since she lived here at one time too. They'll find the killer soon, I'm sure, and then all this will be over."

She sipped her tea, eager to be on her way and was glad when Harold came out with the model. It was blue and white, and very pretty. "You did a great job, Harold. It's beautiful." The Cheerio was gone from the corner of his mouth.

He beamed, then grabbed his jacket, gave his aunt a peck on the cheek and started out the door. Mrs. Bannister intercepted him, taking the airplane from his hand. Harold laughed and was gone.

"He didn't finish his breakfast." She shook her head in dismay and removed his bowl from the table. Her tone softening, she said, "Well, I hope you're right about them finding that monster, dear." She set the airplane on the fridge.

Mr. Denton is a tad older than you isn't he? Not that it matters. My own dear Harlan was twelve years older than me and we had a good life together. Oh, we had our differences, mind you, everyone does, but I miss him. He was a good man, Harlan was. So, you're going to check out your old stomping grounds, are you? Would you like some company? I have a few errands to do downtown."

Caroline begged off. "This is something I need to do on my

own." Her landlady looked hurt, and Caroline confided her reason for going. "I was lost for a very long time, Mrs. Bannister. Fragmented, my doctor used to say. Some of the missing pieces are still back in that house. I need to collect them. Or say goodbye to them, once and for all."

Mrs. Bannister walked her to the door. "I'm having the lock changed on the front door today, Caroline. It's not cheap, but better to be safe. You'll have a new key when you get back, so the old one won't fit. Just ring the bell. And good luck to you, dear."

But luck, in the good sense, would not follow her on that cold January day.

FIFTY-SIX

It was a cold gray day but thankfully Caroline didn't have long to wait before the bus pulled up, and she was glad to step into inside, where it was warm. She slid into a seat halfway down the aisle where she could look out the window, and watch for her stop.

Gazing out at the passing landscape, the houses and stores now familiar to her, she began to relax in the comfortable seat.

At the next stop, a woman and a little boy with curly blond hair got on, and took the seat in front of her. The boy immediately knelt on his seat facing Caroline, and grinned at her. She smiled back and said hi, just as his mother slapped his leg lightly and told him to sit down and behave.

It was not far to Gleneton, and so her bus stop came up before she was quite ready to get off. But there was no help for it. Seconds after she rang the bell, the bus jerked to a stop, air brakes hissing. She stepped down onto the sidewalk amidst the smell of diesel and cold air that carried the briny smell of the bay, triggering a flood of childhood memories.

She looked after the bus as it pulled away, and waved to the little boy was waving to her. Admired her hand in the pretty blue glove Lynne had bought for her. Standing there on the deserted sidewalk, she felt abandoned by the bus, which was silly. Yet a cold dread had settled in the pit of her stomach. She knew it was just being on this street after so many years that was effecting her. Like coming through a long, dark tunnel into the light. She wasn't fully adjusted yet, that was all. She'd be fine.

She drew her coat collar up, glad she'd worn slacks and a warm sweater under her pea coat. She drew her hat down to cover her ears and crossed the street to the corner store. She went inside, heard the bell jangle above the door and at once thought of Natalie's Boutique and how it was all locked up and dark now. But she wouldn't let herself think of that.

This was the street she grew up in, where she had walked to and from school, frequented this store on errands for her mother.

Inside, she half-expected to see the round jovial face of Mr. Jackson, who always greeted her with, "Hey, little Missy, and what can we do for you this morning?" She had not thought of Mr. Jackson in a long time.

But it was a girl who stood behind the counter. She was talking on the phone and chewing gum. She glanced at Caroline. "Hold on, got a customer." She held the receiver in her hand. "Yes?"

On impulse, Caroline asked for a b-b-bat, her favorite as a child when she had a few extra pennies, but the girl said they didn't carry them anymore, and went back to talking on the phone. Caroline spotted a pack of Chicklets in a display, and held them up, reaching into her purse as she did. The girl took the money and rang up the sale on the cash register without looking at her.

"Is Mr. Jackson still here?" Caroline asked the girl.

"Who?"

"Mr. Jackson. He owns—or at least he used to own, this store."

"Oh. Hold on a sec, Wendy," she said into the receiver and Caroline could almost hear her inward sigh. "Mr. Jackson died, Ma'am. But we kept the name. My parents have owned this store for the past five years."

Caroline thanked her for her trouble and headed for the door.

"No *problemo*," she said to her back, and returned to the conversation Caroline had interrupted, neither knowing nor having the remotest interest in the woman who had come here this morning to face her past and try to reclaim a part of herself. Caroline dropped the chicklets into her pocket, and left.

Continuing up Gleneton, she took no notice of the dark grey car parked on the other side of the street, motor running. The driver's eyes were looking straight ahead so she did not feel them on her.

Soon, an eagerness to see the old house again, combined with the cold air stinging her cheeks, made her pick up her pace.

Gleneton Street rose in a slight grade as it made its way to the top of the hill, then stretched down toward the church she had attended every Sunday morning with her parents, and the ball field, beyond it. She wondered if they were both still in existence.

She passed the wooden houses in their faded maroons, green and browns, built in the late thirties and forties. Built closely together, but leaving narrow alleys between some of them. She recalled family names she hadn't thought of in years—the Blanchards, the Walls, the Prestons; she and Sharon Preston had been best friends for a while. They walked to and from school together, played together at recess, even shared their sandwiches. But her father's critical view of any new friend ensured they would soon abandon her for other friends whose parents were more welcoming and less strict. Sharon's eventual rejection of her had hurt terribly, but she understood. Not then, at least not entirely, but now.

Just over the rise she slowed her step, finally standing very still as her old house came into view. Two-story, white with brown gingerbread trim and shutters, set back from the road. It looked smaller than she remembered. Shabbier. An old acquaintance fallen on hard times. Here she had lived with her parents for the first seventeen years of her life. A myriad of emotions welled in her chest and she felt a faint lightheadedness. She fought it off, took a deep breath and walked on.

As she drew nearer, she saw the FOR SALE sign sticking out of the snow-covered lawn. Jeffrey had mentioned he'd thought the house was up for sale.

The gray cement walk was shoveled clear of snow and Caroline made the short walk, as she had done thousands of times before. She peered through the dirt-smeared window to the left of the door; this had been their living room.

There was debris everywhere, paint cans, cardboard boxes and chunks of plaster. A white dust lay over everything that was visible to her from this vantage point, and she could see by the lighter spots here and there on the walls, where someone had sanded them.

The mantle, where once family photos had been displayed, a couple which now hung on the wall in her room, held only a bottle with a plastic daisy sticking out of it. Beneath the mantle, the brick fireplace where, on winter evening, a cozy fire had crackled, sending shadow-flames leaping and dancing on the walls, looked black and cold.

The patched walls suddenly disappeared as her memory re-created the wallpaper patterned with its green and gold leaves, that once was there. Her eye followed the part of the stairs she could see leading up to their bedrooms—her bedroom.

The urgency to get inside was overpowering. With no thought to anyone who might see her and call the police, she tussled with the windows on both sides of the door, then the front door itself, but the house was locked up tight.

There was a phone number of a real estate company on the window. She could walk back to the store and phone them. Say she was a prospective buyer and someone would come and let her in. But they might not be able to come right away, and she needed to get in now.

Unaware of the grey Mustang driving slowly past the house, Caroline slipped into the alley that once had seemed been bigger, and went around back to the small fenced-in yard, tromping through deep snow that managed to get inside her boots, making her ankles ache with instant cold.

Some of the picketed slats were lying half-buried in the snow, and she carefully walked over them, pushing them deeper toward the ground.

The kitchen windows were hung with yellowing newspapers. She tried the window closest to the alley, but it was locked, as was the door, serving only to make her more determined. Crossing to the other window, where she at once that the lock was broken, she tried the window. But it didn't budge.

Removing her gloves and slipping them into her pocket, she tried again. The window was stuck fast, probably due to age and or rarely being opened. I could smash the window out, she thought, but decided to keep that option as a last resort. She needed something to pry it open with. Turning away from the window, she looked about her. In the far corner of the yard, where part of the fence still stood bravely, there was a pile of trash: cans, chunks of wallboard and plaster, a bicycle with a wheel missing, other garbage.

She made her way to the mound, and spotted a large, rusting fork sitting atop the debris, and picked it up; it had a good solid heft. Worth a try. She trudged back through the snow and went to work.

Jamming the fork between the sill and the window sash, she pushed down on it until the heel of her hand began to throb with pain as well as cold. The wood was blackened and rotting now, some of it flecking away. As she worked, a small urgent voice in her head warned her that she was breaking the law and would go to jail if she was caught, but the compulsion to get inside the house was stronger and she ignored it and prepared for another try.

She rubbed her cold hands together to try to bring warmth into them, curled them up in her pockets for a few seconds, then returned to her task with renewed will, prying until her arms and shoulders ached, and her hands began to lose feeling, and the fork began to bend.

She blew out a long breath. Then, finding a surge of strength that hadn't been there a moment before, she gave a final hard push. The window croaked open. A sense of triumph rippled through her. She dropped the ruined fork on the ground and stood quietly for a moment, breathing hard, massaging the pain from her hands. Then she raised the window the rest of the way, and crawled inside.

The kitchen had been painted recently, which explained the strong smell of paint in the house. It was a soft ivory, clean and bright. The old flooring was partially torn up, pieces of linoleum tossed in a corner. Caroline took off her boots, and treading carefully on the old wood crossed to the sink and shook the snow out of her boots. Pulling them back on, ignoring her wet feet, she went through to the living room.

The ghosts of her parents were here with her. She could feel them, faintly detect her mother's Tweed cologne mingling with the smell of paint. Other people had lived here after them, but they had left no part of themselves behind. Not for her. She knew Doctor Rosen would probably tell her she had brought the ghosts with her, that they were inside her head. Maybe he was right. But she didn't think so. Were they still waiting for her to come back home?

Holding onto the familiar wood railing, she climbed the

carpeted stairs. The fifth creaked when she stepped on it, as if a mouse were trapped beneath. Her boots made soft footfalls on the steps, fourteen in all. Just as she remembered.

The bathroom was at the top of the stairs and down a short hallway. At the opposite end of the hallway, a tall window overlooked the street. The bedrooms branched off the hallway. Her own small room was directly across from her parents' bedroom, on the right. Both doors were open, and she stepped warily into her old room, like stepping back into time and her heart seemed to stop.

A myriad of conflicting emotions fought for top place inside her, so powerful she had to place her palm against the wall to steady herself. She closed her eyes. You are okay. You are fine. You can do this. Breathe. She inhaled deep, let the breath out slow and easy. And again. When she felt calmer, she opened her eyes.

A narrow bed much like the one she had slept in stood against the wall. Someone had left it behind. This was the room where she had danced in secret, keeping the radio low so as not to bring wrath upon herself. The room where she dreamed and planned, and finally cried herself to sleep night after night, pining for the boy she loved with her whole heart.

The door was stained brown, and she ran a hand over it. She had pounded on this locked door until her knuckles were raw and bleeding. You'd think there'd be some evidence of her crazed heart here. But there was not. There was no window in this room, else she might have leapt from it all those years ago.

Tears were streaming from her eyes, and wiped them away with the back of her hand. But more flowed, hot and scalding, and she took some tissues from her bag. She should have cried herself out long ago, but apparently not.

I forgive you both. I forgive myself for hating you.

They had done what they thought was right. That they were wrong didn't really matter now. She mopped at her eyes with new tissues, blew her nose. In a little while the tears ceased, and she felt cleansed and whole. She would be okay. She could go on with her life.

At the sound of a car motor down on the street, she turned in the open doorway and looked toward the hallway window. The motor cut and there was silence. Someone had stopped outside. You've broken in. You're a criminal, she told herself.

Fighting a bout of angst, she went into the hallway and looked out the window in time to see a man getting out of a grey car. The car door shut with a solid thunk and the man turned and came up the walkway, head bent so that she couldn't see his face. He wore a green jacket and a cap with the eartabs turned down. The cap looked to have some logo on it. One of the workers?

He had a distinctive walk, head and shoulders thrust forward. Something familiar about that. As he drew nearer the house, he disappeared from her view.

Moving away from the window, Caroline tried to think what she should she do? She'd never make it back downstairs and out the kitchen window in time to avoid being seen.

Was he the owner of the house? she wondered. Well, if it was she would just be truthful and tell him she used to live here and wanted to see the old place again. Or she could lie and say she was considering buying the house, and there'd been no one to let her in. Surely he wouldn't call the police. She hadn't touched anything or done any damage. She decided it was one of the workers, a painter or an electrician. Yes, she'd seen a logo on his cap, though he'd been too far away to make it out.

Taking a deep breath, she forced herself to be calm. Dabbed at her eyes with a tissue. She would simply handle this like a reasonable, mature woman. She would first apologize, then…

Why hadn't she heard a key in the lock, or the front door open?

FIFTY-SEVEN

This realization no sooner struck her, when she heard a footfall on the stairs. When the fifth stair creaked, her heart leapt in her chest like a small animal seeking escape. But there was no escaping the obvious; he had gotten in the same way she had. He followed her footprints in the deep snow through the alley and around to the back yard. She envisioned him climbing through the kitchen window.

Caroline took a tentative step forward until she could see the stranger's shadow on the wall ascending the stairs, huge and frightening. An instant later she saw him in the flesh, though his face was hidden beneath the peak of the cap, but she saw the logo there -BB-intertwined in blue and gold. *Big Bakery.* He wore a black hooded jacket, with the hood down.

Harold? She'd never seen him wearing this coat. He always wore his new down-filled coat. And then, on the second step from the top, he raised his head and smiled at her. "Hello, Caroline."

No. Not Harold. A bigger man than the landlady's nephew. For a long moment she couldn't speak. Then, finding her voice, she said pleasantly, "Hello. You're Harold's friend." She tried to return his smile, but the muscles in her face felt frozen. "You helped him carry my trunk upstairs. Are you working here?"

But she knew of course in her deepest self that that wasn't why he was here. Not even close. She also knew she'd seen him long before that day he'd helped Harold upstairs with the trunk. That realization hit her as she was watching him get out of the green car and walked up the walkway, something in the way he moved had jarred a memory loose, but the memory floated just out of reach. Not answering her question, he just kept coming in those big boots… *Clomp…clomp…*and then was on the landing, turning to face her. "He said you'd be here."

He had large features, longish dirty blond hair escaping the cap. Big, dangerous hands protruded from the cuffs of his jacket. Wide forehead, intense pale eyes.

"Who...who said I'd be here?"

"Harold. He tells me everything about you. I knew that first day you moved in you'd been in Bayshore. Anyway, I just followed your bus. You haven't been quite true, have you, Caroline? But at least I know you haven't laid with him."

"Who? I don't know what you're talking about." She tried to keep the waver from her voice.

"Don't lie. I saw you kissing him before you both went inside the building. I followed you in. I was outside your door last night and I heard you send him away. That was very lucky for you. Not so lucky for him. I didn't come to your rescue just so you could defile yourself with another."

Her heart thumped in her chest. Jeffrey. What had he done to Jeffrey? Oh, God. "How did you get a key to the building?"

She heard only a trace of French accent in his words. She had heard it that night he put Mike Handratty in the hospital, but it hadn't registered. He spoke well, but the rhythm was there.

"A key, of course," he said. "Harold always hung his jacket in the staffroom, the key in his pocket. I had a copy made."

He was bragging, thinking she would be impressed at his cleverness.

"I had planned for us to go last night at midnight. But you ruined that." Anger flared in his eyes like a dark flame fanned. The flame went out. "But what does that matter now? We're together, and that's all that matters."

She remembered that Harold had called him Danny. She didn't remember his last name, only that it was French.

"Yes," she half-whispered. The floating memory snapped into place and a vision of the men at Bayshore shuffling about in the yard below her barred window flashed at the forefront of her mind, like a movie frame. That was where she had first seen him. At Bayshore mental institution. Down in the yard with the other male patients. He didn't shuffle like the others, though, but strode when he walked, shoulders thrust forward, a man with purpose, yet going nowhere. *Like a speared bull looking for the source of its torment.* Those weren't her words, but little Martha Blizzard's. Martha had a different way of seeing things and people. Just like she saw her husband waving goodbye to her after she struck him in the head with the baseball bat. Danny wasn't a particularly big man, but his very presence was fierce and enormous and terrifying. She tried not to let her fear show.

The man who stood before her had been an inmate, just like herself. Why was he here? Even as she asked herself the question, cold fear like spread in the hollow of her stomach, like melting ice. The small voice in her head was urging her to run. But how? Where? He was blocking her path to the stairs. The window was behind her.

She should not have come here alone. She wished she had taken Mrs. Bannister up on her offer to go with her, but too late now for second thoughts.

"All is forgiven, Caroline," he said, moving toward her. She recoiled instinctively, and he stopped, looking hurt. She could see him fighting his natural bent to rage. Slowly, the clenched fists relaxed and he smiled, a chilling smile. "It's my fault, I know. I shouldn't have waited so long, but I couldn't come for you until the time was right. You can see that, can't you?   Did you like your Christmas gift, Caroline? I saw you admiring it in the store."

He'd been looking in the store window, watching her. He killed Natalie Breen and took the pin because he thought she wanted it. Oh, God. He was insane, a murderer. She had doomed that lovely woman to a terrible fate the instant she walked into her store.

He read her thoughts and his face darkened "She was giving your name out to strangers. I couldn't allow that."

"I understand. Please. I have to go now." She took a step to go past him, but he blocked her way.

"Don't make me angry at you, Caroline. I don't want to be angry with you. Believe me, you don't want me to be. Now listen to me. Those other women…I thought they were the right ones too, but I was wrong. They lied. They wanted to take love away, see, so I treated them like the whores they were. And I made sure they told no more lies. They deserved to die. My mother was a whore, you know."

He said this so matter-of-factly, he might have been telling her his mother knitted socks. She said nothing.

And then, suddenly, he slipped a hand under his jacket and withdrew a large knife from a sheath attached to his belt, and the saliva dried up in her throat and mouth. The curved blade gleamed in the cold milky light from the window and froze any words she might have uttered.

"You're not like that, are you, Caroline?" he asked in a deadly soft voice. "You wouldn't take love away."

"No, no, I wouldn't," she said, her voice a strangled whisper. She had no idea what he was talking about, but she knew he was a killer and that she had to be very careful of what she said and how she said it. But it was so hard to think with this din inside her skull, when everything in her wanted to run, screaming. But she knew she wouldn't get far before he plunged that knife into her.

"Good, Caroline. I knew you weren't like the others."

For some reason, she was remembering Harold telling her he was from some little place where the population was largely French. Information that might be helpful to her at some point, though she couldn't imagine how. She thought of William, who'd also been French. A man who'd been good and caring, and would never intentionally hurt anyone. This man before her was a monster. What had happened to him to twist him into this dark, fiendish creature who killed so easily.

Poor Natalie Breen. How frightened she must have been before he killed her. As frightened as I am now.

He had mentioned about his mother, a woman for whom he held only disdain. What could she say that might connect with him? Yet she knew from experience it was possible to turn against one's parents. Maybe she would learn something that would save her. The knife gleamed dangerously in his hand.

She had to try.

"Does your mother still live in Petit Ridge?" she said, her mind suddenly throwing out the name of the place. It was merely a stall for time, time in which someone might come to her aid. But the hope was small.

At her question, a frown crossed his broad forehead. "How did you ...? Ah, Harold. Of course. Well, never mind about my mother. Do you think I don't know what game you're playing, Caroline? You think you can outsmart me? Don't waste your time trying. I've had my head shrunk by the best of them. You're disappointing me. I thought you'd be different. I thought you'd understand."

"Really, it's not a game. You said she was a—a whore. Is that why you hate her?" She made her voice soft and caring, in the way that Lynne had so often spoken to her. If she could keep him talking, someone could still show up here, the owner or one of the workers. She let that small hope get bigger.

"My mother is dead to me. We have to go now, Caroline. Earl is waiting."

"Earl?" Who was Earl?

"Enough questions. The car is out front." He stepped aside to let her pass. "You go first. Don't try to run. If you do, you'll be sorry. Go on now. Walk ahead of me. And walk normally. Smile and talk as if we were old friends. Which we are, you know? We're destined to be together. You and me and Earl. A real family."

FIFTY-EIGHT

Lynne drove slowly up Glendon Street, searching the houses for the one Caroline grew up in. She looked for number 264. There. There it is. She pulled up at the curb. Caroline shouldn't be alone to do this.

Seconds before, Lynne passed a grey Mustang going in the opposite direction, but had no way of knowing Caroline, who Danny had ordered to lie down in the seat, was in it and paid the car little attention. Mrs. Bannister gave her the address readily, even describing the place to her. She was concerned about Caroline, she said. She gone to exorcize old demons. The landlady was concerned about her. She wasn't alone.

Looking up at the house with its brown trim and gingerbread decoration, Lynne thought it had a definite charm. She noted the For Sale sign on the lawn. Caroline had come here to exorcize old demons. It was a good sign. But was she ready for the emotional impact stepping into the past would have on her? She'll handle it, Lynne told herself, but was glad she'd come just in case she needed moral support. Caroline was strong, but this would be tough for anyone who'd gone through what she had.

Lynne had a surprise for Caroline, her reason for dropping in on her this morning. She'd located the family that adopted Elizabeth. Oddly enough, they lived not that far from here. Being a psychiatric nurse gave her access to a couple of friends in important places. Not that she planned to do anything with the information, other than to tell Caroline that her daughter was well loved, and happy. She deserved that much, she thought, as she parked the car and got out.

Assuming Caroline got permission from a real estate agent to go through the house, Lynne walked up to the front door. She rapped once and was about to knock again when the door creaked swung open. Strange.

She went inside. "Hello?" she called out, her voice creating a hollow sound the came back to her. She took another step and her eye caught the woman's leather glove on the foyer floor, palm up, slightly curled like a disembodied hand.

She bent down and picked it up, recognizing it at once as part of the pair she'd given Caroline for Christmas. She felt its buttery softness in her hand, looked inside to confirm the designer's name on the tag, along with the color midnight blue.

The silence of the house screamed at her. Caroline had grown up within these walls. How difficult it must have been for her to stand here, where I am now. All those memories must have come flooding back like a great tsunami.

Lynne went through to the kitchen, boots clicking hollowly on the floors. She felt the blast of cool air even before she noticed that the window was wide open. Who would leave a window open in January? Especially as they were renovating.

A bad feeling began to niggle at her, just beneath her breastbone. She went into the living room. At the foot of the stairs, Lynne called up, "Caroline?" But only the echo of her voice in the empty house, answered.

She looked down at the two sets of damp footprints on the stairs. The smaller prints were quite clear, some covered by a larger set. Both coming and going. Had someone followed her here?

There were footprints in the foyer, too, but they could be anyone's. Obviously men had been working in here, and they might even have showed the house to prospective buyers while Caroline was here. But the niggling beneath her breastbone was becoming a very real fear.

She still held the glove in her hand and now she shoved it in her bag. The dropped glove was no small thing. It was a damn cold day and Caroline wouldn't have gotten far before realizing she had dropped it somewhere. She would have come back here to find it. She'd dropped it deliberately, hoping to provide a clue. The best she could do in her situation. What situation? came the ominous question. You're getting ahead of yourself. Quit it! She's probably home by now.

She remembered seeing a store on the corner. She drove back and phoned Caroline's number. The phone rang and rang. She finally hung up, thanked the clerk and left.

Lynne Addison sped through the streets of St. Simeon, heading for the police station. At the same time Art Lawrence, assistant baker at Big Bakery stood in the parking lot behind the old red brick building that had been there for fifty years, staring with a sick feeling at the empty space where his pride and joy, the '77 dark grey Mustang had been parked while he was away on Christmas vacation, in Hawaii.

Night Corridor
Page 205

FIFTY-NINE

"You say this friend of yours, Marilyn …?"

"Caroline," she snapped at the policeman behind the desk. He had a blond crew cut and looked twelve. "Caroline Hill." He raised an eyebrow at the sharpness of her tone. " Sorry. She's been missing for—less than an hour."

He almost grinned at her and Lynne had to rein in her fury, and the urge to smack him, which wasn't likely to help her cause. She made herself calm down. She had broken all speeding records getting here, expecting to hear sirens behind her at any second. She was sweating under her coat, despite the cold day.

"Listen, please, officer," she said evenly. "My name is Lynne Addison. I'm a psychiatric nurse. I worked at Bayshore Mental Institution for more than twenty years. For nine of those years, Caroline was a patient under my care."

She had his attention. "So what are you saying? You think she ran away…?"

"No. Please hear me out. I've reason to think she is in terrible danger. Two of your detectives have already interviewed her about the murder of the shopkeeper, Natalie Breen. One of the other victims lived in Caroline's building, right across the hall."

All trace of amusement gone from his face, he grabbed up pen and paper. "Go on."

"Thank you. I think someone's been stalking her," she said, her tone softer now that he was listening. "Apparently, the police think so too, or they wouldn't be watching the building." As she was leaving, she'd seen them drive by and slow down.

"Caroline took the bus to her old house on Gleneton, the house where she grew up, and I think he followed her in a car. I believe he has her now." She fought back a rush of panic as she said, "We have to find her. Before it's too late."

The officer was on the phone with someone in charge of the case when Caroline was drawn by a commotion across the room. A man was talking at two cops, hands gesturing wildly as he ranted about someone stealing his Mustang right out of his parking place at his job. Noticing his jacket bearing the logo BB. Big Bakery. Lynne recalled Caroline telling her that the landlady's nephew worked there. Before she could think further on this coincidence, (or maybe not so coincidental) the young policeman hung up the phone, and gestured behind him. "Right down that hall, third door to your left, Ma'am. Detective O'Neal's waiting for you."

SIXTY

Caroline sat beside her abductor in terrified silence as they drove through small villages and towns, past beauty shops, gas stations, stores festooned with Christmas decorations, a small library built of sandstone. She read Halston Library above the big doors before they sped past the building. They drove past a woman walking a beautiful taffy-colored Collie. A few blocks on some kids were playing street hockey and had to scramble onto the sidewalk to escape getting hit. Caroline let out a breath when the last one, a little boy of about nine in a red knit hat, was safely out of harm's way. The kids stared wide-eyed after them. He was speeding and just as she had the thought that he might alert the attention of the police, he apparently had the same thought, and slowed down.

They'd been on the road a couple of hours now. The motor hummed smoothly. She glanced at the driver, at his big hands gripping the wheel. At least he wasn't driving in jerky fits and starts as he had been when they started out, giving Caroline the distinct impression the car wasn't his. He must have stolen it. Either that, or he'd just learned to drive. Maybe both. Her thoughts went back to Jeffrey and she had to fight tears. Was he dead?

"You're very quiet," he said beside her, his voice startling her after the long silence, striking a new chord of fear in her. Though his voice held no immediate threat, she knew if she did not get away from him, she would die. That much she was very sure of.

"Enjoying the ride? I thought you would. Nice car, eh? It's a good day for driving, the roads aren't too bad either. We should be in Toronto tomorrow by supper. We'll rest up at a motel tonight. No need to hurry, eh?" He smiled at her, talking as if they were any ordinary couple and heading for Toronto was the most normal thing in the world to be doing. Wary of drawing out the monster she knew lay just beneath the surface of this reasonable, pleasure demeanor, she said that sounded fine. In reality, just driving in this car with him was terrifying. She had no idea what he might do. Maybe change his mind and drive to some isolated spot and rape and kill her there, as he had the others. All except Natalie. He killed her for a silly brooch Caroline didn't even like. Or did he kill her because she could identify him? But why with such viciousness? The papers said she had been beaten before being strangled to death. Is that how she would die too? Not if she could help it.

He was carrying on with his small talk, and Caroline did her best to give normal, matter-of-fact responses, tried with everything in her to tamp down the mounting panic. She wondered why the people they passed couldn't feel her terror. Why couldn't they hear her silent screams for help? But no one turned around and looked back at the grey car that had just passed them. No one would call the police.

She didn't know why she had thought it would help to drop that glove. No one would connect it to her. The glove could belong to anyone. Only Lynne would know, and there was no reason for her to be at the house.

Ethel will miss me at work tomorrow, she thought, and phone the house. There would be no answer, of course. Will she phone the landlady then? Maybe. Maybe not. It would probably be too late anyway.

Who was Earl? she wondered again.

Tears pressed behind her lids again. I'm just starting to get my life back, to find joy again. Please, God. I don't want to die.

And then it occurred to her that stopping at a motel room might not be the worst thing that could happen. It might even provide her with a chance to get away. They had phones in motel offices, and people in washrooms. Maybe she could pass someone a note. She had a pen in her purse. She could write on a paper towel. Anything.

His hand shot out and clamped down on her wrist causing heart to leap into her throat. She could feel the restrained power in his hand and knew what it was capable of, knew what those evil hands had already done. She glanced down at the back of his hand, matted with black hair, some sprouting from his knuckles.

"I know what you're thinking," he said calmly, as her heart thumped in her chest. "I always know, Caroline. If you try to get away, you'll be very sorry. I told you that. You know I mean it, don't you."

"Yes."

"Good." He smiled at her then, returned his hand to the wheel. Her wrist tingled from his steely grip and she rubbed it lightly, her heart sinking into despair.

SIXTY-ONE

Once Lynne talked to Detective O'Neal, things began unfolding quickly. The first thing the detective did was phone Mrs. Bannister and ask to speak with Harold. Harold was at work, the landlady told him. Although she could hear only one side of the conversation, Lynne was able to get the gist of it. He asked the landlady if she'd mind checking to see if her tenant, Jeffrey Denton was at home. He hung up, said to Lynne, "She said she'd call a Mr. Mason who also lives on the top floor. "It's too hard on her climbing those stairs. She'll call back."

But it was Mr. Mason, who, five minutes later, called back (the landlady was too distraught to talk) to report he'd found Mr. Denton's door unlocked and the man unconscious on the floor, the front of his shirt dark with his blood. He'd already phoned 911. "I thought he was dead," he told him. "He might be by now." Then he said he had to go, the ambulance had arrived.

This, the detective related quickly to Lynne as he was dialing Big Bakery. Harold was indeed at work as his aunt had said. Detective O'Neal hung up the phone, frowning, eyes narrowed as if working out a very difficult puzzle, which of course he was, Lynne thought, standing quietly on the opposite side of the big, cluttered desk, unable to sit and trying not to pace or tear her hair. Caroline's dark blue glove lay on the desk between them in a transparent sealed bag, like a terrible omen.

"Then Harold doesn't have her," Lynne said at the same moment Officer Aiken rapped on the door, and stepped inside.

"Glen, good, you're here." He introduced him to Lynne, filled him in.

"Harold Bannister doesn't have her," he said, "but one of his co-workers, a Danny Babineau didn't show up for work today and another employee just came in and reported his Mustang stolen from the parking lot."

There was already an APB out for the Mustang. Detective O'Neal picked up the phone again and gave an update; the driver was holding a female hostage. Approach with caution. Suspect probably armed and dangerous."

He hung up, said to his partner, "We need to have another talk with Harold Bannister."

"I'm with you."

"They might be working in tandem?" Detective O'Neal said, reaching for his jacket hanging on the hall tree. When he stretched, Lynne saw the black, dangerous looking gun in his holster. She knew nothing about guns but she was gratified to see it there if it could keep Caroline alive.

Danny Babineau. Why did that name seem familiar?

They were headed out the door when the phone rang. O'Neal listened, said they'd be there shortly, and hung up.

"Manager at *Big Bakery*," he told them. "Apparently, Babineau hung around Harold at work. Always chatting him up. Odd since he didn't talk to anyone else. And Harold was a level up; they trusted him with other jobs, even working in the main bakery. Good worker."

"Any background on this Danny Babineau?" Detective Glen Aiken asked.

"Nada. Hired him off the street. He mainly cleaned up, swept the warehouse floor, that sort of thing. He worked casual, traded shifts with another guy; they phoned him when they wanted him. Been there a couple of months. He cleaned out his room at the building where he was living so he's obviously not planning to go back there."

"Seems they did a little investigating on their own," Detective Aiken said.

"I know the name," Lynne said.

They both turned to look at her.

"Who? Babineau?" O'Neal asked with new interest.

"Yes. Danny Babineau. I think he was a patient at Bayshore. I could be wrong but I don't think so. I didn't work in the male wards, of course. But I'm almost sure I heard his name brought up at meetings. Or maybe Dr. Rosen mentioned him to me. It's been awhile ago, before there was any talk of Bayshore closing down."

"Let's roll," O'Neal said to Aiken, who was already three steps ahead of him. To Lynne he said, "Do you think you can find out anything else about this guy?" He opened the door so Lynne could precede them.

"I—I can try. I think so." She still had keys to the files.

"We'll meet you back here in an hour." And then they were gone, tearing out of the police parking lot on squealing tires.

Fifteen minutes later, Lynne drove up the winding drive of Bayshore Mental Hospital, which was presently operating with skeleton staff. As she entered through the big oak doors, she put on her most professional face, produced her credentials to the commissionaire at the door, whose face she knew, signed in, then strode through the long hallway to the big room where patient files were kept under lock and key. What she was doing was probably illegal but she'd take her chances.

She easily found Danny Babineau's file and copied it, slipped it into her briefcase, along with a cassette Dr. Rosen had made. She could have phoned Dr. Rosen for permission, but there wasn't time.

As she was leaving, the commissionaire gave her a smile and a wave.

SIXTY-TWO

Bringing the aroma of baking bread and pies with him, Harold sat in the back seat of the cruiser, looking pale and worried.

In reply to Detective Aiken's question, Harold said, "I told him about her the morning after she moved in. I hadn't seen her yet, but Aunt Greta said she was tiny and pretty with blue eyes and dark hair, and that she seemed really nice. Danny said he had a sister that looked like the girl I described, but she ran away from home when she was sixteen. "When my aunt asked me to take the trunk up to Caroline, I asked Danny to give me a hand so he could see if it was really her. He said it wasn't."

"Did you tell him she'd been at Bayshore?" O'Neal asked.

He was thoughtful for a long moment, then frowning said, "No, I didn't. But he was always asking me about Caroline, even after he said she wasn't his sister."

"Did he ask you about her this morning?" Detective Glen Aiken asked.

"Yeah." Harold dropped his eyes. "He was there when I came out of my building. I told him she was going in the bus to see her old house where she used to live on Gleneton Street."

"Didn't you wonder what he was doing hanging around your building?"

"I – I didn't think he was. We just met up. He said he had things to do and would see me later."

Harold looked angry with himself, and crossed his arms fiercely to keep from crying. Harold knew what had happened. Detective O'Neal still had questions.

"Did you ever give Danny the key to your house, Harold?"

He squirmed visibly in the back seat. "No." He swallowed

hard. "But I think he knew I kept it in my jacket pocket. He saw it that day he helped me with the trunk." Harold looked miserable. "I shouldn't have told him about Caroline. But Danny asked me."

'Danny asked me'. He hadn't known how to lie to him or say he didn't know, and Babineau had used him. It didn't matter; he would have seen her get on the bus this morning anyway, and followed her. He must have parked the stolen car around the corner. The detective told this to Harold and it seemed to make him feel better.

It was not hard to put the pieces together. Danny Babineau had copied the key and used it to gain entry the building and leave Caroline his Christmas gift, the brooch he'd taken from Natalie Breen's shop after he killed her. She must have gift-wrapped for him, thinking he was just a last minute customer, as men often are, not realizing it would be her last act. Why such brutality though? Where did the rage come from? Maybe Lynne Addison could enlighten them. But that wasn't their first priority.

"Some of the workers are saying Danny stole Mr. Lawrence's car," Harold said. "Did Danny do...something. Did he hurt Caroline?"

"We hope not, Harold. Do you know Caroline very well?" Detective Aiken asked gently.

"Caroline's my friend. She bought me a model plane for Christmas. She thinks I'm smart. Caroline said I could learn a new job if I wanted."

Harold looked upset and both detectives knew he had nothing at all to do with what had gone down. He was just a nice kid who was a little slow in recognizing the con and danger in a man like Danny Babineau.

"We think he abducted your friend, Harold. We think he has her now. Do you have any idea where he might have taken her? Did he ever say anything to you?"

Harold eyes were big and his skin was pale as flour. "No. He had some relatives in Petit Ridge. Or at least that's what he said," he added, his face expressing suspicions that maybe Danny didn't always tell him the truth. Then, as if a lightbulb had gone off in his brain, he said, "Danny said he was going to see his father soon. He said he lives in Toronto."

SIXTY-THREE

Lynne was waiting for them when they arrived back at the station. She'd had a chance to scan through the file and listened to the tape in the car. Without preamble, she said, "I'll spare you the psychiatric jargon, Detectives. Enough to know that Danny is caught in a sort of 'time warp' and wants to recreate that time. Like tearing a curtain between present and past worlds, and stepping through. But with certain modifications. Somehow Caroline figures into the picture. I'm a little vague on exactly how. Whatever it is, when his plan doesn't work, he'll kill like her did the others. I want to go with you."

O'Neal argued against it but she held her ground. "If you find Caroline with that man, I may be able to talk him into letting her go without any need for more violence. Psychiatry is my field. And Danny Babineau is insane, Detective O'Neal. By anyone's definition, legal or otherwise."

SIXTY-FOUR

For hours they drove in silence, the car swallowing up miles of mainly narrow roads, past service stations, barber shops, fire stations. More towns and villages swept by, one becoming very like the last one they had just driven through. She guessed he wanted to avoid the main highway. He was worried they were looking for him.

The clock on the dash said 2:10 P.M. She and Jeffrey would have been at lunch now. She had somehow brought this monster in their lives. Into Jeffrey's life. Oh, God, I'm so sorry.

Danny must have followed him upstairs. He must have walked very softly, for she heard no footsteps past her door or on the stairs after she closed her door. Nor apparently did Mrs. Bannister.

He suddenly reached across her and she jumped, her whole body reacting.

"Just turning on the radio," he said, almost apologetically. "You like country music, Caroline?"

She said she did, she liked lots of music. She liked blues best. As his fingers found the knobs, she again observed how large his hands were, the dark mat of hair curling on the backs. The tendons in his wrists like ropes. Hands that had beaten and strangled at least three women to death. She banished the horrid images the thought evoked.

He finally found a country music station. Willie Nelson was singing *You Are always On My Mind*, his voice filling the small space around them.

"Good song," he said, and grinned at her.

"It's nice." He was being pleasant again. She chanced it. "Danny, I have to go to the bathroom."

"My name's not Danny. It's Buddy." He spoke matter-of-factly, but gave no answer to her request, one way or another, just began singing with Willie, his own voice deep and out of tune. She found no humor in it, but was glad his hands were back on the wheel.

Willie Nelson's song over, one by Loretta Lynn began to play and he said, "Country music is Earl's favorite, you know."

An icy chill slid down Caroline's spine, for the words spoken were not in a man's voice, but in a child's, high and thin and laced with excitement. In spite of herself, she snapped a look at him. His profile was set in a childish cast, conflicting with the strong nose with its bump on the bridge, the beetle brows. "Earl sings and plays the guitar," he said, staring straight ahead. "He plays at a place in Toronto called Curly's."

"Curly's?" she managed, unable to tear her eyes from him.

"Yep. It's a bar. I think he's going to be discovered soon and he'll be big as Johnny Cash or any of those guys. He knows lots of songs, *Folsom prison Blues*, Glen Smith's *You're the One*. My favorite song, though, is *You Don't Know Me* by Eddie Arnold. Earl's going to be famous just like the guys.

"He promised to teach me some chords," the child said, smiling, with something close to joy on his man-child face. "Pretty neat, eh. He calls me Buddy."

Caroline could neither breathe nor speak. The hairs on the back of her neck rose and her skin felt like things were crawling over it. She forced herself to stay calm. *You've seen crazy before. You know crazy. You've lived it.* You have to find out who Earl is. Why we're going to Toronto to meet him. If this Earl wanted to be with Danny, why had he needed to search for him?

She took long, slow breath --soundless breaths, before she spoke. "He sounds like a very nice man."

He flashed her a shy smile. A little boy smile, and said, "Earl's my real daddy."

SIXTY-FIVE

Across the country, police and the general public had been alerted to be on the lookout for a 1977 grey Mustang, license number BKR-613, with a man and woman inside. A description of Daniel Babineau was released, and a warning that he was armed and dangerous, with a history of violence. Photos of both Babineau and Caroline Hill would make the evening news. The Toronto police had already been alerted to the abduction and informed that Babineau was headed for their neck of the woods.

Lynne sat in the back of the cruiser, the buff folder containing the copy of Danny's file open on her lap. Glen Aiken drove, while O'Neal rode gunshot.

"I don't know all the details, of course," she said. "But according to Dr. Rosen's notes," (God, she would have to tell Dr. Rosen she'd taken the file) Danny was terribly abused as a child."

"Lots of people are abused," O'Neal said, turning around in the seat, facing Lynne. "They don't go around raping and killing."

"I know. But some abuses are more terrible than you know, Detective. I know you see a lot of the underbelly of the world in your line of work, but so have I in my work over the years. I've seen the results of what that world can do to people. Especially kids."

Neither detective spoke. The tires hummed over the asphalt. The Mustang would be miles ahead of them by now. Please let her be okay, Lynne prayed.

"There aren't a lot of specific details in the medical notes," she said, "most abuses implied, both physical and sexual, enough to get a very good sense of his childhood," Lynne continued. " Anyway, apparently this Earl Parker, who is mentioned in the notes, and I'm reading between the lines, was something of a hero to the little boy that Danny was at the time. He made him feel special, loved. I imagine it was the only time in his life Danny experienced that, so when Parker took off on his mother, disappearing from his own life, he was traumatized. It did something to him. And God knows what atrocities happened to him after that. His mother was an alcoholic. And not a mother you would want, according to all accounts. Anyway, Danny hung onto the dream, determined to find Earl one day, and I guess, bring back that brief time in his life when he was happy. For all intents and purposes, he's still that same little boy.

"You feeling sorry for this creep who has your friend?" Detective Aiken asked, merely puzzled, not angry.

Lynne bristled at the question. "No, of course not. But I think I understand him. Anyway, that's about it. He apparently has a fixation on this man, as I said. He'd go into a rant in Dr. Rosen's office about him being his real father and how his mother sent him away. Sent love away." Took hope away, she thought, but didn't say. "But on the admission form his father is listed as unknown. That's probably closer to the truth."

"Parker's probably the father he was talking about when he mentioned to Harold Bannister that he was going to see him," Detective O'Neal said to his partner. "The guy's a real psycho."

"Incidentally," Lynne said, "you guys brought him in to Bayshore. Well, not you specifically, Detectives, but the police. He'd beaten a woman within an inch of her life. He didn't know her, just saw her on the street one day and something about her set him off. The judge said he was unfit to stand trial. That was four years ago. He was released last spring. Before that, he was in and out of jail. Somehow he kept being sent back out on the streets."

Detective Aiken nodded then braked for a red fox sprinting across the road. Brakes squealed behind him and Lynne braced herself, but there was no impact. "It's the way of the system," he said, stepping on the gas. "On the other hand, if we're placing blame, you people had him in your care for a time, you think you coulda fixed him." He gave her a half-smile in the rearview mirror to soften the words.

"Point taken. But some things, and people, are beyond repair."

Lynne consulted her notes again. "Oh, by the way, there was a sister, but she died. Apparently, she drowned in a bathtub. She was three. Her name was Millie."

"Accident?"

"It was ruled accidental. But who knows? Danny would have been six at the time."

"More reason to hate the mother," Detective O'Neal said.

"Possibly, though I don't think he needed more reason. I managed to track down his mother, thinking I might learn more, but she died a year ago in a nursing home.

SIXTY-SIX

Dolly Parton was singing *Coat of Many Colors* when they entered the brightly lit city of Montreal. In different circumstances, Caroline, who'd only read and dreamed of places outside St. Simeon might have been excited to be driving through these streets.

Danny snapped the radio off before the song ended. "Makes herself up like a whore," he mumbled, in his man's voice. All the way here, every time a country station faded out he fiddled with the dial until he found another one. Now they sat in silence.

Caroline liked Dolly Parton, especially liked watching her on TV. She was like a beautiful big doll. It made you smile to watch her sing and make jokes, mostly on herself. You knew she was real and had a good heart. And you could tell she was smart too.

Traffic snaked slowly along the highway, then stopped altogether. The car idled, its big engine vibrating. Danny yawned. "Must be an accident up ahead," he said.

Caroline had been considering in the past hour or so telling Buddy where she first saw him, try to establish a report with him. She'd tell him she was at Bayshore Mental Hospital, too. Would he know that? Harold did. Would be have told him? Maybe not. She and Harold were friends, after all. But there were other ways he could have found out things about her.

The urge to jump out of the car and run for all she was worth was overwhelming. They were stopped here in traffic. Why didn't she? Because he would be faster, she answered herself. She wouldn't get one foot out the door and he'd have her. Maybe stab her to death right here. Splatter her blood all over the front seat.

The awful imagery shattered as suddenly the car broke from the line of traffic and veered left onto a narrow side street, throwing her against the opposite door. Straightening again, Caroline glimpsed the police car up ahead, dome light flashing. The policeman appeared to be handing out some sort of flyer to the driver. Then he was gone from her view as they left the scene behind them. She should have tried to get away.

Sometime later, maybe half an hour, she saw a McDonald's coming up on their left on the edge of some small town or village. He glanced at her and as if reading her thoughts, asked, "Hungry?" Or maybe he was hungry himself.

"Yes."

"Good. We'll eat here, then find a motel."

She said nothing. And then they pulled into the line at the McDonald's drive-through. Without giving her a choice, he ordered cheeseburgers, fries and Pepsis for both of them. After he'd given the order, she said, "I need to use the bathroom."

He looked long and hard at her. "Yeah, okay." Hope rose in her. She would tell someone to call the police, that she'd been kidnapped. She would be saved.

She had set one foot on the sidewalk when he grabbed her arm, hard enough to make her wince, hard enough to leave bruises. He kept his voice soft, friendly, as he held her with his riveting eyes. Those strange pale eyes. "You've got two minutes. If you try to talk to anyone or leave a note or do anything else, I'll slit your throat. And I'll kill anyone else who gets in the way. You know I will. Don't try me."

"I won't say anything. I promise."

He let her go. Her arm throbbed where he had gripped it. "Okay, then," he said.

She hurried inside the restaurant, into the warmth and normalness of the environment, and went on through to the washroom. She was shaking. He'd given her a similar warning when they stopped for gas earlier, even though he hadn't let her out of the car then. The attendant, a middle-aged woman wearing an orange baseball cap turned around backwards, had smiled in at her, but Caroline did not smile back nor try to communicate her distress in any way, lest she put the woman in danger. Instead she stared straight ahead, knowing he would do what he said without a second thought.

Finished her business, she now she stood in the washroom, with another chance to get away, but was afraid to dare. As she washed her hands, she stared at the mirror and thought of writing a note in lipstick, but then immediately imagined him just flinging this door open to check. He would do that. He could think ahead of her, almost like he had supernatural powers. The woman in the mirror looked back at her with large frightened eyes. There were dark shadows beneath them.

When Caroline came out of the washroom and stepped back into the crowded, noisy restaurant again everything in her wanted to break into a run, or start screaming that she was being held hostage by a madman, but she knew if she did that he would start wielding his knife and people would die. Maybe this nice waitress behind the counter, or the teenage girls sitting and laughing together by the window, dipping their french fries in ketchup, eating them in small bites. Or maybe that little blond boy who sat with his mother, coloring in his book. She would want to die too if that happened.

A horn blatted. She knew it was him. Seconds later, the door opened and there he was in the doorway, head thrust forward, eyes wild, expression grim, and she was out the door, walking past him to the car.

"There was someone in the washroom," she said, regressing to the small obedient child she had been, and tried not to cry. He hadn't checked the washroom after all; she could have written the note on the mirror. He had known she'd be too scared and he'd been right. She would just have to try to get away when they were alone. She would find the courage. Or she would die.

Caroline felt as if she was trapped in some awful movie, with herself cast in the lead role. Or dreaming. Can you get hungry in a dream? She didn't know. She couldn't remember. But she was starving, and the food he'd ordered smelled delicious. She ate every bit of her cheeseburger, the last tiny burnt fry, and drank her pop down to the last drop. You can only be gripped by terror for so long. Terror was exhausting. Her hunger satisfied, she now wanted only to sleep. Even as she drifted off, she could feel his pleasure beside her. He was taking care of her. He was in control. The thought brought a welling of anger. And then it ebbed, like a murky tide as sleep took her in.

***

She woke just as they were pulling into a motel on the outskirts of the city. She saw the VACANCY sign in red neon above the office door. *Tony Greer's Inn.* She couldn't have said where they were, exactly, but she knew that this was the place where she would try to make her escape. She would be putting no one else at risk. She would open the door to the office just long enough to tell whoever was in there to lock the door and call the police, and then she would run. She had no plan beyond that.

She would wait until he was asleep; he had to sleep sometime. She thought he looked tired. Good. That was good.

He opened the passenger door. "C'mon," he said. "Remember, don't try nothing."

"I won't." He let her precede him into the motel office. Once they were inside, she stepped off to the side and pretended to be interested in the rack of postcards.

The desk clerk was a heavy-set man with thick iron-gray hair, wearing a caramel and beige striped sport shirt that strained over his stomach. He'd been leaning back in a swivel chair watching a hockey game on a small black and white TV set and smoking a cigar, his profile to them. The sweetish smell of cigar smoke was strong in the room. The man stubbed his cigar out in an ashtry beside him and left his game. The chair complained at his leaving. "Evening, folks. How long you stayin' for?"

"Just tonight."

He nodded and pushed the register at Danny. The pen made a scratching sound on the page as he signed them in. Caroline wondered what names he had used.

"Weatherman calling for snow," the man said. "Supposed to be a big one. You were smart to get off the road." Danny grunted in answer. The man made a second try at small talk, and after receiving another quick, non-answer, he gave it up, but apparently taking no offence. Caroline thought he probably got his share of strange people in here. One night stands. That's probably what he thought about them, if he thought anything.

"That'll be Fifty-five dollars plus tax."

Buddy pushed some bills across at him. Caroline felt the man's eyes on her, but kept her own averted.

"Room Ten," the man said, handing them a key from those hanging on the wall board behind him. He had a gravelly voice and Caroline wondered idly if it was from the cigars. As if her thoughts had transmitted to him, he grinned at her. She managed a weak smile and turned her head away, fearful of Danny...Buddy thinking she was trying to pass him a message.

"One door down," the man said. "There's makings for coffee in the room. If you need anything else, just give a holler. Although all I can provide you with is today's paper. Some postcards." He laughed at his own joke and returned to his game, his latest guests all but forgotten.

SIXTY-SEVEN

Once inside the motel room, Danny flicked the switch on the wall and the light went on, revealing a beige room, two windows with heavy nicotine-colored drapes. The only color was the ashrose bedspread on the bed. Even the carpeting was brown tweed, better to hide the stains. The furniture was dark, two stuffed chairs and a table. A TV facing the bed.

He crossed the room and glanced out the window, then closed the drapes, shutting them in.

A painting with a pastoral scene hung above the headboard, jersey cows in a pasture. One of the brown stuffed chairs sat in the corner by a small round table. On it a brown plastic tray held the makings for coffee the clerk had mentioned. Just enough for two cups.

Buddy took off his coat and flung it over a chair. Standing in the middle of the room, taking in his surroundings, his very presence made the room seem even smaller than it was. She could smell him from where she stood, reeking of sour sweat and danger. A rabid animal momentarily calmed. He raked a hand through lank and greasy hair, that was badly in need of a wash. He wore the same faded cords and plaid shirt he'd had on the first time she saw him coming through her door hefting one end of the trunk. The collar of the shirt was frayed, and he looked like he'd lost weight even during the drive, which was not possible. He turned his eyes on her and seeming to read her mind, flicked off the light, leaving only the dim light of a small lamp in the room.

"You want coffee?" She kept her voice friendly, unafraid.

He looked mildly surprised at her offer, her friendliness. She pretended not to notice as she went about making the coffee. Then he smiled. The boy's smile but thankfully not the voice. "Yeah, sure. That's be great."

"There's hot chocolate here."

"No. Coffee's good."

The coffee perked, the *put ...put ...put* ...reminding her for some reason of oatmeal bubbling in a pot in the kitchen at Bayshore. Soon, the aroma of the coffee filled the room. She poured two cups. "Sugar? Cream? There's just this powdered stuff." She could hear the hockey game faintly through the wall.

"Black's good, thanks." He sat down in the brown, stuffed chair and looked at her. "We need to get an early start in the morning, Caroline. Drink your coffee, then get into bed. I'll just doze off in the chair here. You get a good night's sleep. I know it's been a long day. I want you to look your best when you meet Earl."

She could see that he was very tired. His body had begun to sag into the chair.

"I'd like to take a shower first if that's okay."

She wasn't afraid of him sexually assaulting her. He seemed to have no interest in that direction, for which she was grateful. But he did get up and check out the small bathroom. When he was satisfied there was no window, no means for her to escape, he said, "Yeah, go ahead. I want you to know how much you've pleased me, Caroline. I don't mean to be hard on you, but I know you're scared, and I have to protect you against yourself. I'm starting to feel I can really trust you now though. You get how important this is for all of us, don't you?'

"Yes." She had no idea what he was talking about.

"This is your destiny. Mine too. You can't imagine how excited I am that our journey is nearly at an end. But you do know, don't you. You're excited too; I can tell. We'll all be so happy, Caroline. I promise you."

She smiled at him. "Yes."

She had many questions, but she knew if she started asking them he would change back again. He was lulled for the moment, happy. This was the best she could hope for. And her unanswered questions would just have to remain that. It was not important. She would be gone from here the instant he fell asleep.

Please let him go to sleep.

She quietly locked the bathroom door, then ran the water in the tub as she frantically looked around the small space for something she could use as a weapon if she needed to. Other than a tiny cake of soap she could always wrap in a towel and swing at him, there was nothing. Odd she should think of that now. Anyway, so much for a weapon. She gave herself a quick wash, brushed her hair and went back into the room.

Since she wasn't really worried about him forcing himself on her now, she could only guess that he was saving her for the man named Earl, which while equally frightening, but at least gave her some time to think.

He kept talking about their destiny, and how they would all be happy together.

Had those other women done something to make themselves unfit for …what? His mentor? Someone he knew as a boy, the boy he sometimes became when he spoke to her. She must be careful not to upset him. She feared the child in him almost as much as she did the beast the child had become.

She couldn't pretend to understand it all, but she understood enough to know he was a ticking time bomb that could explode at any moment. She must be very careful.

She could no longer hear the hockey game through the wall; it must be over. Buddy looked at her. He had the TV remote in his hand. A silence hung in the room. She tried to close it up with conversation. "There's a little coffee left. If you don't want it…"

"Go ahead." he said, apparently no longer so set on her going straight to bed.

There was a quarter of a cup left, lukewarm now. But she sipped it anyway. He turned the TV on, ran through a few channels and was about to flick it off when they both froze at the sight of his face filling the screen. It sent a jolt of shock through her, a similar response reflected on Buddy's face.

"…Danny Babineau has a history of mental illness," the newsman was saying, "and is believed to be armed and dangerous." Then they flashed a photo of Caroline below his. One taken at the hospital. They took everyone's photo in case of runaways. They were both ex-patients.

"The woman in the photo is believed to be traveling with Babineau. She was recently released from Bayshore Institution, where Danny Babineau had previously been a patient. Her name is Caroline Hill and police believe she was abducted, although that's not been established. It is unknown whether they knew one another. Babineau is also considered a person of interest in the recent killings of three women in St. Simeon, and possibly others."

A clip followed, showing a scene on a Montreal street where a policeman was handing out flyers to drivers, with their pictures on it. So that's what she was looking at when they veered out of the line of stalled traffic.

"...Anyone seeing a grey Mustang with the licen..." He switched the TV off and stood up. The vein in his jaw pulsed dangerously.

He reminded her of a cornered a dog with its hackles raised. "We've got to get out of here. Get your..."

"Wait..." She was about to call him Danny, then thought better of it. This was her chance to gain his trust completely. "Buddy, I think we'll be safer here, don't you?" She kept her voice calm, reassuring. "I don't hear the TV next door anymore so the man must have turned it off. He didn't hear the news. No one else knows we're here."

She saw him thinking, wondering if she was trying to trick him. Deciding she wasn't. Maybe because that's what he wanted to believe. "But the car..."

"It's dark out. Who would see it?" she said, though faint light still bled at the edges of the curtains.

"The cops. They'll be checking all the cars, especially at motels. They have powerful flashlights."

"You could drive the car around back," she said reasonably. "Keep the lights off."

Beads of perspiration had formed on his forehead, darkened the underarms of his already stained shirt. There was a wildness in his eyes, yet he looked ready to collapse. "No. That just might draw someone's attention." He set the remote on the table and sagged back down into the chair. "Let me think about it. Maybe later, when it's darker."

Caroline rinsed the cups in the small sink in the bathroom, returned them to their brown, plastic tray on the little table. Danny still had his eyes closed. She had a flash of him waking and finding her gone, then smashing through the office door in a rage and killing the desk clerk. No, you have to think positive. You have to believe that's not going to happen. She went over her flimsy plan in her mind. You'll stop long enough to tell him Danny is a crazed killer, to lock the door and phone the police, and then you'll run, and keep on running till you put a safe distance between yourself and Danny Babineau. Just like you planned.

Caroline set her boots and socks on the floor by the bed, draped her outer-clothing over a chair within easy reach, and set her bag on the chair. Then she slipped into bed and pulled the blanket over herself.

As she listened for his even breathing that would let her know he was asleep, it occurred to her he'd not been the least surprised to hear that she'd been a patient at Bayshore. So he already knew. Harold must have told him. It was Harold who first bought Danny into her life. Not that she blamed him. He didn't know. How could he?

Suddenly the lamp went out.

"Good night, Caroline," came the disembodied voice from the darkness.

SIXTY-EIGHT

The call came in from the dispatcher relating that a female gas station attendant had called the police department in Montreal a couple of hours ago to report a man identified as Danny Babineau gassing up at her station. "Grey Mustang," Detective O'Neal said. "She confirmed the license number, and is positive the woman with him was Caroline Hill. She had just finished putting the flyer in her window when they drove up."

"Did Babineau catch that she made him? Did he see the flyer?" his partner asked.

"She's pretty sure he didn't. She stayed cool, said the woman in the car refused to look at her, just kept staring straight ahead, but she looked very frightened."

Attuned to his partner, Detective Glen Aiken stepped on the gas and the car shot forward. It was beyond dusk now, and Glen switched on the headlights. Coming up on a mini-van, he hit the siren.

"Maybe we can still get lucky," Tom said.

"If Danny filled up the gas tank, Maybe he's planning on driving straight through to Toronto," Lynne said from the back seat.

"Maybe. But I wouldn't count on it," Tom replied.

SIXTY-NINE

Caroline had one advantage over him. She'd been able to sleep in the car, and he had looked exhausted. Even so, it was 1:37 a.m. by the glowing red numbers of the clock on the night table, before she finally heard his soft snores from across the room.

Slowly, Caroline reached a hand across to the chair and felt for her clothes. She dressed in the dark, trying not to make a sound. She eased her feet in her stockings and boots. She could see nothing in the darkness of the room but she knew where the door was, and lock in the door, and the chain. She would have to be very quiet. Not a sound. Not a breath.

She sat on the edge of the bed for a good five minutes, afraid to get up, afraid there would be a squeaking or some other sound from the bed, when she did. Suddenly, hearing an abrupt change in the rhythm of his snores, her heart knocked against her ribcage. She didn't move. When his breathing returned to normal sleep sounds, gradually her heart settled down.

Satisfied he had not wakened, she got slowly to her feet. The bed did not betray her, but remained silent. Dizziness assailed her and she came dangerously close to falling back down on the bed. The dizziness passed. It's just the long tension, she thought, taking a deep breath, letting it out without sound.

Her blood thudded in her ears as she crossed to the door. Her fingers felt for the lock, found it. She realized that when she turned it, there would be a click and he would hear it. Undo the chain first.

Slowly, slowly, she released the chain, taking care not to make a sound. Despite her best effort, she heard a soft, metallic creak and froze there in the darkness, her throat closing. She tried to still her breathing, certain he could hear it. But there was no stirring behind her. Sweat was slick on her brow, her hands were damp.

The door would relock when she closed it behind her, giving her a few seconds head start. But now she knew there would be no time to warn the desk clerk. Barely enough to make her escape. With luck, he'd already have seen their pictures on TV and phoned the police. Get ready. Okay... unlock, open, run...

She eased the door open. Ironically, it was not Caroline who wakened Danny, but the sudden clunk, wheeze and rattle of the air-conditioning kicking in.

In a blind panic, she tried to run, but there was time only to feel the cool air on her face as his hand clamped over her mouth and he dragged her back into the room, the heels of her boots raking over the carpeting. Just as her heart had begun to rejoice in the anticipation of freedom, it was over.

He turned the lamp back on.

"I—I couldn't sleep," she stammered when he took his hand away from her mouth. "The man said he had today's paper. I thought I'd read..." But her voice held no conviction, only pleas that fell on deaf ears. Transparent excuses for her betrayal.

He stared at her, disappointment etched on his face. "You're lying." He didn't look angry, just sad. "You want to take love away, just like the others. But I can't let you do that, you see." Tears sprung to his eyes. "You are the right one, Caroline, I was not wrong this time. You just refuse to accept it. I don't want to punish you, though you deserve to be punished. But you understand that I can't trust you anymore not to run away?"

"I wasn't going to run away. I was..."

"Stop it," he growled. "Do you think I'm a fool?" The tears dried quickly. "Well, I'll just have to make sure it doesn't happen again." This he said more to himself than to her and she felt a terrible sense of dread at his words. Before she could even wonder what he would do next, he rushed into the washroom and came out with a washcloth which he stuffed into her mouth so quickly she had no chance to protest, or cry out for help. Then he threw her down on the bed, and bound her hands and feet with duct tape. She flailed and kicked, but she was no match for him; she might have been a rag doll he was handling.

"You'll be fine. I won't hurt you," he said, as he wound the duct tape around her neck, securing the other end to the bedpost.

Seeing he had run out of duct tape, he looked momentarily surprised. Frustrated, he tossed the empty roll in the waste basket. Glancing around the room, his eye stopped at the curtain tie-backs hanging loose beside the closed drapes. Seconds later, he was using it to secure the gag in her mouth. He knotted the length of cloth at the back of her head. She cried out, but her voice was a muffled moan, barely audible, except inside her own head.

"I need to get some sleep," he said. "You be a good girl."

But he didn't sleep. For only a moment did he go back to the chair, springing out of it almost instantly, and walking the length of the floor and back again, mumbling to himself, running his hand through his hair. Once, he stopped and looked down at her and Caroline wondered if he was deciding it might be best to save himself a lot of trouble and get rid of her. But he turned away abruptly and left the room. Seconds later, she heard the car's motor running. The backlights shone through the heavy drapes into the room.

Was he going to leave her here?

The answer came swiftly as he burst back in and immediately wrapped her in the faded rose chenille spread she lay on. "This is your own doing, Caroline," he said. "You need a lesson. And I don't need to be worrying about you taking off again."

He carried her outside and deposited her in the open trunk, closing it with a satisfying thunk on her muffled scream…*mmmph*…*mmmph*…

He smiled and straightened. Then looked quickly around, suddenly edgy, thinking someone might be watching, but all was silent.

The lights were dimmed in the office. It looked to be locked up. He shivered in the cold air. A few lights glowed faintly from behind curtains of other motel rooms, but there was no sound and gradually the tension eased from his muscles. There was a rightness to his mission; everything was back on track now. Soon they would see Earl, and everything would be good again, and they would all laugh about Caroline's resistance to her own destiny, as they sipped their hot chocolates with the tiny marshmallows on top.

He had chosen right this time. She was perfect, even if she didn't know it yet. Danny had known from the instant he'd stepped into her room holding one end of a trunk, that she was the one. Maybe he even knew it when Harold told him about her. She was the one who would complete his family.

You thought the other girls were right too. And then you killed them.

He clapped his hands over his ears to keep out the voices. Shut up! Shut up!

Soon the journey would end. Earl would be so happy to see him again. He'd be overjoyed that Danny had never forgotten him, indeed had searched and searched until he found him. Earl would ruffle his hair, tell him he did good. *Well done, little Buddy.*

He was just testing me, Danny thought, and felt proud that he had passed the tests. He slid into the driver's seat and without turning the headlights on, drove the car around back, which turned out to be not much more than a vacant lot.

He got out of the car and scooped up a handful of dirt and smeared it over the license plates. The cops were on the lookout for a Mustang with a man and a woman inside. There'd be just him now. Maybe this had happened for a reason.

She was rolling about in there, making a racket but there was no one to hear her. She'll tire soon enough, he thought. Leaving her there, he made his way back to the room on foot, staying close to the building in deep shadow.

He needed some shut-eye. His eyes burned and he was sweating through his clothes. As he walked, the sweat cooled in the frigid night air and he shivered.

When the trunk lid closed on Caroline, throwing her into complete darkness, it was like being shut up in a coffin. Terror rose in her throat, but she made no effort to scream, knowing it would be futile. She sensed the silence and isolation around her, and knew from the short distance he'd driven, that he'd taken the car around back of the motel as she had suggested, though she hadn't meant with herself inside the trunk. But at least she was still alive.

She wondered for how long. She tried to calmly assess her situation, and figure a way out of it, which, at the moment, seemed impossible. Wrapped in the bedspread, she could barely move, nor could she dislodge the cloth he'd stuffed in her mouth, that threatened to strangle her, making her gorge rise again and again. Panicking just made it worse.

Despite her best efforts, a tear ran down her cheek, and then another, threatening to become a flood. Don't. It just makes it harder to breathe. The tears under control, she began humming an old hymn remembered from Sunday School—*Jesus loves me this I know, for the Bible tells me so*—filtered through the gag, the tune sounded more like the keening of an animal in pain then it did a song, and she stopped and the tears came again, making her nose run and her breathing shallow. She gagged on the cloth in her mouth, and took a few deep breaths through her nose.

She grew acutely aware of the knot from the strip of cloth that held the gag in place, digging into the back of her head. By turning her head from side to side, then working it up and down, it finally slipped down toward her neck. She thrust her tongue against the washcloth, and pushed it out. It fell away and she gratefully gasped in air.

She lay quietly for several minutes.

She needed to get free of this blanket. Her knees were bent, with no room to straighten them. With her feet pressed against the metal, she could feel the cold seeping in, even through the soles of her boots. She began a rocking motion, back and forth, back and forth, as much as was possible in the small space. If she could just get her wrists free, she might be able to find a way to get out of here. At least he had taped her wrists in front of her. But that wouldn't help unless she could free herself from this bedspread, which was like a straight-jacket, something she'd managed to avoid in all her years in Bayshore.

Did he go back to the room? Or simply walked away into the night, looking for another car to steal. A different woman to fit into his bizarre plan.

As she lay there, she heard a train whistle far in the distance. A lonely sound that somehow made her feel even more helpless and alone. Fight, Caroline. You're a strong woman, you can get yourself out of this. You have to try.

She began moving about again, rolling back and forth, struggling to loosen the spread that wrapped her like a mummy. She managed to push holes in the flimsy cloth with the heels of her boots and make long tears in the fabric. The ripping sound gave her hope. She kept it up, relentless. Then she seized an edge of the blanket with her teeth and folded it back. After what seemed like hours, though she knew it was probably twenty minutes or so the spread finally began to lose its hold on her. She could raise her hands several inches against the fabric, which she now began to tear with fingers.

SEVENTY

Their photos were on the front page of the morning paper, which arrived at eight a.m. Tony Greer, owner of the motel was on the phone to the police department two minutes after he put the paper down.

"They stayed in room ten, last night," he told the female officer on the phone. "I knew it was them as soon as I saw their pictures." Jesus, freakin' killer in my own place, he thought.

"I figured he looked a little...Tony...Tony Greer," he replied to her question. Then he had to spell his name for her. His impatience spilled over. "Tony Greer's Inn. Yeah, get it? It's a play on words. Listen, I'm trying to tell you, I think the poor woman is dead in there and I'm damned if I'm going in there without a cop."

"What makes you think she's dead, Mr. Greer?" the officer asked him.

"I booked them in. And I saw that son-of-gun drive out of the lot about four this morning, and he was alone..."

She wanted to know if he remembered the make of the car? He might have had a few last night, which was why he fell asleep in the chair, but there was nothing wrong with his memory.

"Course I do. It was a Mustang. Just like the paper reported."

He gave directions to his place for a second time, and hung up. He'd already locked the door, but kept going to the window, scared the guy might return. He was a wreck. Where the hell were the cops?

Five minutes later two cruisers pulled in front of the office, and four cops got out, guns drawn. The sight both unnerved Tony, and at the same time washed relief through him, as he hurried to let them in, feeling as if he'd stumbled onto the set of S.W.A.T. He half-expected to see Robert Urich step out of one of the cruisers.

"He's gone hours ago," he said. "I told your dispatcher he drove out of here at four this morning. The woman wasn't with him. I think she's in the room, dead. I think he killed her."

They re-holstered their guns. "Take it easy, Mr. Greer. How do you know it was Babineau?"

A case of the left hand not knowing what the right hand was doing, Tony thought, but didn't say. "He slapped the front page of the paper on the desk, tapped the photos with a chubby finger. "I recognized the pictures as soon as I saw them. It was them, no question. Like I said, she wasn't with him when he drove out of here. He was alone."

"When he registered, did he say anything, tell you where he might be headed, for example?" a big, red-haired cop said.

"No. He wasn't one for talk, and from what I could gather, she was afraid to open her mouth. Made a pretense of looking at the postcards."

Tony unlocked the door of room ten and stepped off to one side to let the police go in. They told him to stay back, which was fine with him. He wasn't in any hurry to see no dead girl. Though when the door opened, he couldn't resist a look. The first thing he saw was a piece of duct tape hanging off the bedpost. The room was empty, the key on the dresser.

They'd drawn their guns again; he couldn't figure why. He already told them the guy had vamoosed.

After a check in the closet, the older cop, and apparently the guy in charge, put his gun away. The others followed suit. "No one here. Either playing some rough games, or the lady is in trouble."

"Bedspread's gone," Tony said from the doorway.

"People take things, don't they?" a big redheaded cop said.

"Not that old spread; couldn't have stood another wash."

"You sure then, Mr.Greer, that it was them."

"Yeah. I'm sure. Ya know, I had a bad feeling about that guy even before I saw the picture in the paper. Woman seemed pleasant enough though, nice looking, quiet, like I said." Tony was beginning to warm to being an important witness in the case. "Maybe he killed her and buried her out back. Ain't nothing but back there but an empty lot."

Three of the cops went round to check it out but found no

evidence to support his suspicion. While they were gone, the big, red-haired cop bent down near the waste basket, and hooked a finger into an empty roll of duct tape, which he dropped into an evidence bag and sealed closed. Seconds later slid out a woman's leather bag from under the bed. The I.D. inside confirmed that it belonged to Caroline Hill.

SEVENTY-ONE

From his latest intelligence, it looked to Detective O'Neal like Caroline Hill's time was running out, if she wasn't already dead. So she was either in the trunk, or Babineau had pulled off the highway somewhere and dumped her body.

The weatherman was calling for heavy snowfall in the Toronto area, which would make their search for the car all the more difficult.

O'Neal fought the tension inside him as the cruiser bulleted through the early morning light. They would be there soon.

SEVENTY-TWO

Toronto is a city of over seven hundred thousand citizens, but Danny, who thought of himself only as Buddy, honed in on the only one he was interested in, Earl Parker, with relative ease. Leaving the car parked in the corner of a small parking lot off Yonge Street, with Caroline in the trunk, Danny went in search of Curly's, found it twenty minutes later, with little trouble.

Curly's was a small, dark hole reeking of booze and cigarette smoke. There was a small adjoining room where two customers were playing billiards. Both looked to be in their twenties, one a black guy with dazzling teeth. The white guy wore a gold earring in his ear.

The man behind the bar was round and bald, apparently inspiring the name of the place. He was wiping a glass with a wad of cheesecloth when Danny slid onto a stool. He smiled and asked if Earl was around.

"Earl don't come in till around nine," he said, in answer to Danny's question. He glanced at his watch. "Probably half hour or so?"

Danny ordered a beer. Looking around, he noticed the small stage with the microphone already set up, in a corner of the room.

This might not be Nashville, or Curly's bar Grand Ole Opry, but as far as Danny was concerned, Earl Parker was a star. Anticipation built inside him, he could barely contain it. His heart was beating double-time, he was so happy. Another twenty minutes or so and he'd be here. The place was already starting to fill up.

Someone put money in the old-fashioned jukebox at the back of the room and Loretta Lynn began to sing her song about being a Coal Miner's Daughter.

"You say he's a friend of yours?" The bartender asked, flipping off the caps on two Moosehead, and sliding them down the counter to a couple of patrons.

Danny's heart swelled. "He's my father." The name was sweet in his mouth and brought a lump to his throat.

"No shit. His son, eh? Earl never mentioned he had kids. He stays over at Seaton House. That's on George Street, not too far from here."

We'll probably go there after, Danny thought, maybe just shoot the breeze, get to know one another again. He smiled. "No, no, that's okay, I'll just wait here."

"Yeah, well, make yourself at home. He won't be long. Beer's on the house, kid. Earl expecting you?"

"No. No, it's a surprise."

The man nodded, grinned, and went to wait on other customers.

Danny sipped his beer, and watched the door for the arrival of his hero, while in the background billiard balls clattered, customers talked and laughed, and Loretta Lynn wailed on about the shabby life of being a coal miner's daughter.

***

Inside the trunk, Caroline slipped in and out of consciousness. When she was awake, it was like being in a dream state. She could no longer think clearly. She could hear traffic, the occasional car horn, but it all seemed so far away. Her cramped body ached and throbbed, yet at the same time seemed a thing apart from her, like the gassy cold air she breathed in. She had peed herself at some point, and the cold, wet seeped through her panties and slacks. Shifting about, she tried to find a less painful position, one that did not catch her legs in a cramp, sending needles into her back.

The bedspread lay in shreds around her. Over the past hours, she had somehow managed to tear the tape off her wrists with her teeth, then undo her ankles. But there was no way out of the trunk. If he had stopped somewhere she would have screamed for help, kicked at the trunk lid to draw attention of anyone nearby. But he didn't stop, and she remembered that he'd filled the car with gas before they left Montreal. She yelled out now, but her voice was raspy and weak, no more than a whisper.

She wondered where she was. Toronto? She had wakened when the car came to a stop and the engine fell silent. Then drifted away again. Now back in her body, all the aches and pains and the cold returned full force, leaving her feeling lost, wretched in spirit. Still, the will to survive was strong, and the small familiar voice urged to her fight to stay alive, to try to save herself. She gave a feeble kick at the trunk and tried to cry out, but then the darkness that filled the tomb-like space around her, moved into her.

And silenced the voices.

SEVENTY-THREE

It was just before nine o'clock when Earl Parker walked through the door of Curly's bar. There was a smattering of clapping and 'Hey, Earls', and he grinned and gave a little wave to his fan club. The man at the bar, and Earl's boss, looked at him with a big secret grin on his face. He opened a beer and set it before the big guy who had slid onto the stool, a couple away from Danny. He removed his well-worn cowboy hat and sat it on the bar.

Curly watched the two men, waiting for the big greeting. Odd, Earl never mentioning he had a kid, Curly thought.

Danny took no notice of the barman; he was too busy drinking in Earl's face, every line, the smile, the crinkles around the eyes. He was older now, hair turned gray, whiskered, gut spilling over his belt, with its fancy copper buckle, but Danny didn't care about any of that. It was Earl right enough. He would know him anywhere. His heart was pounding so hard he was afraid it might just burst out through his shirt. Like Curly, he was waiting for Earl to recognize him, to throw his arms around him in a warm embrace. But Earl seemed the old-fashioned type, and probably would just give his hand a hearty shake, maybe pat him on the back, like they did in the movies and that was okay too.

Once, Earl looked in his direction and looked away again, giving no sign of recognition, and Danny felt his joy slipping just a little, like skidding on an unseen piece of black ice. I've changed, that's all. He kept grinning at Earl, at once shy and at the same time wanting to rush at him and hug him, never let him go. He always knew Millie would still be alive if Earl had been with them then. He would have taken care of them, wouldn't let nothing bad happen to either of them. *I should have saved Millie. But I couldn't...I was afraid...*

Why was he thinking bad thoughts? This was the best day of his life.

Danny had just gotten up the courage to speak to him when Earl finished off his beer, wiped his mouth with the back of his hand and stood up. Curly, a puzzled look on his face, handed him his guitar from behind the bar. There was a chair behind the mic, and Earl Parker walked over sat down to a scattering of applause. "Evening, folks, how's everybody tonight?"

A chorus of cheerful replies. Earl struck a couple of chords, spoke over them, filling the small room with a voice that was deep and rich, despite too much booze and a hard life. "You folks all know this old favorite," he said, and his voice was exactly as Danny remembered it. Earl acknowledged the smiling faces with a grin of his own and Danny didn't mind sharing him with his fans. He was proud of his father.

"*Together again*," Earl announced, and was rewarded with more applause and a couple of hoots. "This one was written and first recorded by Buck Owens in the sixties," he said

It was obviously a crowd favorite, and Danny, quite naturally, took it as a sign that Earl was singing straight to him, giving the words special meaning, and his eyes stung with tears, his heart swelled with love. He was home. He was finally home.

Earl performed half a dozen songs, all of them made famous in decades past. *Oh, Lonesome me, Crying Again, Release me*. At the end of his set, he returned to his stool at the bar where another beer awaited him.

"That was really great," Danny said, smiling at him, not shy anymore.

Earl took a sip of his beer, turned and nodded. "Thanks. I try, Buddy. Glad you enjoyed it." He went back to his beer.

"I knew you'd remember." Danny batted a tear from his eye, embarrassed, but so overcome with emotion he couldn't help himself.

"Hmmm?"

"That you'd remember me. I knew you would."

Earl looked at him for a long moment, then said, "Sure. Sure I do. We did a road trip a couple of years back what town ...?" Earl was small time, but still accustomed to dealing with overly zealous fans. He forced another smile. "You want an autograph? I'm happy as hell to do that. Ya got something I can write on..."

"St. Simeon," Danny said. He heard his voice crack. "That was the town." His happiness flickered like a candle-flame blown by a cold draft. Threatening to go out, and bring the darkness. No, Earl was just teasing. Earl liked to tease. "I'm Buddy." He was shy again, tentative.

"Earl calls everyone Buddy, young fella," said the bartender, whose curiosity had drawn him closer to the conversation, despite his being busy with customers. "Says he's your kid, Earl. Your boy." He wasn't grinning now.

"My kid?" He gave a soft chuckle that sounded mean. "I ain't got no kid."

"That's your story, ain't it, young fella?"

"You lived with me and my mom. Don't you remember?" Now he understood why Earl was acting this way. He was still mad about what happened. He didn't blame him, but it wasn't Danny's fault. He was just a kid when she kicked him out. "I'm sorry she sent you away, Earl. She wasn't no damn good." He remembered Caroline again. He left her in the trunk; she'd be cold. But she'd be okay. They'd go get her together. "I got you a present, Earl. You'll really like it."

"You're freakin' me out, kid. Look, I don't know you, okay? I've never been to the place you mention, as far as I know. Though it's not impossible, I been a lotta places in my time, shacked up with a few mommas, too." He laughed. "Now, I'm trying to get a little break here if it's okay with you. You wanna hang around and listen to the songs, that's good. Otherwise...well...just back off, okay?"

He'd waited so long. All those years, waiting. No, he had to make Earl understand. They were meant to be together, a real family. "You said you'd teach me some chords on the guitar," he said, desperate to jog Earl's memory. "You loved me." Unknown to Danny, his voice had risen to the point where people were turning in their seats to see what was going on. Conversations fell silent.

Curly said quietly, "Hey kid, take it easy. You heard what the man said. Now am I gonna have to ask you to take a hike or are you gonna settle down?" He had this fixation on Earl, nothing else you could call it. This sort of thing happened now and then, but Earl could usually handle it. He'd been his floorshow for three years now and it worked out for both of them. Earl worked for food, beer and a few bucks and also served as a bouncer, a skill he rarely needed and when he did, he usually handled the problem with a hail-fellow, well-met approach. Curly also liked the guy and didn't take well to his being harassed by a customer, nut case or not.

"No, you don't understand. Earl, you know me. I'm Buddy…please." He practically dove at him then, embraced him, spilling Earl's beer in the process. Earl slipped off the stool and backhanded him across the mouth, sending him reeling. "Get the hell away from me, you little faggot."

Danny staggered backwards, stunned. He stared at Earl, his face on fire. No, no, this can't be. A mistake. "You don't mean it. You…"

"I damn well do mean it."

Danny put a hand out, a childish gesture, an apology, a plea for acceptance, and Earl grabbed his hand, whipping it up behind his back, and frog-marched him out the door. A final push sent Danny sprawling onto the snow-covered sidewalk. Then Earl Parker went back inside.

Laughter drifted out to Danny from behind the closed door.

SEVENTY-FOUR

Danny sat on the sidewalk, the heavy wet snow mingling with his tears. The cold snow fell on his heart, smashing the dream, obliterating his path to home. Inside his head, the voice was screaming...screaming...he pressed his hands over his ears to block out the sound, but he couldn't.

He took his hands away and at last the screams died away. The snow fell, softly, silently, and for a long time Danny didn't move from the place where he sat on the sidewalk. The snow turned him white, as if he were a sculpted likeness of himself. Pedestrians hurrying past, glanced in his direction then stepped into the gutter to avoid him. At last, his face like stone, eyes glazed with madness, he rose to slowly to his feet, his hand reaching inside his coat where the hunting knife with its gleaming curved blade, waited.

No one saw it coming. One woman later told police it reminded her of Norman Bates in Psycho the way he came at poor Earl with that knife.

Earl was sitting with his back to the door when it was flung open and the cold snow blasted in along with a knife wielding man with crazed eyes. A woman screamed, but before Earl could turn around the man flew at him, and with a bone-chilling primal howl, plunged the knife between his shoulder blades.

Earl shot up straight in the chair and arched his back, hand flailing behind him as he tried to reach the source of his pain, so excruciating it was like he'd been kicked by a horse.

Danny's strength was that of the madman he was, and he pulled out the knife as if it were buried in butter, and brought it down again and again and again, until Earl slid from the stool, boneless, and now lay in a heap on the floor, dead. The cries and screams in the room had fallen silent. Curly Burrows, the owner of Curly's, stood frozen behind the counter, not quite believing his own eyes as he watched the life go out of his friend. Patrons looked on in shock. Someone had slipped away and called police. A woman was weeping softly. It had begun and ended in less than a minute.

His rage spent, Danny looked down at what had once been Earl Parker. He cocked his head, looked mildly puzzled, like a dog, listening. Then he turned and left the bar. He was still holding the bloodied knife at his side when he walked back out into the storm.

Like a zombie, he plodded through the snow to where he'd parked the car. When he got to it, he sagged down on the ground with his back against the driver's side, crying, and let the knife fall from his hand. The white swirling world swam through his tears.

"I'm sorry, mommy. I'll be good," the child Danny whimpered into his chest. "Don't let the man hurt me. I won't be bad no more."

SEVENTY-FIVE

Sirens wailed through the streets. This was not just another killing in the big bad city of Toronto. This was serial killer, Danny Babineau they were honing in on. Dozens of sightings had been reported of a man walking blindly down the street through the storm, a knife clutched in his hand.

The blood drops from the knife and stopped a short distance from the bar, but the cops were able to follow his boot tracks to the small parking lot off Yonge. They found Danny sitting with his back against the Mustang, now blanketed with snow so you couldn't have told what make it was. A dozen cops leapt from their cars, and scurried behind the open car doors for cover, guns drawn.

"Lie face down and put your hands behind your back," one cop bellowed. "Down. Now!"

A sane part of Danny understood and obeyed. They were on him at once.

Danny was eight years old again, back in his little bed, filled with terror. He could smell the stink of the mattress, the man pushing his face into it, his whiskey breath on his neck. Pain ripped through his small body. No, no, he wailed.

The cop pressed his knee into the small of his back, and roughly grabbed his left wrist to snap on the handcuff, sending a lightning bolt up through Danny's shoulder. Danny's other hand frantically felt in the snow for the hilt of the knife. His hand closed around it and he thrust the blade swiftly behind him, wanting only to stop the pain. To make the man go away. He found flesh. The cop shrieked and fell backwards, clutching his leg.

"Shit, he stabbed me. He's got a knife."

Danny had begun to sit up, still holding the knife. The popping of bullets knocked him back, made his body jerk about on the ground and sent sprays of blood over the pure white snow.

The uniformed men looked down at the still body, silent now. Others came to look, were told to get back. Two cops had their guns still drawn, as if the fallen man might only be feigning his death and would leap up at any second, wielding his knife.

Three of the faces in the small crowd that was fast growing belonged to Detectives Tom O'Neal, Glen Aiken and Lynne Addison. They were at the police department when the call came in from the bar that a man fitting Babineau's description had just killed Earl Parker.

One of the officers broke from the group and walked over to a cruiser, reached for the microphone inside and spoke into it. Another officer put on a latex glove, picked up the knife and slipped it into an evidence bag. It was then that he heard the faint knocking. He turned head. "What was that?"

"The trunk," Lynne cried out. "Oh, my God, someone open the trunk."

Now the others heard the knocking, too. Faint, very faint. But definite. The officer found the key in Babineau's jacket pocket, and opened the trunk.

"Help me," the young woman inside whispered up at him. "Please, help me."

SEVENTY-SIX

One Year Later

Caroline smiled at the woman. "This is a great book, Mrs. Tompkins," she said, as she rang in the sale. "You'll love it."

"Thank you, dear," the woman said. "And thanks for the recommendation; you've never let me down yet."

Caroline had been working in Mr. Goldman's bookstore for four months now, and she loved it. Mr. Goldman was training her in all aspects of running a bookstore. He came to the hospital to visit her and offered her the job, telling her he'd thought she was the perfect person to take over for him when he went to Florida next winter, and the winters following, with an option to buy down the road, if she was interested. Because she'd needed physiotherapy after the long hours in the trunk during which she had been unable to straighten her legs, she couldn't accept the job right way. But he'd waited for her.

Now and then she still had faint stabs of pain in her legs, though not for a while now, and the limp was barely noticeable. Sometimes she still had bad dreams of being locked in the trunk of a car, or being chased with a knife, and woke up in a panic, soaked with perspiration, her heart hammering, but the bad dreams too came less and less as time passed. She had many people to thank for her recovery.

Detectives Tom O'Neal and Glen Aiken were her first visitors in the hospital the day she'd been transferred back to St. Simeon General. They'd been so kind to her. She'd received hundreds of cards offering good wishes, and 'get well soons' from friends and strangers alike.

Last week, she'd been both surprised and pleased to see Detective O'Neal's engagement to Gloria Clark-Breen in the paper. She hoped they'd be happy.

Caroline admired her own lovely diamond in the light from the window; Jeffery had given it to her on Valentine's day. They would be married in June. Jeffrey had come very close to dying from the stab wounds he'd received, but thankfully recovered, though it was a slow process. He lost a lot of blood and the surgery was major. They were in the hospital at the same time and visited one another's rooms, shuffling up and down the corridors, until they were both well enough to go home.

Jeffrey's mother was a lovely woman and Caroline got on well with her. Jeffrey said she was thrilled with the upcoming wedding. She was much better these days, but Caroline thought that probably had more to do with the gentleman friend she'd been seeing, a retired school teacher, then any wedding. Love could work powerful magic.

She also had a new kitten to love, Misty, one of the latest balls of fur with blue eyes. Caroline shared her room and her heart and didn't worry anymore about someone taking her away.

Caroline was feeling particularly good today, if also on pins and needles, but for a different reason. She would be seeing her daughter this afternoon. Lynne had arranged with the adopted mother to bring her daughter into the store. There would be no formal introduction, the woman had said, but she wasn't closed to a meeting when Beth (she had kept the name Elizabeth) was older, and ready to make that decision on her own. Beth had known from a young age that she was adopted.

Oddly enough, she'd been watching the evening news a couple of months back and saw William, Elizabeth's father, on the screen. He had become a prosecuting attorney. He still had the same kind face, if made slightly sterner by his vocation, though most of his lovely fair silken hair was gone. She felt only that pleasant sensation one feels upon seeing someone you've known and cared for once. A very long time ago.

Caroline knew neither the last name of Elizabeth's adoptive parents, nor where they lived, and that was fine with her. The woman was being more than generous, and Caroline was grateful for the blessing she was being given. She would, of course, give no sign that she was anything but a clerk in a bookstore. Nothing to give away what was in her heart.

It was a relatively busy afternoon, the door opening and closing, but she knew the instant her daughter and the woman who had raised her as her own, walked through the door.

The sight of the girl made Caroline's breath catch. Her long hair was lighter than Caroline's, the color of caramel, but other than that, looking at her was like looking at the photo of herself that hung on the wall in her room, come to life. This is my child, she thought, the baby girl the nurse snatched from my arms that morning, while we both protested, little Elizabeth with her doll's fist striking the air. She looks happy, she thought. Lynne had said she was.

Elizabeth (Beth) set a copy of Jean Auel's Clan of the Cave Bear on the counter and smiled up at Caroline. Her eyes were very blue, and there was a light dusting of freckles across her nose and cheeks. "I'd like this book, please."

"She's a great little reader," her mother said.

ABOUT THE AUTHOR

As well as penning Award-winning suspense novels including Chill Waters, Nowhere To Hide and Listen to the Shadows, Joan Hall Hovey's articles and short stories have appeared in such diverse publications as The Reader, Atlantic Advocate, The Toronto Star, Mystery Scene, True Confessions, Home Life magazine, Seek and various other magazines and newspapers. Her short story, "Dark Reunion" was selected for the Anthology, Investigating Women, published by Simon & Pierre.

Joan also tutors with Winghill Writing School and is a Voice Over pro, narrating books and scripts. She lives in New Brunswick, Canada with her husband Mel and dog, Scamp.

She is currently working on her latest suspense novel.

ALSO PUBLISHED BY BWLPP

Chill Waters
Nowhere To Hide
Listen to the Shadows

NOTE FROM THE PUBLISHER:
Thank you for purchasing and reading this BWLPP Book. We hope you have enjoyed your reading experience. BWLPP and the author would very much appreciate you returning to the online retailer where you purchased this book and leaving a review for the author. To show our appreciation we will send you one of our BWLPP eBooks for your enjoyment. To receive your free eBook send us an email with the link to your review. Visit http://bwlpp.com to browse our eBooks. Once you have made your selection email your review information and your choice of eBook to bwlpp@shaw.ca

Best Regards and Happy Reading, Jamie and Jude

BWLPP and BWLPP Spice
The Beverly Hills Boutique of eBook publishers.
Vintage and New from award winning authors.
Top quality books loved by readers,
Romance, Mystery, Fantasy, Young Adult
Vampires, Werewolves, Cops, Lovers.
Looking for Something Spicier
for Sexy Spicy Selections
Try BWLPP Spice

Made in the USA
Charleston, SC
09 May 2011